# The Balance of a Soul

D.S. Daniels

Cover art: "Camille the Helper Cat," by the author.

Author photo by the author's sexy wife

First Edition: November 2016

Second Edition: February 2017

Copyright © 2016 Daniel Sloper

ISBN:0692794573

ISBN-13: **978-0692794579**

# DEDICATION

To my wife: Once again, thank you for indulging me and my insanity.

I know I may not be the nicest person.

But for you, I'll always be sweet.

You are the best part of me.

I Love You.

# ACKNOWLEDGMENTS

The Author would like to acknowledge all those literary agents and publishing houses for refusing his work. Thank you for making me do this myself; I've learned so much about how the system works.

Thanks to CreateSpace for letting me try.

# 1.

Now it's down to just me and you. Out of everyone I know, hang out with, work with, trust, or thought I could have come to love; it turns out you are the only one who might actually believe me. Let me show you something which no one else has seen. No one else has seen it because it turns out they didn't believe me, to begin with, which meant we didn't even get to this point.

Before you start rolling your eyes, yawning and stretching, I am going to show you something. Here it is. It would look normal enough to any person. But I know what it really is, what it does, and most importantly from whom it came. Yeah, it looks normal, but there is no way it is, not this one, no way. Sure, at first glance, even second, well at every glance given to it by anyone who I might have shown it to, but again I never made it that far for reasons you're about to hear. You are the only one who has been able to lay eyes on it, and I have no idea how it appears to you.

It is according to the business standard two inches high, by three and one-half inches long, by maybe a millimeter thick. A regular looking business card. The life of a business card is to be ordered and printed, bought and sold. The card is then given to someone. The final stage the card can be stuffed into a pocket, Rolodex filed, circular filed, stuff into a Costanza-esk wallet, used, never used, lost, found or some version of all the above options. There maybe some options which haven't be thought of yet. That would be the life of the usual business card. However, this one may look like one of those cards, yet I would surmise there are very few if any like this one. Why is that you ask? What makes this card so unique? Well, I'll tell you.

On this plain white card of normal appearance and construction is the sentence in a generic san serif, probably Arial font, printed in black ink, "Owed, One Favor of Your Asking." and a phone number. That's all. No crazy bas relief.

4

No odd smells or colors or even maybe sounds. It was nothing like I would expect a business card to look like considering where I was when I got it and who gave it to me. Where was I, and who gave it to me you ask? Well, I am glad you did. Also, you need to understand now, that this a true story. So, sit back, relax and here we go.

## 2.

Andrew's day had started out just like all his usual days started, in their usual manner. The usual waking up to the alarm, the usual turning off the alarm, the usual getting out of a warm, comfortable bed, down to the usual quite internalized passive-aggressive lamenting about having to get up and go to work. It wasn't that Andrew hated his job, in fact, it was just the opposite. However, it was the tedious process of waking up and getting ready to go to work which irritated him. Andrew, in fact, enjoyed his work and had the bonus of it being what he went to college and received a degree. Unlike some of his college acquaintances who had majored in history and philosophy. As far as Andrew knew, they were still waiting tables and bartending.

Andrew earned a decent salary which allowed him to pay off his debts as they occurred, as long as he didn't try to live in a lavish of a means. It allowed him to live a certain lifestyle that was not "rock-star" or "big time Hollywood actor." But his life was also not "starving college student, first time away from home eating ramen noodle and Chef Boyardee." It was an all-around good job. Andrew was comfortable and sometimes in life that's all that mattered, at least to him anyway.

The job itself was not really all that exciting. Andrew worked as an advertising copywriter. He didn't feel the need to dress it up with fancy names or titles. He worked at the advertising and marketing agency Total Package. Which sometimes was renamed, usually by the people working there, with variants usually vulgar and jocular in nature. Life in a cube farm wasn't bad. It wasn't great, but it wasn't bad; sometimes the office bantering became as tedious as it was soothing in its' commonplace normal, usual manner.

At the end of the day, his job provided money for everyday living. It had several 401K options for his retirement, reasonable health insurance coverage, the usual holiday and time-off accruement plan; it was in all foci and facets an average everyday run-of-the-mill job that was to be both loved and hated in the same synoptic breath. Why just the thought of it made him think in long run-on sentences where the rumination about his job and his place in the world would consume Andrew with such distraction that only the forced bodily reflex indicating oxygen was a physical requirement for continued life could break the monotonous spell.

Andrew continued those same said and a variety of other contemplations through his morning bathroom routine which consisted of the usual shaving and showering. The making of breakfast was a much simpler affair. It entailed heating water in the microwave and pouring it over the package of instant oatmeal to which he added a sliced-up banana.

The last action made Andrew pause a moment. Because just the other day he had wasted the usual amount of time at work reading a senseless web factoid blurb about food superstitions. Besides odd ideas such as the devil will sit on your rising bread dough and ruin the loaf if you don't cut the top or something like that, there was another one saying slicing a banana was bad luck. He thought about that particular odd belief as he put together a ham and cheese sandwich and dumped some potato chips into a baggie for his lunch. He did this as he ate his oatmeal with the sliced banana and drank his coffee.

Andrew packed up his backpack did a quick time check to make sure he was neither too early nor too late; he was right on schedule. As he poured the last of the coffee into his thermal to-go mug and checked the weather app on his phone to see if he needed a coat; he did not. It was a reasonable late April morning which according to the predicted digital forecast on his phone was to become a very nice afternoon. Andrew picked up his stuff said goodbye to his cat Camille and left for work.

Andrew walked out the front door of his condo, turned around, took out his keys and locked the deadbolt on the door. He turned back around and went down the one, two, three steps to the sidewalk which deviated left and right. Just like all the other several hundred thousand million tedious and forgotten times he had done it before, Andrew turned left. He followed the designated Home Owners Association sidewalk which was always swept clean of any and all offending dirt. He HOA sidewalk was flanked on either side by the meticulously groomed, and please keep off of the Home Owners Association grass. The HOA sidewalk ended at the No Solicitors/Residents Only Home Owners Association gate. Opening the HOA gate, Andrew egressed out onto the littered and unkempt world of the public sidewalk. From his condo, Andrew had a leisurely three and a half a block walk to the bus stop. From there he would take the morning commuter bus to work.

That was the usual everyday routine. There were, of course, possible alterations affecting the usual everyday routine. Such items could include really heavy rain or really bad cold and wind-chill. There were the various dentist and or doctor appointments as required. Sometimes Andrew felt like driving his car instead of taking the plurality of public transportation.

But today was one of those countless and endless times where the universe maintained and observed what seemed to be the greater of the two options. As Andrew strolled down the sidewalk, he was mindful of the uneven and raised portions of the sidewalk. This damage to the sidewalk caused by the various elm and oak trees. These were the boulevard trees providing shade and beauty to the neighborhood. Along with wrecking the sidewalk. But Andrew did care. These trees were beginning to bud with new spring leaves. Andrew noticed but rarely looked at the various brownstone and red brick houses and apartments along the way. Only if there was something different about one would he mentally pause and note that detail. But there were none of those on that day, and fifteen minutes later he arrived at the bus stop.

Andrew stood waiting at the bus stop with casual indifference. The kind of indifference found in any large gathering of people who have come together for a nonsocial but necessary reason. Everyone established a small designated personal area where they stood. Everyone else did their best to respect those boundaries, and that same courtesy was returned. Some of the people stood inside the plexiglass bus stop shelter. Others gathered to sides around it. Except for the smokers who all seemed to politely gather off several feet to one side away from the main group. Several of the benches were used to hold bags and briefcases because the majority of the people didn't want to sit on them. Kids would often sit on the back of the bench and put their dirty feet on the seat. No one wanted a dirty shoe print on their butt from the bus stop bench.

Andrew sipped at his coffee and adjusted his backpack which contained his lunch, notebooks, and general miscellaneous life. As he waited, Andrew made unconscious and indifferent silent visual notes of the fellow bus riders. There were men and women dressed in everything from baggy pants and a sports team jerseys to variations of suits and dresses. Some wore bandanas and chains, and some wore ties and scarves. Some carried plastic bags or lunch boxes and some carried backpacks or briefcases. All of which represented a nice demographic swath of the American and more locally, the St. Paul, Minnesota culturescape. Andrew found this type of people watching helped him in his job. He reasoned, how could someone try to advertise and sell something to someone if they didn't know their audience? Andrew would always make mental notes of not only what the passengers said, but also how they said it. Always know your audience.

Andrew was happy to fall in the middle of the appropriate for work fashion dichotomy. He wore the business casual attire of light colored khaki pants and a short-sleeved button-down shirt, and some general purpose brown leather shoes. These were the usual Monday to Thursday clothes. On Friday's it was casual, and blue jeans and athletic style shoes were acceptable. The exception to the usual dress code policy was client meetings. Then no matter the day all the guys wore shirts and ties and jackets, and the women wore slacks and blazers or dresses.

On that bright spring, Thursday morning in April, Andrew stood there at the bus stop next to Hey Susie and What's up Bill. They were several of the people Andrew had come associate with, in a passive conversational way, while waiting for the bus. Andrew had mentally nicknamed Susie as "Hey Susie." He gave her that name because that was pretty much the extent of their conversations. A simple, not quite mono-syllabic, more of a tri-syllabic "Hey Susie." She would mimic his greeting with "Hey Andrew." He couldn't remember how they initially struck their acquaintanceship, probably a comment about the weather. Andrew honestly wasn't sure if he would even recognize Susie outside of the context of the bus stop.

This situation was also true for the other person Andrew had become casually, in a bus stop sort of way, acquainted with, "What's up Bill." What's up Bill was much the same as Hey Susie except instead of saying "Hey" it was "What's Up?" They would on occasion banter about sports, politics, or the weather. Minnesotan's loved to talk about and subsequently complain about the weather. In the course of those discussions, Andrew never made the mistake of mentioning the Wind Chill Factor because that discussion could go on for days.

Andrew took another drink of his morning coffee. He quietly stood there waiting with Hey Susie, What's up Bill and the other gathered plurality of commuters waiting for the Metro express bus to arrive. Over the years, Andrew had observed a routine, a sort of ritual that came with being a bus rider. As everyone waited for the bus, they would absently look at watches and phones to check the time. After doing that, they would then look down the street to where the bus should be. Then they would look back at their watches and phones to confirm the time. This action performed with an almost synchronized movement by everyone at the bus stop. One slow morning and wanting to test his theory, Andrew made a distinct action of looking at his watch and then to look down the street. Before he had finished looking at his watch and was able to look up and down the street, several other people started to do the same thing.

It was like the "Wave" at sporting events. All it took was one person to start it. The next thing Andrew knew everybody started looking at the time and then for the bus.

But on that auspicious morning, the usual routine waiting for the Metro bus ritual was broken. The breaking off the ritual was done by an almost cliché' long, almost cliché' black, with almost cliché' dark tinted windows; this almost cliché' limousine pulled up into the spot where the bus was supposed to stop. This unexpected disruption of the normal morning routine brought unwelcome chaos to the situation. The disruption caused everyone en masse to look at their various watches and phones. Then they looked past the limo down the street to where the bus should be coming. Then looked back at the almost cliché limo. And concluded the action by once again checking the time. The almost part of this cliché limo was because it wasn't just another cliché limousine. It didn't carry a cliché, somebody, who thought themselves better than everyone else just because they were in a limo.

Sure, Andrew thought, there was something like that about it. But every limousine carries such a stigma. However, there was another vibe to this limousine. This limo had something new, something very different. Andrew contemplated the limo and found it difficult to describe. Then he thought of the *Fonz*. The Fonz, from the television, show *Happy Days*. The Fonz was the coolest ever. Why? He just was. He couldn't be defined. It was just how the Fonz was, cool. That is how Andrew came to see the limo. It was cool. It looked like a limo, but it had an aura or air of distinction. It radiated something more than just a limo with some idiot inside who thought it would be funny to park in the bus zone. The black wasn't just black. If the light hit the paint just right, the black flashed with a shade of fire brick red. But when Andrew thought he could see the red shade, the color immediately went back to black. It was almost mesmerizing trying to see that red color through the black. Andrew started to feel hypnotized by it. But he looked away to see if anyone else was experiencing such a strange effect. Andrew looked questioningly at Hey Susie and What's up Bill. They looked at him as if they didn't see anything accept the limo.

Andrew turned back to look at the car. The almost cliché black windows looked like cliché limo windows. They had the typical dark black tint. In the windows, Andrew could see his dark tinted reflection of the world and people around him. Andrew looked a little longer and a little harder as if by doing so he might see through the windows to whoever was inside the car. As he did, Andrew was caught by something more.

It seemed like there was a special effect green screen behind him and the windows were the computer monitors displaying the virtual background image. At first glance, Andrew was standing there at the bus stop. Then looking again the reflection suggested he was standing alone in the desert surrounded by shadows. He performed a quick double-take looking around to see if it was somehow true. Andrew looked to his left and right and only to see he was just standing at the bus stop surrounded by Hey Susie, What's up Bill, and the other waiting passengers.

Andrew started to feel the entire situation was on the verge of not quite normal. Then the back passenger window opened, and the situation went at light speed from the verge of not quite normal in a direct line too far from normal. From there the situation didn't stop or slow down. Instead, it kept going and went right over the cliff of far from normal, and down into the WTF ravine.

# 3.

"Mr. Andrew Wheeler?"

A voice called out from the dark and seemingly empty interior of the limo.

"Our records indicate there is a Mr. Andrew Wheeler in this group. Would Mr. Andrew Wheeler please be so kind as to step forward?"

It sounded like a question, but it wasn't. However, it also wasn't quite a command. It was a sentence which couldn't be ignored. But no one who was there and heard it would have been able to explain why.

Then it became the gag bit from the movies. When a volunteer is asked to take one step forward, and everyone except for the punch line guy takes a step backward. In a parody of said gag, Hey Susie and What's up Bill without hesitating stepped away from me. At the same time, everyone else around me stepped sideways, back, or several steps from in front of and then to the side of me. I stood alone. Whoever was in the limo now knew who I was and I didn't have to do anything to identify myself.

*-Thanks, everyone! Bunch'a douche bags!-*

The bus that should have been pulling up right at that moment, with possibly a traffic cop to ticket the limo, was nowhere to be seen.

*-Stupid bus-.*

Well, I decided I had two options. First, I could step up to the limo and go to the window where it was so black that it almost seemed like the window was still up. No light went in; no light went out. Albert Einstein or Stephen Hawking or that Brian Greene guy from the PBS special on String Theory might have had an issue with that. I could step up to that window and say, *"Yes, I am Andrew Wheeler"* and then see where life took me. Or my second option which was to run. Run like, well like any metaphor involving running like something really fast, like a cheetah made out of wind and light chased by an evil Superman who decided to become a poacher. Since at that time I had no reason to run I went with the first option. The second option came later.

Andrew was enjoying a cold beer while telling his story. He had arrived at Al's Bar via a taxi instead of his usual walk from the office. He thought a nice cold beer would help him get his sense of taste and smell back in sync. Although he almost felt normal in his skin again, everything still smelled and tasted like cardboard. Andrew rationalized beer should be the panacea for such an ailment.

Andrew had, "found" Al's Bar about a year earlier. A sudden afternoon rainstorm slammed into Minneapolis on his way to the bus stop. Looking to escape the deluge Andrew ducked into the nearest location, which happened to be Al's Bar. He had never gone in even though he passed it every morning and afternoon when going from and to the bus.

Andrew had always been a bit curious and sometimes imaginative about it. The front and exposed left side wall, under all the dirt, dust, and some faded graffiti, the original old Minneapolis red brick. The right-side Andrew guessed was also still the original brick, but there was a newer building built next to it which blocked the view. Andrew looked at the about one-foot wide gap between the buildings and thought if they ever needed to do any renovations it was going to be difficult.

The only indication the building was a bar was because of the sign. Above the single door hung a medium sized illuminated white plastic sign with red letters stating *Al's Bar*. The front wall was nondescript. It had long narrow rectangular windows and a solid looking metal door. The windows were set high up, about six feet Andrew thought. He had estimated the height of the windows based on his physical height, which was about six feet.

However, even though could see the windows, he wouldn't have been able to see into the interior. The windows were tinted a dark black. That tinting didn't let passerby's spy on any of the going on's inside the building. The door was constructed of heavy gauge sheet steel with the massive hinges and door handle riveted in place. The lock looked like something belonging to a prison cell or bank vault. These imposing looking features made Andrew imagine it was a new version of old nineteen-twenties speak-easy. Out front Andrew had seen a gamut of vehicles parked; Ferrari's and Porsche's to groups of Harley Davidson motorcycles.

Out of curiosity, Andrew would sometimes think about going in for a beer. To see what the bar was like on the inside, and who might be in there. However, he always came up with an over-rationalized counter argument. Andrew imagined as he walked into the bar all the music would stop playing with a screeching sound. Then everyone would turn and stare at him with dead flat eyes and with a unified expression of, *"wha'da you want?"*.

But caught in the midst of the afternoon downpour with no umbrella or raincoat, Andrew was fated to take refuge at Al's Bar.

Andrew never understood why he hadn't done it sooner.

"So why would you go up to an almost weird looking limo if you didn't know what it was about?"

Not only was Al a good bartender he was also the owner. Andrew hadn't realized when he first started going to "Al's Bar"; there, in fact, was an Al who owned "Al's Bar." However, the current Al, whose full name was Alexander Boyd, was not the original Al. As Andrew became an occasional regular at Al's, he came to learn the history of the place.

The bar had been around for quite a long time, since the 1940's, although there was some conjecture as to the actual date. The current Al, quoting from the building abstract, said it was 1947, but the dated foundation stone on the corner had 1943 etched into it. Whichever date was correct, it didn't matter because the building had always been a bar, and it had always been called Al's.

The fact that the building had always been a bar was evident from the interior. Andrew was fairly certain the central bar around which everyone stood, sat, and rested their drinks upon, was the original wooden bar with brass foot rail. The areas of variation in the color of the wood stain suggesting it may have been restored once or twice. If the bar had been restored care had been taken to leave the top as it was. For there were still spots on the on it where previous customers had decided they needed to carve their names, or initials, or some memento from the past for future patrons to ponder.

The back of the bar with all the shelves and cabinets was also wood, but they didn't match the central bar. The wood was different, and so was the stain. The back area all looked newer, lacking the character given to wood over time. The bar went almost the length of the building on one side with a row of tables down the middle and several private high-backed booths along the opposite wall. Despite a grimy exterior and having only two windows Al kept the inside clean and well lit. The original name never changed always staying "Al's Bar." The current Al repeated the reason for this, as explained to him by the previous owner Earl Peterson. Who was also known as *Al*.

"Because it was easier to maintain the liquor license, insurance, and other paperwork."

Initially, Andrew found Al to be sort of, off-putting. To be completely honest, Andrew found Al to be a little bit scary. Al had long black and gray hair that went down his back and braided in a ponytail. Al's face was road leathery from spending years on a motorcycle. He was a bit shorter than average. Andrew figured Al stood around five six. Al was also burly. He wasn't fat but stoutly built with a roundish but solid looking midsection. It could have been a beer-belly, but Andrew didn't really want to find out. Andrew's initial reservations about Al might have been because Andrew knew Al also hung out with a local motorcycle "club."

That, of course, didn't make Al a bad guy, but at first glance and with hasty judgment it did skew Andrew's initial impression.

However, on that original raining afternoon, Al was working as the bartender, and with a slow stretch Al walked over to Andrew and introduced himself. Soon he and Andrew started talking about all manner of topics. Andrew had originally thought, as he ordered a beer, the short, brutish looking guy behind the bar was just an employee. That he was the bartender and bouncer all wrapped up in a pair of old blue jeans, a well-worn Harley Davidson T-shirt and a faded black leather vest full of motorcycle patches.

Despite the gruff and off-putting appearance, Andrew found Al to be a very intelligent and thoughtful person. Al asked straight forward questions and answered questions asked of him with a worldly thought provoking insight. Al was a bartender straight out a Hemmingway story.

"I don't know why I did it," replied Andrew. "I guess it's just the passive-aggressive good mannered Minnesotan upbringing. It compels us to do things we don't really want to do. We act like it's okay and we don't mind, but secretly we hate it. That's the best answer I have because honestly, I don't know why I walked up to that limo. It was like I had a strange compulsion that I couldn't resist, yet I knew it was wrong."

"So, what happened? Who was in there?"

Andrew looked at Doug sitting on the bar stool to Andrew's left. He was one of the after-work, happy hour barfly's Andrew had gotten to know. Doug was an average guy of normal appearance and height with sandy brown hair, glasses. He was wearing his favorite *Duluth Dukes* baseball cap. He had found it while hiking along the North Shore of Lake Superior and decided to keep it. It wasn't because he liked or supported that particular bush league baseball team, but it was the hat itself. When asked about the hat, Doug always responded with "Lake Superior doesn't give up her dead, but she does give up her hats."

Doug worked as a social worker and group home caretaker for the mentally challenged. He explained it as, "the people aren't full 'tards. They just aren't high functioning; think Forrest Gump but a bit stupider and with more drool." Although he seemed crass about his job, Doug had a genuine concern for the people he worked with and cared.

"As I walked forward, the weird blackness was still there, but once I got right next to the car, it seemed to drift away. It reminded me of those "transition" eye glasses. The kind that just changes from clear to dark from UV rays. I looked in, and sitting there was the strangest looking man I have ever seen. He was perfect. Everything about him was perfect. His dark ebony skin was perfect with no blemish. His short-cropped hair-perfect. His teeth-perfect. His looks-perfect. His suit-perfect. His speech-perfect. No one is perfect. We all have little flaws; one eye is a bit lower than the other; a nose is a bit too big or small for a face; teeth crooked or discolored."

"Yeah, like women complain my dick is too big" interjected Doug with a half-laugh."

"Hey pipe down and let Andrew tell his story. I want to know about the perfect guy in the limo."

The comment came from Zev sitting on Andrew's right. Zev was another of the happy-hour crowd. He also happened to be the marketing executive at a local internet company. Andrew liked Zev. He was always enthusiastic. There was never a boring meeting with Zev. He was one of those people who went through life with an exclamation point attached to them. Unlike himself and Doug, Zev wore suits or dress shirts and ties to work. He wasn't short, but not quite an average height. He had shaved his head to alleviate the burden of dealing with what remained of his hair. Seeing a family photo from Zev's teenage years; his hair was almost orange red.

Andrew first met Zev when his internet company InterWeb came to Total Package to help with the development of an advertising campaign. The account was assigned to Andrew. The two of them often met usually after work at Al's to go over new ideas and slogans. Andrew didn't know it when he and Zev first started working together that Zev hung out at Al's. After they had met several times at the office, Zev suggested they go for a beer after work. To Andrew's surprise, they went to Al's.

They sat in one of the booths and what started as a casual beer became a brain-storming session about new ideas. From then on, the two of them would meet there instead of the office. Zev would pay for everything and write it off as a business expense. Andrew was getting paid to drink beer.

"Thanks" Andrew replied to Zev.

"Well, not this guy. He was absolutely perfect looking, and it was suddenly very terrifying. He looked at me a bit bemused with this perfect half smile. Then he took out a scroll from inside his suit coat. It was rolled up on both ends, and it kind'a looked like one of those Hollywood Egyptian mummy movie props. It even had a red ribbon around it. He unties the ribbon and opens the scroll and sort of mumble-reads through it. He does it perfectly. Suddenly he stops and turns to me and says in this almost pompous, but perfect English lord sort of voice.

"Forgive me my poor manners for not providing a proper introduction of myself. It is not my intent to appear as crass as to overlook the simple civilities to which all creatures should strive. It would go far to make this a much more pleasant place for all."

Andrew paused, waiting for any comments from his audience. Hearing none, he continued with his story.

Not sure how to respond, I just said something like, "Yes, I suppose it would. I guess."

Andrew took a drink of his beer. He did this because he was thirsty, and also trying to build an idea of suspense.

I looked in the car at this man. I wasn't sure if he was alone or not. Because although the weird darkness was no longer around him, it still sort-of, well it hung for lack of a better description, in the rest of the car like a black fog."

"Okay that is weird." said Zev with a questioning tone.

Al standing on the other side of the bar was leaning against the wooden shelves listening. He looked between both Zev, and Doug and Andrew. His eyes were squinting, and he seemed to have a distant look on his face.

"Did it smell at all? You know what I mean? Cigarettes, Weed, booze, women, new car smell, anything like those?"

Andrew thought about what Al said for a minute. Then for the first time that day, what Al had said hit him.

"No, it didn't smell at all. There was nothing like that at all now that you mention it and I think about it a bit. There was no smell, and there was no sound except for our voices."

"That's fucking weird" exclaimed Doug.

"Yeah and it's about to get weirder" replied Andrew.

So, I'm standing there and looking at this perfect guy, and something starts to click in my head. There was something about that whole situation that wasn't right. It nagged at my brain like I was supposed to remember something. The perfect looking guy turns away from the scroll, then to me.

"As we are not acquainted with each other, and I have you at a social disadvantage, please allow me to introduce myself. I have many names, several of which would be both unpronounceable and unintelligible by your kind. However for our purpose today, you may simply refer to me as Mr. Cadwallader".

Suddenly the idea came to me that this was some kind'a elaborate YouTube video prank like a *Punk'd* or *Jackass*. This guy was setting me up.

Suddenly and in a fit of excitement Doug drummed his hands on the bar and finished the sentence, "for some sort'a practical joke to be posted on some website! Dude! You should 'a gone through with it. You could'a gone viral!"

"Yeah, I thought about that for a moment. I even wondered what the set-up was supposed to be. But it just so happened that before the conversation could go any further, the bus pulled up and honked at the limo."

"Well, sorry Mr. Cadwallader, but you seem to be blocking the bus. Which also happens to be my ride to work, where I need to go. It has been nice meeting you, but I have to go now."

Which was true because the other people at the bus stop, the ones who metaphorically threw me in front of the bus were now getting on it. However, the perfect guy in the limo wasn't going to let it go. As I was stepped away to leave, he spoke again.

"Mr. Wheeler we do have a contract here which requires our final signatures before it is closed. Please be so kind as to permit me to offer you a ride to where you are going. Thus, allowing us the leisure and might I add, a certain amount of comfort and privacy in which to complete your transaction."

"Look, buddy, I have no idea what you are talking about, but I have to go, and you now get to talk to the traffic cop instead of me. Have a great day."

It was impeccable timing because the traffic officer had not a moment before I stood, parked their squad car in front of the limo blocking it, and the officer walked up as I walked away and stepped onto the bus for work. Out of voyeuristic curiosity, I had to watch the guy get a ticket as the bus pulled away.

But instead of having their ticket book out and asking the driver for their license and insurance, the officer was just stuck there stooping over and looking in the back of the limo. The last thing I was able to see before the scene was out of sight was the traffic officer had turned sort of ashen with big round eyes and I could have, and would still swear that I think the officer's black hair started either turning white, falling out, or both. I have no idea; all I know is that as that bus pulled away, a puddle started to form on the sidewalk around the officer's feet.

I wasn't on the bus for more than five minutes before my cell phone rang. I looked at it to see who was calling. The phone number and picture that came up said it was my mom. I couldn't think why she would be calling me at seven-thirty in the morning, but she probably had some reason. Of course, that reason would take the entire bus ride for her to tell me. So, out of my polite curiosity, I answered. And, yes, I know you are all thinking it anyway; no, it wasn't my mom.

"Hi, Mom. What's up?"

The voice on the other phone responded in a perfect almost pompous English lord sort of voice, but his time it had a perfect touch of peevishness to it.

"Mr. Wheeler, I am certainly not your mother. For had I been your mother I would have instructed you in better manners and civility than the ones you poignantly just displayed."

Doug made a *guwhuf* laughing sound at Andrew. "He didn't really say that, did he? I mean no one really talks like that.

29

He must'a been reading from a script for that internet prank or something."

Andrew looked over at Doug who was staring at him with a questioning expression.

"No, those are pretty much his words and as close as I can come to imitating the way he said it."

"Mr. Wheeler, we have a business transaction to conclude, and my dear boy, there is no escape clause here."

That last sentence he sorts of chuckled-snuffled laughed, and it was the first time it wasn't remotely perfect. In fact, it wasn't remotely anything identifiable. It was very unnatural sounding like it wasn't coming from a human.

"At that point, I felt it best not just to hang up but to turn off my phone. I don't know how whoever this person or those people were and how they got my mom's cell phone number…"

"…unless she was in on it too?" suggested Zev.

I don't know all I know is that it became a very long express bus ride to work. I kept looking around me to see if there was some quasi-perfect looking person waiting and watching from a different seat on the bus. I was giving every cell phone a paranoid stare thinking it was part of the prank set-up and they were streaming me live to some internet site in China or something. But nothing like that took place; I can say that now in retrospect. I thought it was all behind me and I would go back to having just a regular day."

The MTC bus pulled up at the usual Nicollet Avenue stop. I got off the bus and walked the block to the office. The walk helped me relax. I was no longer paranoid as I rode the elevator up to the eighth floor. The elevator opened, and a group of us existed. I casually strolled down the hall to the office opened the door and started to think about the projects I had waiting for me. I walked down the row of the cube farm to arrive at my desk at the usual eight o'clockish thinking about freshening my coffee. Then I turned to put my backpack down, and yes there he was, Mr. Cadwallader as he called himself, and he was sitting, perfectly, in the extra chair in my cube.

"He didn't sit in *your* chair; he sat in the other chair? Seriously? I mean if you want to intimidate or violate someone you take over their space, like their chair, or their spot." Al's tone of voice and body language suggested he might have done something similar to someone once or twice in his life.

"Or piss on their leg when you are both at a urinal, and the other guy has finished up and can't do it back." interjected Doug with a sort of far-away thoughtful face.

"What is wrong with you? Seriously Doug, that is, I don't know what that is but wow, man, I mean how do you come up with this stuff?", responded Zev with revulsion.

"Didn't anyone else say anything about this guy in your space?"

"No. That was it. No one said anything about the guy even being there. It was like I was the only one who could see, or talk to him."

"But the other people at the bus stop all heard him, and you said the traffic cop's hair fell out and he pissed himself when he looked into that limo. What gives? I'm starting to think you're making this shit up", said Doug.

Andrew knew he had to keep them going. He was getting close to the critical point. But, he wondered to himself, what was going to happen when he got there?

"Just hang on, and I will get to the best part here."

So, I walk into the cube, and there he is. He politely stands up and gives me this slight Japanese style bow, which for some reason I return."

Al laughed, "Probably your good, passive-aggressive Minnesotan manners."

He then pulls out my chair and turns it for me suggesting I sit down. Through all of this, I hav'ta say the dude does have impeccable and dare I say, perfect, manners.

"Mr. Wheeler. I must say this morning has not gone according to schedule. Your lack of civilities in the finalization and conclusion of this transaction has become a bit vexing for me. I am a patient being, but even I have my limits. So now that we are here and it is just the two of us, we can close the file on your contract and take your payment in full."

"I am sorry Mr. Cadwallader, sir, dude, whatever, but I really don't know what you are talking about, and I am at work, and I really don't want to get fired, and I have no idea how you got in here or why no one seems to notice you, and I don't know what television, or internet, or whatever prank-practical joke show this is a part of but I really don't want to do this anymore and can you please just end this now so I can get on with my life?"

This Cadwallader guy just sat there in the chair, unblinking, staring at me. He didn't move. He didn't flinch. I wasn't sure if he was even breathing because his nostrils didn't flare even a little to suggest air was being exchanged. Finally, after what seemed to be hours, he pursed his lips a little bit, blinked once and sort of leaned his head to the right as if in contemplation.

"Mr. Wheeler, are you aware of what you just said?"

"I don't know? Maybe? Yes? I, mean what?"

I didn't know what to do next because I wasn't sure what this Cadwallader was talking about. Cadwallader leaned forward a bit and sort of made a tent with his hands touching the fingertips together. As he spoke the index fingers on his hands would move and gesture to support the inflection of his voice. He was like some stage actor, and he did all of it with perfect timing and poise.

"You spoke in one long fused or run-on sentence. Although I will admit, you did it quite admirably requiring only one breath. However, it is not what would be considered proper grammatical construction. Your sentence, in fact, should have been broken into several individual clauses. Doing such would have allowed for more nuance, emotion, and subtle points of punctuation. Mr. Wheeler, you have been using this form of English for your entire life. Despite your advanced education and current employment where you have to display more than a proficient understanding of the subject, you have still to become its master. I would submit a modicum of leniency is due you. After all, you are only human."

Now the situation was becoming ludicrous. The guy was giving me English lessons like he was one of my college professors, and also inferring he wasn't human. Then Cadwallader did the alien sounding laugh that made all the tiny hairs over the entirety of my body stand up and sent an actual shiver down my spine. I still had no idea what was going on so; I figured I would ask. I tried not to be too sarcastic about it, but his whole good manners shtick was getting on my nerves.

"What do you mean my entire life and only human? Umm, I don't know what you are talking about, and I don't know why you think I do. But for civilities sake, how about *you* pretend *I* don't know. Maybe if you start at the beginning, I will better understand this situation."

"Mr. Wheeler this is a bit unorthodox, and I well understand you may be vying for more time here. However, it is protocol to go over the contract in full before the final signatures are captured, and the contract closed."

Once again, he pulled out the scroll again from his suit pocket. I didn't understand how it was in there and not sticking out somehow. He unrolls it on my desk and looks at me and said,

"You remember this, of course, the contract for your soul."

"I knew it," shouted Zev. "I knew I knew this and that clenched it. You ripped off *The Twilight Zone*!"

Doug with his beer glass half way to his mouth looked over at Zev, "Huh?"

Zev's normal exclamation mark level of enthusiasm increased to a two or possibly three exclamation mark level. "*The Twilight Zone*. Greatest show ever!"

Doug took a drink of beer before replying with an irritated, "Yes, I know *The Twilight Zone*. I think everyone does, especially the theme song."

At this point, all three of them start going, "Do-do-do-do, Do-do-do-do." To which Al added, "You have just crossed into the Twilight Zone."

"What are you talking about I ripped off the *Twilight Zone*?"

Looking between the three of them Andrew could start to see the skepticism forming. He had just arrived at the moment of truth.

"There was an episode where a guy was a hypochondriac. He was afraid of dying, so he sold his soul to the devil for immortality. Just like your story the devil appeared to him out of nowhere and called himself, Cadwallader."

Andrew felt his stomach drop. It dropped down to the bottom of the pit of unreasonable and undeniable. No one from that point on was ever going to believe him. He had already been warned this very situation was going to happen. Andrew wasn't sure why he was surprised or disappointed by their reaction. But despite being told this was going to happen, Andrew had already decided he had to try. It was his way of trying to prove to himself what happened was real.

"No really guys. My story is real!"

Andrew could feel them start to slip away from the story. Al turned away to check on a group of women who had just come into the bar. Zev suddenly turned to his phone and started furiously tapping a message to someone who had become more important than Andrew and his story. Even Doug lost interest in the story. He was usually very attentive to what was being said if for nothing else just to drop in some non-sequitur comment. Doug rose from his bar stool and downed the remains of his beer. He pushed the glass to the inside edge of the bar and absently said in Al's direction,

"Gonna empty this one" with an open-handed gesture towards his groin, "how about a refill on that one" pointing back towards his glass.

Andrew sat alone. His now considered blatant rip-off, or re-versioning to put a Hollywood spin to it, of the classic *Twilight Zone* story, was now forgotten.

"So, I finished my beer and caught the bus home. The guys at the bar yesterday afternoon never got to hear how the rest of the story unfolded."

# 4.

Andrew was at home. He was sitting in his favorite leather wingback chair, with Camille on his lap. He gently rubbed Camille's furry head between her ears. With an approving response, she raised her head upwards, firmly pressing it against Andrews's fingers. She hinted he was to scratch just a little bit harder. Andrew yawned. He glanced at the kitchen clock; it read ten minutes past eight. Even though it was still early in the evening and a Friday, Andrew was tired and was thinking about going to bed. The past two days had been, to quote the Grateful Dead, a long strange trip. But he could never refuse a furry request from Camille. He put his feet up on the footstool, continued to rub and scratch Camille's head, and tell her his story.

"Mr. Wheeler, are you denying that this spot of blood and signature are in fact yours?"

Andrew didn't know what to do. He was sitting in his office with some guy who called himself Cadwallader. He called himself Cadwallader because he said Andrew wouldn't be able to pronounce his other names.

Besides an odd name, which apparently he stole from the *Twilight Zone*. Cadwallader was also unnaturally perfect. Despite Andrew's current irritation he had to admit, secretly to himself, that this Cadwallader guy was both smooth and suave. The two words formed a perfect mash-up to become the new word, *smoove*.

Smoove'ness, aside, this Cadwallader guy who Andrew had left at the bus stop about thirty minutes earlier, somehow arrived before Andrew, to Andrew's place of work. The last he had seen, Cadwallader was talking with a traffic cop. Who as Andrew voyeuristically gazed in delight was about to give the guy a ticket. Instead, the cop started to lose their hair and wet themselves. Then Andrews's phone rang and his mom was calling; it was not his mom, it was Cadwallader. Then he finally made it to his office. Where to Andrew's surprise and dismay, Cadwallader was sitting in his cube. Sitting there waiting for him. Not just waiting for him. But waiting to tell Andrew that he was there to collect Andrew's soul. That he, Andrew, had apparently sold it. The whole thing sounded ludicrous. Even if a soul did exist who would buy it, the devil? To Andrew, despite Cadwallader's weird smoove like perfection, he certainly didn't look like the devil. Should the devil be real?

But now Andrew was sitting in his cube at work, with some perfect looking guy. A perfect looking guy who was showing him a scroll with what Andrew had to admit, did look like his signature. There was also a dark crusty looking spot next to what was supposed to be his signature, which apparently was supposed to be his blood.

"Seriously Mr. Cadwallader or whoever you are, I have to get to work. I have projects to finish, and you're going to get me fired. I don't know anything about this. I don't know who put ya up to this gag. If it was some radio, or TV or internet joke thing? But it's gone on long enough. I did not sign that contract. I did not put a spot of blood on it. I certainly did not sell my soul to you. You should know that since you're apparently supposed to be the devil!"

Cadwallader smiled at Andrew. It was his perfect smile, and it was at the moment very irritating to Andrew. It was just so smug and perfect. Andrew felt the desire to make that perfect expression, not so perfect.

"Mr. Wheeler, I understand you are not familiar with the complete intricacies of a soul transaction. First and foremost, I am not, as you put it, the devil. I am at the moment in charge of soul collection. Your initial confusion is to be understood because this is the first time we have met."

Andrew was now not just irritated, but also confused. The story just kept getting weirder and convoluted. Andrew just wanted it to end so he could start work.

"Finally, something we can both agree on; we have never met. So, whatever dude. I just want to work and not get fired. I don't care anymore about the prank or the video; it's over. Go home, or back to the studio, or even Hell. I don't care. Besides, if you weren't there to make the deal in the first place, how do you know if you even have the right guy? There are a lot of twenty-eight-year-old white guys, about six-foot-tall, normal length blackish hair, brown eyes, with a medium build. In fact, don't trip over one on your way out. You screwed up. Bye now."

Andrew had done it. He had turned the whole situation around and stuffed it back in the face of the Cadwallader person. This whole stupid little escapade was over. He picked up his backpack and set it on his desk next to his monitor. Andrew was about to turn his chair around and get to work in a flagrantly rude gesture. It was to be a way to signal to Cadwallader "Get out, we're done." But, before Andrew could carry out his plan, Cadwallader raised his perfect eyebrows, perfectly, of course, leaned back in the chair while maintaining perfect posture, and took a deep breath. To Andrew, it looked like Cadwallader were collecting his thoughts on how to proceed next, now that Andrew was calling an end to whatever gag was going on. It was almost like fate that Nancy from the next cube over walked by. Cadwallader stopped her.

"Excuse me, Mrs. Nystrom; I am in need of your assistance for, just a moment."

Without pausing to think about it, Nancy stopped what she was doing, and walked into Andrews cube. She didn't say "good morning" to him as she usually did. In fact, Andrew wasn't sure if Nancy even noticed he was there. Instead, Nancy stopped in front of Cadwallader with a sort of blank sleepwalker look on her face.

"Yes?"

"Please, Mrs. Nystrom put your right index finger over but, do not touch the document."

Cadwallader passed the so-called contract for Andrew's soul over to Nancy. She reached out her right hand over the document, specifically over the area where the blood spot was. There was nothing. Nothing happened. Nancy just stood there as if in a trance. Andrew thought if Cadwallader had told her to stand on one leg and cluck like a chicken, she would have done it.

"Thank you, Mrs. Nystrom. You may return to your affairs."

As if being dismissed, Nancy turned and left the cube and continued on her way. Andrew, with disbelief, watched her go.

"Now, Mr. Wheeler, will you be as kind as to put your finger of the document?"

"Why? What's gonna happen?" How'd you do that by the way? Did Nancy even know what was going on, or that you were even here?"

Cadwallader looked at Andrew with an expression of impatience and mild irritation. His expression was, of course, perfect, thought Andrew.

"Mr. Wheeler if the blood on this contract is not yours, as you claim, then nothing will happen. However, if it is your blood on the contract, we will both know immediately. To resolve this situation to the satisfaction of us both, please be so kind as to repeat the process your lovely coworker just demonstrated."

Andrew wanted to say no. He wanted to tell Cadwallader to get the hell out of his cube, and out of his workplace! But after witnessing the mornings events, Andrew had a suspicion such a course of action was not going to work out as he might have wanted. Andrew wanted to end the whole stupid situation and get to work. He figured the only course of action he had was to put his hand over the paper as Mr. Cadwallader said. So, he did.

"What the crap!"

As Andrews' hand passed close to the blood spot, the paper came up off the desk and stuck to his finger. He tried to shake it off, but it was stuck.

Not just stuck, but stuck. Andrew grabbed at the scroll with his left hand not caring if he tore it. He pulled at the scroll. But it didn't tear or rip. It did not let go. This stuck scroll was worse than the great Crazy Glue mishap.

"Whatever joke this is I'm done! I don't know how you are doing this but stop it now. I'm calling the building security. "

Cadwallader didn't flinch. He sat there regarding Andrew. He sat there with a quiet, perfect smile. There was just a hint of white teeth contrasted against his dark lips.

"There we have it, Mr. Wheeler. There can be no denying the result of the approximation test. The blood on that contract is yours. If you were to doubt it still, we could test every person in this office. We could test every person in this building. We could test every person on this entire planet. And at the conclusion, you would find this contract will only stick to you. But neither do I have the time, nor the inclination for such and endeavor. It is time to go, being blunt in my manners and speech."

Cadwallader stood and looked down at Andrew who was still trying to get the contract off his finger. Andrew amazed, watched as Cadwallader, with ease and somehow impeccable style, simply took hold of the scroll, and it dropped from Andrew's finger. Cadwallader then rolled it back up and slid it into the inside pocket of his suit coat where it disappeared once again.

"Come along Mr. Wheeler; we shall now be on our way."

Andrew then decided it was time for the second option. Which probably should've been the first option he chose that morning when all of this began, instead of trying to be polite. Andrew stood as nonchalantly as he could muster and took a deep resolute breath. He looked around the office noting where people and objects were currently positioned. Then Andrew ran.

# 5.

Andrew's first action was to knock over the table next to his cube stacked full of miscellaneous office supplies. He pushed it over as he bolted from his cube. The table dumped the contents of notepads, pens, pencils, and envelopes, all of which landed in front of the opening to his cube. Andrew hoped that mess would slow down and distract Cadwallader long enough for Andrew to make it to either the elevator or the stairwell.

As fortune, would have it, the elevator had just arrived, and other workers were exiting. Andrew jumped in and pressed the close button. He quick looked as the door was closing, but Cadwallader was not in sight. Andrew had made it! Of course, Cadwallader would expect him to go to the ground floor and out onto the street. But, Andrew knew he could exit on the fourth floor, go down the one flight of open stairs, into the skyway system, and make his escape that way. It was always good to know all the exits thought Andrew. In the meantime, he had pressed the buttons for the fifth, fourth, third, second, and first floor.

He didn't care how much that particular action may have irritated anyone. He was trying to escape from whatever was going on, and whoever the Cadwallader person was.

Andrews' heart was still racing as the elevator stopped, and the doors began to open to the fifth floor. Just in case it was needed, Andrew had clenched his fists and was ready to fight and run. The elevator doors slid apart. There was no one there. He jabbed at the door close button. The fourth floor was the same, only this time he did exit. He went down the hallway to the staircase looking at everything, and especially everyone, around him the entire time. There was no one. Well, there were lots of someone's, but not *the someone*, specifically the Cadwallader dude, looking for him. Andrew tried to slow his pace and walk normal, but he found it was difficult. Fortunately, the skyway was

busy with morning rush-hour foot traffic. With the hustle and
bustle of the crowd around him, Andrew didn't look as out of place
as his somewhat furtive demeanor might otherwise have been at
other times of the day.

Andrew knew he needed a place to hide out. He walked
the two blocks following the skyway system. The network of
walkways led him through several buildings above the streets until
he came to the Nicolet Avenue exit. He knew there was a coffee
shop on the other side of the plaza. Because it was still early
enough in the morning, the place would still be busy with people.

As Andrew walked across the mall, there was dirty faced
homeless man dressed in the remains of what might have been a
winter jacket. He was standing next to a broken looking box,
holding a sign asking for donations. For some reason, and Andrew
didn't know why he paused. Andrew took a dollar from his pocket
and dropped it into the box.

"God bless." was the invocation given to him by the man for his
good deed.

Andrew started to feel maybe some good karma, and a little
blessing even from a homeless guy would be appreciated about
now. He walked into the coffee shop. The place was almost filled
to capacity with patrons. Most of the people were waiting in line
for their takeout order. Others looked more like lazy hipster
college students. The majority of them were monopolizing all the

tables and outlets just to use the free Wi-Fi. Andrew didn't care about any of the minutiae; he only cared about getting away. In case, by some stupid chance Cadwallader might be looking around the area for him, Andrew decided to hide in the one place where no one should be looking. He made his way to the toilet stall.

Andrew's luck held it was empty. He thought maybe giving the bum a dollar did help? He went into the stall, shut and locked the door. Not caring about sanitation at the moment; he sat down on the toilet and tried to calm his nerves. He took several deep breaths to try and steady his shaking hands. How had his day that had begun so normal, so routine, in just a couple hours have gone so wrong?

*"How wrong had it become,"* Andrew mentally asked himself? It had gone so wrong that he was, at that moment, hiding in a coffee shop toilet stall. Hiding from a man who claimed Andrew had sold his soul to the Devil. Now that person was there to collect Andrew's soul. How the Cadwallader person did the trick with the paper, Andrew didn't know and didn't care. He just wanted the day to end, even if it meant spending it right where he was, on the public toilet in the bathroom of a coffee shop.

He didn't want, whoever that Cadwallader person was, stalking him everywhere he went. *"Wait,"* thought Andrew, *"that's it! He's stalking me, and there is something I can do about it."* Andrew reached into his pants pocket and took out his phone.

When in trouble call the police.

Andrew touched the screen to activate the phone, and nothing happened. He held down the power button to restart the phone, and nothing happened. Andrew knew his phone was charged. He was sure of it because it worked because the Cadwallader person had called him on it earlier. When Andrew had been on the bus and Cadwallader pretended to be his mother. Then Andrew knew what was going on. He didn't want to believe it because the whole thing was just, well it was just unbelievable. But he couldn't deny something crazy was going on. Despite his irritation and anxiety and although he didn't want to admit it, fear; Andrew could only respond in similar fashion to Jerry Seinfeld when he would see his nemesis Newman: *"Cadwallader."*

The timing was perfect. Just as Andrew was making his mental exclamation, the door to the bathroom opened. Andrew leaned next to the metal walls. He made furtive glances through the separations in the metal panels in an attempt to see who had just entered. But the narrow field of vision didn't allow him to see anyone. He almost considered looking under the stall for shoes, when there were three sharp knocks on the stall door.

"Occupied, sorry," exclaimed Andrew.

The door opened despite the lock, and Cadwallader stood there looking at Andrew. Cadwallader wore a perfect expression of *I have better things to do than chase after you.* He was holding an odd-looking metal object. It appeared to be an oversized metal handcuff, with an oversized strange looking latch. There was a thin metal chain attached to the cuff. There were also odd squiggly lines etched all over the outside of the silver or pewter metal looking cuff. Andrew thought it looked like it had come out of a *Lord of the Rings* or *Game of Thrones* prop locker.

"Mr. Wheeler as patient a being as I am, even my level of courtesy and politeness has limits. Today you have certainly done your best to test them."

At that moment, Andrew wished he had taken the time to lower his pants. That was because his stomach was starting to make some very unpleasant noises. Although his stomachs hinted at revolt, Andrew's brain kicked into an adrenaline-fueled high gear. How had Cadwallader found him?

Andrew knew he hadn't been followed to the coffee shop. Now his phone wasn't working when it had been earlier. And, and he was hiding out in the bathroom of a busy coffee shop, and no one was coming in to use it. Not even the lazy, free WiFi using, hogging all the power outlets, hipster wannabe, college students. All of this wasn't right! Andrew was now becoming fatigued by the whole situation. The whole loony, crazy, wacked-out insanity of, of the situation and everything happening to him. His fatigue gave way to frustration. The frustration grew and became anger. Andrew without thinking, being fueled by his antagonism rose up and threw a hard punch straight at Cadwallader's face!

Where there should have been Cadwallader's perfect looking face, being violently punched by Andrew's very angry fist, there was nothing. Andrew connected with the empty air. Instead on Andrew's right side stood a calm, a perfect calm, looking Cadwallader. With a simple, quick movement, Cadwallader deftly put the cuff of the strange metal thing around Andrew's wrist. There was a very sharp snapping sound, and suddenly Andrews's right arm went numb and fell to his side. A moment ago, what was about to be a good old-fashioned ass whooping, quickly became something else. Now a weird metal handcuff thing was locked around Andrew's right wrist and arm. And instead of victorious exit from the toilet, he was now figuratively going into it. Either the weird metal handcuff thing was becoming heavier, or he was becoming weaker. Andrew could no longer hold up his arm. It became such that Andrew had to use his left arm to support his right.

"What is this thing? What have you done to me?"

Cadwallader watched as Andrew felt the need to sit back down again. Andrew for the second time that day began to wish he had lowered his pants before sitting down on the toilet. Everything was beginning to become dizzy, and he began to feel weak.

"Mr. Wheeler, due to your misbehavior, your lack of manners, and your pathetic attempt at fleeing, I have been left with no recourse.

Thus, I am withdrawing your soul here in the public restroom of this coffee shop. When discovered your body would appear as if to have suffered a form of stress-induced heart attack. You are, at this moment feeling the effects of the mortal coil. It is currently separating your soul from your body. Soon your soul form will be permanently bound to the coil until I release it. Mr. Wheeler, I will only release you when we arrive in Hell."

Andrew looked at Cadwallader with a frustrated desperation. This situation, this whole situation wasn't right; it wasn't fair. Andrew didn't know why this was happening, or what was going on. However, at that moment he was very sure of one thing. Andrew knew he was in fact, at that moment, dying.

"Should you have any last mortal words I would suggest you speak them now, for soon you will lose the capacity."

Andrew slouched on the toilet, struggling to keep himself upright.

"How…how did you find me?"

Instability and weakness continued to wreak physical havoc on Andrew. His strength continued to wane, and sitting was no longer possible. He slid from the toilet to sitting on the floor and leaning against the wall. The coil thing was becoming too heavy, his body too weak.

"Your blood is on the contract, Mr. Wheeler. There is no place on this planet where you could hide from me. Your blood will always lead me to you."

Andrew heard Cadwallader speaking, but the words started to sound like the adults from the old *Charlie Brown* television show, and all he actually heard was "wa wa wa wa." Andrew was becoming desperate; he had to do something. His soul was going to be removed from his body, his soul! Once extracted this Cadwallader person was going to take him to Hell! Hell, of all places!

Up to this point in his life, Andrew had been philosophically wrestling with the idea of should he feel bad about not going to church on Sundays instead of sleeping. Or if he was with Monica, other things. He was now forced to step past that paltry dilemma. Instead, he went right on over to learning both Heaven and Hell were real.

After being bitch-slapped in the face with that information, Andrew's iconoclastic epiphany continued with the absolute and undeniable fact of; he had a soul. Not only did Andrew have a soul but, he had without knowing how sold it for some unknown service which was rendered. Now the devil had come to collect his payment.

However, the person here was apparently not "The Devil" but some associate of sorts named Cadwallader. Even if he wasn't the actual "Devil" Andrew was certainly frightened enough that he wasn't sure if he could handle meeting the actual one. Which meeting the actual Devil was about to happen. Unless, in the next instant, Andrew figuratively pulled something out of his ass which could literally save it.

Cadwallader locked a smaller cuff at the other end of the chain to his wrist. Andrew then experienced the unique and terrifying sensation he had ever felt. Andrew felt his heart stopping. It became a labored forced beating like hard, single hammer strikes, against the inside of his rib cage.

"Parlay!"

Andrew was desperate and uttered the first word that flashed into his head.

"I beg your pardon, Mr. Wheeler."

"Parlay. I want a parlay, and you have to take me to someone, to talk this over. That's the rules of parlay."

Cadwallader did his unnatural snuffling laugh that made Andrews flesh, his dying flesh, crawl.

"Mr. Wheeler, parlay is only a silly word from an over-rated movie. It was used as a comical transition device to move the weak plot forward. It has no actual litigious advantage."

Andrew felt cold; his breathing was now shallow, forced. He felt his last gasping breath of air. His oxygen deprived brain made one last series of synaptic links. It was a last desperate series of events and memories were retrieved, processed, and constructed into a sentence. He could feel the burn of the cold metal band around his arm. He started to feel something pulling him upward as if he were a puppet on a string. What he said next, this would be his last desperate act. As the world went dark, with everything Andrew physically had left, he shouted his whispered last words.

"I request mediation with a third-party arbitrator to resolve this dispute."

Without warning, Andrew's lungs burned with air. His heart began to beat with the force of jack-hammer as blood began to surge once again through his body. After several gasping breaths, his breathing became easier, less labored. His heart began to slow its frantic pace, and he started feeling warmth in his fingertips. Cadwallader looked at him with flat dead eyes. In fact, at that moment Andrew couldn't be sure if they were real eyes.

"Mr. Wheeler if such a request is granted, whom do you wish to act as mediator? Since I will regard myself as the transgressor against whom you are seeking the mediation."

Andrew was still trying to get his body to work again. The sudden reperfusion of oxygen to his brain was making him both dizzy, and a bit nauseous. At the moment, Andrew was doing his best to keep his stomach from returning the morning oatmeal, banana, and coffee to the mouth. Although Andrew was very happy he had stopped the dying process; he was trying to figure out how he had done it. Andrew had become caught-up in all the physical and mental confusion of the situation. So, the first words spoken weren't necessarily in the order they should have been. In fact, they were words Andrew, under normal circumstances, probably never would have said at all. However, do to the unfortunate final conversation before almost dying; they were some of the last thoughts and words his brain had processed. Because they were, they lingered near the surface. They were, unfortunately, to be the first words to fall out of his mouth.

"The devil."

The effect of the words leaving Andrews' mouth resulted in a shock to his entire body. Similar to a defibrillating device on maximum charge. He was suddenly very much aware of everything around him, and the utterance, the mistaken utterance of those two words. Adrenaline once more flowed hard through his bod.y. The brain, realizing its fatal mistake, tried to rebound and provide a solution to get him out of it.

"No, wait. That wasn't right. I meant to say, um God. Yes, God. I want God to, ahh mediate."

Andrew knew it wasn't going to work. As he lay there on the bathroom floor, trying to bring life back to his almost dead body, he knew he had just messed up. His eyes once again were focusing as they should, and he could now clearly see Cadwallader standing over him. Cadwallader was looking down with the perfect smile of one who was sitting in the catbird seat. He leaned down slightly, unsnapped the metal cuff from around Andrews' arm, and in a calm, but adamant demeanor replied, "The first option is accepted, Mr. Wheeler."

Andrew felt the cuff snap from his wrist, and he suddenly felt brand new. He felt like an Olympic weightlifter, who had been standing on him while lifting weights, decided to step off his chest. It was too late now to take back his verbal blunder. Andrew felt like the proverbial saying of "out of the frying pan and into the fire." *Maybe this would still work out; maybe?*

Andrew wiped away the drool which had run down his face as he lay on the floor dying, or dead. Andrew wasn't sure which one it may have been and really didn't want to think about it. Cadwallader stood over him. He stared down at Andrew like he was an errant, misbehaving child.

"Mr. Wheeler, I have agreed to your request for arbitration. From this time forward I will trust you will honor your request with respect. You will cease in your futile attempts to flee. Also, matter the ruling you will from this point forward, release and relinquish all further claims and appeals. Do you give me your word?"

Andrew stopped feeling great and mentally processed what Cadwallader just said. Andrew knew this situation; this whole I sold my soul to the devil thing was a mistake. It was just a matter of getting this Cadwallader or somebody else to listen, even if that somebody were going to be the devil. Andrew thought, at least, he would get his day in court to plead his side of the case.

"Cadwallader, can I be sure the devil will be impartial and not automatically rule against me because, well because he's the devil and evil and all that?"

Cadwallader for the fist time since Andrew had met him showed a not perfect, but natural reaction and emotion.

"Mr. Wheeler, Satan is always fair."

Andrew was able to sit up against the wall now. He was still shaky, but his strength was returning. To his pleasure, the stomach decided to keep the breakfast where it was. Andrew sat there on the floor of a toilet stall. He preferred sitting on the floor of a public bathroom much better than lying on it as he had just been. Andrew realized dying was nothing like he had expected. Especially dying as he had just been doing, in a coffee shop bathroom stall, with a weird metal handcuff around his wrist. And dying of a heart attack anywhere close to a toilet; people might have mistaken him for a wannabe Elvis impersonator.

Even if he did have to talk to the Devil, at least he would get a chance to present his side of the situation. Part of this chance hinged on what Cadwallader had said was true. As ludicrous as it sounded to Andrew, that Satan was always fair; because Andrew seemed to recall his Sunday school teacher and the church minister, well all of humanity saying things to the contrary. But his memory of the situation was back twenty some odd years ago when he was eight, and his parents forced him to go to church. Maybe he should have paid better attention back then. The problem, well his problem anyway was, you can't force a person to do something and then expect them to remember anything said other than goodbye.

However, as he sat there willing his almost dead body to return to life, Andrew realized he had no other choice. Cadwallader was standing there staring at him, waiting for Andrew to respond. Andrew had to do a mental double take; Cadwallader had been wrapping up the handcuff thing, and now it was nowhere to be seen. Where did it go? But he put aside the crazy magic trick and gave Cadwallader what he wanted.

"I give my word." Although the crazy now missing handcuff had not again been put around his wrist, Andrew would have sworn he heard it snap shut. Once again his heart skipped a beat.

# 6.

Cadwallader opened the door to the stall and gestured to Andrew. "Shall we be on our way?" Cadwallader's tone suggested t wasn't so much a request, as it was a course of action.

Andrew used his hand against the wall to steady himself, He stood on still somewhat shaky legs and exited the bathroom stall. Andrew allowed Cadwallader to guide him from the coffee shop; none of the waiting customers, or the lazy, free wifi using outlet-hogging wannabe hipster college students, seemed to notice their passing. Once outside, they walked the short way to the street where Cadwallader's limo was illegally parked, but no one seemed to notice or care.

The back passenger door opened despite no one opening it. Or at least no one Andrew could see. Just like the first time he looked inside that limo, which was probably less than two hours ago, the inside was inky black, and no light prevailed. Cadwallader gestured for Andrew to enter.

"Mr. Wheeler, guests are always first."

Andrew turned and looked at Cadwallader with an expression of "*gee, thanks a lot.*" Not knowing what to expect, he stooped down and climbed into the blackness. They rode in silence. Andrew tried to look around inside the limo, but there was the weird, pervasive black fog thing going on. Andrew didn't understand how it worked and decided not even to try. All he could see was Cadwallader sitting across from him, and that was it. Even the door he used to enter the limo was no longer visible. He wasn't even sure if what he was sitting on was a seat? He could see his legs and feet, but what was under them was nothing but impenetrable darkness.

Andrew wasn't sure how long they were in the limo, or even if it was moving. Despite the baffling and unnerving nature of being in such a situation, Andrew had to admit to himself it was a *smoove* limo. It fit the personality of this Cadwallader person or being, or whatever he was.

The silence of the ride also gave Andrew time to contemplate the epiphany which came to him while dying in the bathroom. The first item was, he could not under any condition deny, he was in some serious shit. This shit wasn't the normal speeding ticket brush with the law sort of shit. This shit wasn't; I screwed up at work sort of shit. This shit wasn't even close to the stupid High School antics of getting busted while mooning the afternoon English class sort of shit. This shit was on a biblical level.

Those thoughts led to the second item of internal dogmatic contemplation. Andrew had a soul. It was now a fact to him. It couldn't be denied or rationalized away. It also meant if he had a soul, then everything else about it was also real. There was a Heaven. There was a Hell. And if there were a Heaven and Hell, there was also a God and a Devil. He didn't want to accept those hard facts. But he had too because he was, in fact, going to meet the Devil.

Also, there was no way he could deny he was, at that very moment, riding in a car which had no internal light of any kind. Yes, he could see his body with absolute clarity, right down to the laces on his shoes. But he could not see the floor under them. He couldn't see the seat on which he was sitting. Pretending this wasn't happening was not an option because it was happening and he had better figure out how to resolve it. Because, when the car stopped at wherever they were going, Andrew had to talk with the Devil, and his soul was on the line.

Apparently, they had arrived, and the car had stopped. For without any warning or indication, the passenger door opened. Andrew had the odd pleasure of seeing the outside world through the pervasive darkness. It reminded him of looking at the world through heavy tinted welder's glass. The midmorning sun shone onto the limo, even right at the open door, but there was no illumination of the interior. Andrew could only see himself, Cadwallader, and the sepia-tinted world outside the open door. Einstein would've had kittens.

"Please, after you Mr. Wheeler."

Cadwallader gestured for Andrew to exit. Andrew stepped out onto the sidewalk. They were in front of a plain-looking office building, in a plain looking part of town. Andrew wasn't sure if they were still in Minneapolis, over in St. Paul, or some suburb in-between. Nothing looked familiar. There were no street signs or building numbers. There was nothing which might have at least given him a suggestion of their location.

"What're we doing here?" asked Andrew with casual indifference and asperity.

"What are we doing here Mr. Cadwallader, would not only be the correct but also, the more social and polite phrasing of your question."

Andrew gritted his teeth. Cadwallader was still all about being polite and with good manners. Then part of his limo ride contemplation came back to Andrew, and he thought about it a moment. He, Andrew Jackson Wheeler, unequivocally right at that very moment was entangled in some *no kidding this is some really serious supernatural shit sort of on a biblical level* situation. And maybe, just maybe, when in such a situation, perhaps not upsetting those around him might be the correct action to take. So instead of acting like a petulant ill-mannered child, perhaps being a polite and well-mannered adult might not be a bad thing to do. With a slight, forced, internal attitude adjustment, Andrew started again.

He turned to his right, where Cadwallader was standing after getting out of the limo.

"Pardon me: Mr. Cadwallader, what are we doing here?"

Cadwallader gave Andrew a perfect smile of approval.

"That would also be acceptable phrasing. To answer your question, although I feel it will not initially be to your liking; this is where we will be depositing your physical body while we go to Hell.

Andrew thought he might have peed himself a little. "Hell!?!?"

"Yes, Mr. Wheeler. Hell, is where the arbitration is to take place. You didn't expect Satan to come to you, did you?"

Cadwallader started walking towards the office building expecting Andrew to follow. But Andrew's feet suddenly didn't' want to move. He also realized except for those bodily functions he had no direct control over; all the rest seemed to stop. Although he wasn't sure, he thought maybe, for several seconds his heart had stopped, again. A sudden cough and gasping reflex told him he had stopped breathing. So maybe his heart decided to stop again as well.

He was very happy his sphincter decided to clench, instead of relaxing.

"I'm going to Hell?
Cadwallader realized Andrew was no longer beside him. Instead, he was several feet behind, leaning against the limo, and looking semi-catatonic.

From the perfect and smoove way Cadwallader handled it, Andrew was certain Cadwallader had dealt with similar situations before. He hoped today's situation; his situation would be a bit different. Because, besides the soul stealing and body killing handcuff thing, and the crazy, not-obeying-the-laws-of-nature limo, Andrew was certain Cadwallader had other methods at his disposal. Any of which he could use in difficult situations. Andrew was very, very pleased Cadwallader maintained his civility and temper. With the calm of a lazy summer day, Cadwallader strolled back to Andrew. Andrew, who now had a bit of drool starting to run from the corner of his mouth.

"Mr. Wheeler, I must politely insist you keep up with me. We are on a schedule. Please believe me when I say to you, to keep Satan waiting is not an action you wish to undertake."

Andrew looked at Cadwallader through vacant eyes and a vapor locked brain. But one sentence made its way into the last bit of his conscious mind and stuck there, "We don't want to keep Satan waiting."

Andrew's brain recovered itself and started rebooting the rest of his bodies systems.

"...and if you feel like you might vomit or soil yourself please inform me before, rather than after the act."

It was Cadwallader finishing whatever he had been saying.

"I'm..." Andrew was trying to get his mental feet under himself again. He took several very necessary deep breaths, and physically and mentally steadied himself.

"I'm sorry, about that, Mr. Cadwallader. I guess, I just freaked out a little bit, there for a moment or two. I should be good now."

Cadwallader regarded Andrew for a moment. Andrew thought Cadwallader's expression might have been a hint, a small one, but just a hint of compassion.

"Very well Mr. Wheeler. If you feel you will no longer suffer from these mild paroxysms, we shall be on our way."

Cadwallader walked up the several gray marble steps to the building door. He opened the left side of the glass double doors, held it open, and gestured for Andrew to enter. As Andrew walked into the building his footsteps, even with rubber soled shoes, echoed down the vacant hallways. There were no people, no desks, no plants, no chairs, no tables, no anything in the lobby of the office building. The lights were on, and that was the only indication the building was occupied in any fashion.

Andrew wasn't sure if the doors were locked or not; Cadwallader didn't use a key to open them. Instead, Cadwallader just pulled them open. But the world worked just a bit different where Cadwallader was concerned so that Andrew couldn't be sure about the locked or unlocked doors question. Cadwallader led him forward to a wall with an elevator bank. The elevator obviously worked because the door dinged, and opened as soon as Cadwallader stepped in front of it. Again, Andrew noted Cadwallader's world worked a bit different because no one had pressed the button for the elevator. It just opened on its own.

Cadwallader extended his right arm gesturing for Andrew to precede him into the elevator. Andrew pondered the act of courtesy with imaginative suspicion. Maybe, Andrew thought to himself; Cadwallader thought he would try and run away again.

He would trick Cadwallader into the elevator, and then make a break for the doors. Andrew knew such a hackneyed plan wouldn't work. The first reason was that he didn't know if the building doors were unlocked, or if they would even open for him. A second reason the plan would fail was that he had no idea where he was. Sure if, if he made it outside where would he try to go? Just run down the street screaming like a madman?

There was one detail that kept Andrew from than just considering the fleeing option. Andrew had given his word to this Mr. Cadwallader. Andrew had promised that he wouldn't try to escape again. Besides he had already attempted that option, and it was eminently obvious from the morning's incident in the bathroom stall, he couldn't escape even if he wanted. There was nothing more he could do than to try and remain calm, stay cool, and remember he had not, in fact, sold his soul to the devil. Up to this point in his life, Andrew hadn't even realized such an act was possible. He had just thought it was some weird script plot and sketch from the old *Muppet Show* when Alice Cooper was a guest star.

"Please Mr. Wheeler, guests are first."

Andrew couldn't help but be terrified and flattered.

"Thank you, Mr. Cadwallader."

"It is my pleasure, Mr. Wheeler."

As they stepped in Andrew turned to face the door. It was the normal reflex action taken by everyone when stepping into an elevator. Cadwallader did not. He instead turned to face the back-left corner. Cadwallader stepped into the elevator and took his place. The doors slid shut and became a seamless wall. The elevator started to move despite no button being pressed for a floor, or plane of existence. In fact, there was no panel with buttons to be pushed. After the door closed, Andrew wouldn't have known there ever was a door. Currently, Andrew thought there was nothing in the now seamless cube except him and Cadwallader.

"Excuse me Mr. Cadwallader but, well, how? Where?"

"Mr. Wheeler, please control your thoughts and voice. Satan will no more enjoy rambling participles than I. First, always compose your thoughts into a coherent and eloquent sentence. Then and only then, speak in an articulate and respectful manner."

All Andrew could muster in response was "Yes, Sir."

"Now to answer your poor attempt at a question; I choose where this elevator goes as it is my personal elevator. Ah, we have arrived."

# 7.

The elevator stopped moving. Andrew waited and watched for the seamless wall to separate; to once more become the elevator doors, but they did not. Instead, there was a sound behind him where Cadwallader was standing and facing. The back left corners of the elevator started moving. The walls, the roof, and floor began to open. Andrew turned and watched as the large square panels folded along unseen axis points and became part of an extraordinary looking room which started to make Andrew feel dizzy. Was he looking at Hell? Because it certainly didn't look like any Hell Andrew had heard of.

Andrew was looking at the inside of what could only be, something like a mind-bending, five thousand sided, icosahedral polygonal sphere thing. Andrew thought he was standing inside a diamond and looking out. The geometry was impossible, well at least to him anyway. The walls, or facets, had an odd crystalline glowing light the likes of which Andrew had never seen or experienced. He was confident no other living person had either.

As Andrew was trying to guess how many sections or facets there were, he started to hear an odd humming sound. At first, it was very low and almost inaudible, but Andrew knew he heard it. Didn't he? Andrew determined there was a sound because not only did hear it; he could also feel it. The sound was not just sound, but there was also an impression that came with it. It wasn't just an impression. Andrew realized it was an emotion. Then, after the emotion, Andrew felt an actual physical sensation. The humming wasn't like the thud of a deep bass sub-woofer. This humming he was hearing wasn't just auditory, but it was also substantial, tangible. The sound, the light, the weird physical sensations were all becoming too much for him. Andrew had to reach for the walls. He hoped the walls were still walls. Because, at the moment, for all he knew, he might have been standing on the walls and steadying himself against the floor or ceiling. Then there was the voice of Cadwallader. The sound of Cadwallader's voice was able to negate the nausea Andrew was feeling because of the room.

"I suggest you focus on the desk, Mr. Wheeler. It will help with vertigo you are currently experiencing."

Andrew hadn't noticed the desk at first because of the aberrant geometry and the peculiar sound of the room. He forced himself to look beyond, or behind, or through the room, unsure of how the physics of the room worked. But once Andrew was able to focus his attention, there it was. As desks went, it wasn't much of one. Especially a desk that resided in the center of the room of inconceivable geometry, it was by Andrew's imaginative and rational mind, very disappointing. The desk seemed out of place for being in Hell.

What Andrew thought should have been a grand throne looking thing, imperious in stature made of gold covered diamonds; this one was not. The desk looked like it was previously used, bulk purchased government surplus office furniture. It had the hard, sharp corners of folded sheet steel on which a person would routinely scratch and cut themselves. It was covered with a nineteen fifty's enamel gray paint, probably only used for just those desks and U.S. Naval ships. Andrew was sure all of the drawers protested with a hideous metal screech when opened and closed. And of course, one of the drawers would refuse to open or close without some level of physical exertion and verbal threats. The desk was so mundane that it was completely absurd. The harder Andrew concentrated on the desk picking out the little details; the more his brain calmed down. Soon the room didn't seem quite so impossible.

"Mr. Cadwallader, where are we? Is this Hell?"

"This is not Hell Mr. Wheeler. We are in Purgatory."

"Purgatory?"

"Yes, to repeat, Purgatory. Are you familiar with the general human religious concept of this place?"

Andrew was still standing inside the elevator and unsure what he should do, or how to respond. He vaguely remembered something about Purgatory. These memories were from long ago church when he was younger, fidgety and didn't care. There were also references to Purgatory from various works of fiction he had been required to read in college. In the books such as Dante's Divine Comedy. He also remembered a reference to Purgatory in books he enjoyed reading in the Fantasy genre. It wasn't that the classics were bad; they were just boring and could become tedious. Andrew felt they needed more swordplay and young buxom maidens.

So yes, Andrew sort of knew about Purgatory. Although it was in a round-about religious, but mostly in a non-religious way. Andrew was still concentrating on the desk, and attempting to fight the allure of the veridical Purgatory. He didn't trust himself to answer Cadwallader's question verbally, so he just nodded his head in an affirmative manner. However, Andrew failed to notice that Cadwallader had stepped out of the elevator and standing and into the geometric room of Purgatory.

"Mr. Wheeler, your silence suggests you answered my question with an absent-minded affirmative nod of your head. However, before doing so, you should have first noted where I was standing."

Andrew shook the cobwebs from his head. He struggled to keep his focus only on the government surplus looking desk. But the room fought him. It kept grabbing at the edges of his eyes, ears, and mind with its song.

"Sorry, Mr. Cadwallader. It's this room. It's this or Purgatory place. I feel like I'm being pulled off into every direction at once. It's hard to keep on the topic."

Even that brief sentence caused Andrew to begin to lose focus. Then without warning, as if out of nowhere, Cadwallader appeared in front of Andrew. Cadwallader's abrupt appearance made Andrew's heart skip a beat, and also made him lose his assiduity of the desk. Andrew's concentration broken, Purgatory once again began to tantalize and confuse his mental reality and physical senses. Andrew noticed Cadwallader now standing in front of him, but he was at the moment having difficulty seeing or hearing him.

"I understand our dilemma. Your physical being is not quite capable of understanding what is before it. However, your spiritual being, your soul, is capable of not just cognizance of the room, but also what lies beyond it. Do you understand Mr. Wheeler? A simple nod of your head will suffice this time if that is all you are capable of providing?

Andrew gave a brief turning of his head in a negative response. Doing this caused the room around Cadwallader to shift. The color spectra and the humming changed in response to the movement of Andrew's head.

"Very well, I will explain the situation for you in terms you should be capable of comprehending."

Andrew nodded up and down. In fact, Andrew wasn't sure if he had ever stopped moving his head. He had become enthralled by the room. It now seemed like a living blur of color, and an oscillating crescendo of sound.

"Purgatory is a transition area between life stages. Where we are now is the first room of Purgatory. From here there are the other layers of existence. The balanced results of your physical flesh life will dictate your next step in existence. Because this is the first room, your physical body can enter and remain here for a time without permanent damage."

The words, permanent damage, did not sound appealing to Andrew. He tried to keep his focus on Cadwallader. The problem was Cadwallader kept moving his arms and hands as he explained Purgatory. These actions caused psychedelic color waves to swirl about him.

"But, should your body venture any further than this room, it would not survive. Thus, we are going to leave your flesh body here for the time being, while we go to Hell."

Andrew started to get the woozy feeling again. He wanted desperately to sit down. Since he was still in the elevator, he figured the floor would do nicely. Andrew's knees started to win, and he unceremoniously plopped onto the ground.

"Mr. Wheeler, please take a moment then."

Andrew stared at Cadwallader's perfect looking shoes and made a nodding grunt of acknowledgment. It was as if Cadwallader decided that he gave Andrew permission to sit down, instead of Andrew just doing it. The colors were now reaching out and were all around him. He also felt the weight of the humming. The sound wrap around the outside, and the inside, of his body. Then the cocoon of light and sound were torn asunder by Cadwallader's voice.

"Take a deep breath and hold it for a moment, Mr. Wheeler."

Andrew did.

"Now exhale and hold the pause."

Again, Andrew did as Cadwallader told him to do.

"Now repeat the process several times."

Andrew continued the simple process of breathing, and soon he started to feel better.

"You hadn't noticed Mr. Wheeler, but for a moment you forgot to breathe for a moment. The effect of Purgatory upon you if greater than I had anticipated. If you have recovered, please rise and move to stand behind me. When I start to walk forward, you will do the same. When I stop, you also will stop. Keep your focus only on my back and the trip should be without further incident. Do you understand?"

Andrew nodded his head in an affirmative manner, his strength returning now that he was breathing again.

"When we get to the desk, I will take out the chair for you to sit upon, please do."

Andrew nodded yes again.

"Are you ready then Mr. Wheeler?"

Andrew stood, and was finally able to speak again, "Yes, I guess so."

Andrew stepped into place behind Cadwallader. As he did so, Andrew thought Cadwallader suddenly seemed taller and much broad shouldered than before. Andrew tried not to think about it. He tried not to think about anything other than concentrating completely on Cadwallader's back. Andrew didn't have any inclination to repeat the mind and sensory altering Purgatory-style acid trip from which he had just come down.

To help prevent such a reoccurrence, Andrew raised his hands and cupped them along each side of his head and eyes. He made them into stop-gap blinders blocking his peripheral vision. He hoped this would help to keep the crazy purgatory room from again distracting him. Andrew also tried to make his thumbs reach his ears, to try and block out the sound. But they just weren't long enough. He had to keep his focus and block out whatever it was about the room that scrambled his brains. The last thing Andrew wanted to do was to kick or step on the back of Cadwallader's leg or foot because he didn't stop in time.

"Let us proceed then."

Andrew followed Cadwallader as they stepped forward out of the elevator and into Purgatory. Andrew thought the effect of the room had been bad before when he was still inside the elevator. But to actually be inside Purgatory was even worse.

Andrew squinted his eyes and pulled his hands in tighter to the point where he could only see a small portion of Cadwallader's perfect black suit coat. But still, the pervasive lights and sounds assailed him on all levels. His body and senses assaulted by the full effect of the weird otherworldly sounds, but without the visual portion of the sensation, he was able to maintain his concentration.

Despite his attempts to ignore and block out everything, the strange sounds started to become like a Siren song. Some of the sounds became familiar, and he now could recognize them. It was like picking out a friend's voice over the verbal cacophony of a party. There were other sounds, which were alien, and unlike anything, he had ever heard. The song of the room started to become compelling. Andrew just had to uncover his eyes and look. There were flashes of possible images that grabbed at the corners of his vision. They tried to lure Andrew into looking at them. Andrew responded by closing his hands tighter around his eyes. Now all Andrew could see was a small section of Cadwallader's suit coat. Then Andrew felt something new. He could now feel everything. It was as if emotions, sound, light, all had become physically tangible.

Andrew thought he could, in fact, be punched in the stomach by laughter; that love could crush his heart. Andrew also thought he could now be scared to death by fear. He fought the allure and cupped his hands even tighter than before around his eyes. He tried to block out the sound. He kept focus only on Cadwallader's back. Andrew desperately wondered how much further it would be to the desk?

"Remain focused Mr. Wheeler; we are almost to our goal. Please be prepared to stop."

Andrew was for the second time that day thankful for the sound of Cadwallader's voice. It was able to counter the pervasive sensory miasma of the room. Then Cadwallader stopped. Andrew was, with success, able to do the same without stepping on or kicking Cadwallader. There was a sudden pressure against the back of his knees and legs as if something were pressing against him.

"Mr. Wheeler, please sit down. The chair is right behind you, as you can now feel."

Andrew wasn't sure how that worked. Cadwallader was not only still in front of him, but also behind him? Andrew decided it was best not to question, but to act as instructed and sit down.

Cadwallader stepped away, and the total and vast enormity of Purgatory assaulted Andrew. He was confident if not for the chair he would have fallen down, or up, or sideways, or every direction at once because in that room it probably would have been possible. Andrew's mind, body, his everything began to hum with the colors and vibration; he succumbed to the seduction of Purgatory's song.

"Stephen Hawking's gonna love this place."

Cadwallader's voice echoed out from somewhere, and Andrew thought if he were able to reach in the right direction he would have been able to grab the words in his hands.

"Mr. Hawking will never see this room, Mr. Wheeler. It is here only for problem situations, similar to the one in which you are currently embroiled."

Andrew hadn't realized he had spoken out loud. He thought he had been just saying it in his head. Or maybe he had said the words in his head, but they escaped using a different way other than his mouth. But once again Cadwallader's voice was greater than the Song, and it freed Andrew from Purgatory's Siren grip.

"Oh sorry, I guess I didn't realize I spoke out loud. I thought I was just thinking it."

"Yes Mr. Wheeler, I understand. This next part will seem odd to you, but please do as I instruct. By doing so, your confusion caused by Purgatory will be negated. Please put your hands on the desk."

Andrew hadn't realized he had slid the chair forward, but he was indeed sitting at the desk. Andrew didn't fight the overall oddness of the situation. He only wanted to resolve his mental confusion. So he reached out and put his hands on the desk.

"Palms down please Mr. Wheeler." Cadwallader's voice was a knife cutting through Andrew's mental chaos.

Andrew turned his hand's palm down, and suddenly the room made sense. His combination of vertigo-nausea-confusion was gone, and he felt normal. In fact, he felt better than normal. He felt light and fast, and strong, and smart; he felt like how Superman is always described. Then Andrew realized he was standing over his seated body, and his world became vertigo-nausea-confusion again. As Andrew was once again trying to come to terms with his new situation, he noticed Cadwallader standing off to the side watching.

"Mr. Wheeler, I see you have vacated your biological body and are once again having problems. Is this situation such a foreign concept to you?

Andrew steadied himself for a moment, and his anxiety dissipated. The simple explanation of what was going on became fantastically clear to him. In fact, everything about the room seemed logical, and he didn't understand how he had missed it before.

"Mr. Cadwallader, I think, no wait, I do get it now. I understand all of this. How?"

Cadwallader smiled his perfect smile in a pleasing manner.

"Mr. Wheeler you are at this moment, not encompassed by your flesh. Despite your lapse in proper sentence structure. The soul functions more efficiently without being surrounded by your biological body."

"Then why do we have them?"

Andrew very much felt like having a long-term philosophical discussion with Cadwallader about the merits for and against the human physical flesh form. As part of the discussion, each of them would take a side and debate the other. When they finished, they would switch viewpoints and repeat the whole process.

"That, Mr. Wheeler is not my domain. My immediate purpose is to bring you to Satan for an arbitration ruling. However, before we proceed any further, you will need to make an adjustment. Please look at your seated body and think about it. Consider how you would normally perceive yourself when you look at your reflection in a mirror."

Andrew at first didn't understand what Cadwallader was asking him to do. Andrew was supposed to think about his body? He had to make an adjustment? Instead of doing as Cadwallader had said Andrew did the opposite. He looked at himself starting with what should have been his hands. Andrew wished he hadn't and had done what Cadwallader had told him. With his new and improved mental acuity, he understood the situation, but there was still a part of him that wished he hadn't looked down. Andrew was naked and sort of blurry or fuzzy looking. The new improved rational part of his brain explained the situation. The body was only a shell for the soul. Once the soul vacated the body, the soul did its' own thing until a new form was selected.

"Please Mr. Wheeler, we are on a schedule."

Andrew still a bit taken aback from his current appearance and all around nakedness took a calming breath. Did he still need to breathe? Or was it just an ingrained reflex he didn't know how to stop? Whether he needed air or not, Andrew found the idea of breathing and a calming breath worked. He looked at his body sitting there at the desk. Then thought about making his current amorphous body look like his old solid one. He concentrated on what he was wearing and how it all sort of felt, he guessed.

There was a subtle change, like a very mild electrical current, or static charge, over his body or soul. Andrew looked at his hands, and they once again became his normal looking hands. He looked down and saw he was once again wearing a pair of khaki's, and button down shirt. It was all so strange and new. He thought about changing his clothes to something more stylish when Cadwallader interrupted.

"Shall we go Mr. Wheeler?"

Cadwallader gestured for Andrew to move along with him. Andrew found the thought of meeting Satan was still a bit, well a bit frightening to him. But with his newfound mental clarity Andrew felt, no not felt, he knew he would be able to explain the situation to his advantage. He was Super Andrew. He was confident and strong. But that was before Cadwallader reached into one of the ethereal crystalline panels of Purgatory and opened it like a door. That was before Andrew took his first step into Hell.

# 8.

It wasn't what Andrew had expected. In fact, it was nothing like he had been told about or imagined it to be. The door opened, and there was nothing before him, literally nothing. Andrew looked at that darkness. He thought it was nothing like the darkness inside of Cadwallader's limo. Somehow, and Andrew didn't know how; the darkness before him was darker than in the limo. Andrew followed Cadwallader into a dark closet looking space. Cadwallader closed the door, and everything became something more than just blackness.

It wasn't that the dark was dark, it was also emptiness. Andrew thought of the closet he would hide in when he was a kid, playing hide-n-seek with his friends. In that situation, in that dark, there was still some light. He knew on the other side of the door was the world in which he was playing with his friends. Also, there was his family, and pets, and toys, and all those things that made his life, well, his life. But this was different. Where he stood now was not the sensory overload of Purgatory. This darkness was not the hiding closet from his childhood memory with a door that he could open and close whenever he wanted. Andrew wasn't filled with the usual anxious and exhilarating feelings of anticipation while waiting to be found. That maybe the seeker would find him and call "*It*" for the next round of the game.

This room, this hallway, this, whatever this was, was the absence of all of those things amplified. It wasn't empty; it was emptiness. It didn't lack hope; it was hopelessness. There was no love; there was only desperation. All of those positive emotions which had been part of Andrew's life were being stripped away. Andrew began to understand the nature of Hell; it was a great Absence. And Andrew was beginning to feel crushed by it. It couldn't have been more than several seconds by Andrews estimate when without warning a light broke through the overwhelming darkness. Cadwallader who could apparently move and see just fine had opened another door. With the opened door a flood of light streamed into the dark hallway. As the light cut through the darkness, Andrew started to feel the soul-crushing Absence recede into the shadow. Andrew turned to his right, and there was Cadwallader several feet away from him and waiting in an open illuminated doorway gesturing for him to come over. Andrew didn't think he had ever been so happy and relieved to be found.

"Mr. Wheeler, please be on your best behavior and manners. That is unless you would prefer Satan to refuse to consider your side of the arbitration."

They stood in what appeared to Andrew, to be a reception office. It was lavish, but not gaudy. It was tasteful with some simple art forms and pieces which Andrew didn't know or understand. But the room was certainly not something he would have expected to find in Hell. Especially an office so lavish and tastefully decorated. In fact, to be honest, Andrew didn't know Hell would even have an office. He had expected more caves, and lakes of fire, and other more biblical type depictions.

"Please wait here, Mr. Wheeler. Feel free to look about, but do not wander from this room. If you do, I cannot guarantee your safety." Cadwallader walked to a large oversized wooden looking door, knocked three times, opened the door, and entered the room.

Andrew remained in the reception area where Cadwallader had told him to wait. Andrew by his nature hated waiting. Being forced just to sit there, waiting for someone else to get around to seeing him. It was tedious. That was probably one of the reasons he rarely went to the doctor. But, at that moment, he relished in having to wait. Andrew needed a personal moment or two; honestly, Andrew needed several moments. After leaving the room or hallway or gateway, between Purgatory and where he was now. Andrew still felt emotionally scrambled and was dealing with the effects of what he termed the Absence.

Once he stepped out of the gate or passageway area and into the office Andrew's emotions, all of them and especially the good feeling ones, all returned at once. The resulting effect was a bit overwhelming. So, when Cadwallader had asked him to wait in the reception area, Andrew was, for the first time in his history of having to wait, happy to do so. As he regained his composure, Andrew started to look around the office area trying to take it all in. He was in Hell after all. He didn't have any plans of revisiting it, so it was best to take it all in now. Andrew was also mindful of Cadwallader's warning, to not wander off somewhere in Hell. After what he had just gone through to get to where he currently was waiting, Andrew knew he didn't want to experience whatever else may be out there.

But as Hell went, well at least a reception office in Hell, it was very much just like a person would find in a non-Hell reception office. There was a nice looking wooden if it was, in fact, wood, desk. The chairs were all wood with leather bound cushions. Again, the wood question came up. He also thought about what kind of leather the chairs were upholstered with and cringed a bit at his speculative imagination of the possibilities. The floor was carpeted with a red colored fabric with a gold latticework print which complemented the chairs and desk. There were rows upon rows of bookshelves which Andrew went over to inspect. One shelf was filled with classic literature by Voltaire, Plato, Tolstoy, Kafka, Keats, Dostoyevsky, Steinbeck, and Hemmingway, being able to identify those authors out of the many books.

The further curious inspection revealed the majority of the shelves were dominated with volumes and volumes of legal texts. In fact, there were so many leather-bound tomes, Andrew pondered the possibility that in front of him might have been the greatest law library in the world. Then Andrew remembered he wasn't in the world; he was in Hell. Andrew meandered from the book shelves. He was looking at a painting which could have been either Picasso or Dali when the office door opened and Cadwallader walked out.

"Mr. Wheeler, I have presented my details and findings to Satan. He has considered my side of our situation. He is now prepared to hear your argument. Please come in."

*"Said the spider to the fly."* Andrew bit both his tongue and inside lip to ensure he kept that expression to himself. One of the last things he wanted was for Cadwallader or, Heaven forbid, Satan to

hear his sardonic retort. He walked over to door Cadwallader was holding open and entered Satan's office.

# 9.

Even though Andrew expected the door to close behind him, the resulting sound startled him. Andrew was even more startled to not having Cadwallader standing next to him. Since the day began, it seemed Cadwallader had been stuck to him like glue. Now the one time it might have been nice to have Cadwallader there, at least for introductions or something, he leaves. Andrew wasn't sure what to do. So waiting where he was, seemed like a very good idea. He took a quick mental note of the office. It reminded him of something he had seen or read about, before but he couldn't place it.

Then Andrew noticed the desk somewhat offset to his left. Behind it sat, a man who Andrew had to guess was Satan. He looked like a fortyish human male with rugged good looks. From what Andrew could see, the man had normal looking short blond hair and white skin. Andrew had mentally prepared himself to see the stereotypical looking Satan. The demon being with burning red skin. His head that of a goat with oversized horns, a human body with goat legs with cloven hooves. Of course, he would have a long sinuous tail with a barbed end. The usual stereotypical Satan depicted in the movies or described in the Bible.

Instead, this actual Satan was wearing an impeccable suit which, somehow, made Cadwallader seem slovenly. Before seeing Satan, Andrew would have sworn no one wore a suit better than Cadwallader. Andrew stood by the door and with a nervous anticipation, waited for the man at the desk to acknowledge him. This man was looking down at a scroll, and Andrew was certain it was the contract for what claimed to be his soul. Not sure what he should do; should he try to introduce himself? Instead, Andrew opted to wait by the door. It wasn't bad being there. He figured it would be better than being over next to Satan. So, Andrew decided to maintain a passive voice and wait to be recognized. However, the length of time wasn't as long as Andrew thought it might have been. The man behind the desk looked up from the contract and over to where Andrew was standing.

"Mr. Andrew J. Wheeler I presume? Please come in old boy and have a seat. Don't just linger there by the door."

Satan had a curious accent. It was sort of British sounding but not as proper and Lordly as Cadwallader's. Satan's accent was a more common everyday person type. Andrew started to wonder if the English ran Hell. Having had Satan address him, Andrew could no longer passively hide. He turned and nodded in acknowledgment, and walked over to meet the ruler of Hell. Satan but rose a polite bit from his chair and gave Andrew a slight nod of his head. Andrew thought that must be Satan's way of greeting him. Satan gestured with his right hand to the two, high back leather covered chairs facing the desk. Since Andrew was being offered a choice, he opted for the one closest to the door.

"So, you sold us your soul and then claimed it wasn't you despite your signature and blood being on the document."

Andrew both nervous and excited immediately forgot the advice Cadwallader had given him regarding Satan. Andrew instead engaged his mouth before activating his brain.

"But I didn't' put my blood on the document, and I didn't sign it. I've never even seen that thing before today!"

Before the words finished coming out of his mouth, Andrew knew he had committed a serious breach of social etiquette. Satan sat straight in his chair, rested his hands on his desk and interlaced his fingers, and regarded Andrew with a cold piercing gaze. Andrew started to feel more uncomfortable than he had been if that were somehow possible. After an infinite-seeming brief pause, Satan relaxed his solemn posture and once again looked down at the document and continued.

"You were granted your expressed desire in exchange for your soul. You agreed to subsequently relinquish said soul when said contractual desired request was carried out. There is of course much more lawyer-esk legal jargon and clauses, but none of those are important to us right now."

Andrew wasn't sure if Satan had heard him make his blunt exclamation or not. Andrew was foolishly thinking about interrupting again. Then he remembered what Cadwallader had said about manners and decorum. He was to be on his best behavior if he wanted Satan to hear his side of the story. Andrew held his tongue, though he was sure his facial expression was speaking for him.

"Mr. Wheeler, may I call you Andrew? Let's try to keep this more relaxed and not so formal."

Andrew, unsure what to do or how to respond, he nodded his head in an affirmative up and down motion to Satan.

"Oh, come now Andrew, you can speak. I'm not going to bite your head off. I literally have others to do that for me."

Andrew wasn't sure if his soul had a heart, but whatever it had, it started to sink low.

"That was a joke, Andrew. Relax. Despite what you may have heard about me, I am here to be fair and listen to your side of this argument. After all, it was you who asked for me to mediate this conflict."

Andrew still couldn't believe he said that; even if he was just recovering from being almost dead! What manic asks for the devil to mediate a dispute?

"So please, relax, take a breath and tell me your side of this situation from the beginning. Leave out no detail; I want to hear it all."

Andrew paused a social moment to ensure Satan had finished speaking. Satan just told Andrew he wanted to hear Andrew's side of the story. Despite having a mouth which felt like it was full of cotton; which led Andrew to wonder, how could a soul still experience physical sensations and reactions? He took a breath, collected his thoughts. He built those thoughts into coherent sentences as Cadwallader had instructed him to do. Then Andrew worked up some saliva, cleared his throat, and began the story of his Thursday morning adventures.

"Which bring us up to where we are now sir."

Andrew finished. He hoped it wasn't too long or too much detail. Andrew even including a third-person style narrative about what he was thinking at the time. But Satan didn't stop him or wave him off. He just sat there listening intently, occasionally jotting down a note or two. He would sometimes even smile. It was an easy, casual smile. It was relaxing and friendly and made even more so by his soft blue eyes.

"Andrew, please call me Satan. There's no further need for dramatic formalities here. And please relax, try smiling; this isn't a hanging, yet."

Andrew didn't appreciate the hanging comment. However, it sounded sarcastic enough that he almost felt less terrified. Andrew took the advice he was offered and tried out a smile. It was a small nervous smile, but it was still a smile, and he started to relax.

"Okay. Thank you, Satan."

"There now much better. Andrew, please be so kind as to sign your name for me."

Satan slid a pen and piece of paper across the leather cornered blotter on his desk toward Andrew. Andrew was about to pick them up when he hesitated and looked at Satan. Satan smiled at Andrew and nodded his head in an approving manner.

"Very quick of you Andrew, a signature is part of what got you here. However, there is no need to worry about it this time. The signature is for comparison purposes only. I will destroy it once our business is completed. Place a signature using the dominate and then with your non-dominant hand, please."

Andrew picked up the pen with his right hand and signed once. Then using his left hand signed his name once more as best he could. He put the pen down and passed the paper back. Satan picked up the paper and looked at Andrew's signatures in comparison to the signature on the contract.

Satan took hold of the scroll and placed a curious metal looking ring over the blood spot. The color of the metal and the small markings on the ring reminded of Cadwallader's handcuff. He started to hope the bathroom situation was not about to repeat itself. Andrew didn't have too long to wait because Satan turned the contract to face Andrew passed it over to him.

"Andrew, would you please be so kind as to put the index finger of your right hand just a bit above the blood spot on the contract and leave it there for several seconds."

Andrew remembered the crazy approximation test thing Cadwallader had performed earlier that morning in Andrew's cube at work. He knew he had told Satan how the paper, the contract, jumped up off Andrew's desk and stuck to his hand. Andrew wanted to once again tell Satan about how Cadwallader had already done something like that and to ask why they were doing it again. Then Andrew remembered the withering stare Satan had given him the last time he interrupted. Besides, Andrew thought maybe things would be different this time. Maybe he would pass the test this time. Maybe the always perfect Mr. Cadwallader had done something wrong? But ultimately Andrew realized it probably wouldn't be a good idea to make argumentative comments, especially negative sounding ones to Satan.

Andrew held his finger directly over the dried blood spot and waited. He expected the contract to once again not wait for his hand to get there but fly up and stick to him. Or the odd ring to fly onto his finger and kill him like the handcuff did. Or maybe even something more dramatic, which would be the first two options but with lights, music, and fire. Andrew expected something on the scale of a biblical level event. But as Andrew held his hand waiting none of those imagined events occurred.

"And please now lift your hand straight up."

Andrew did and stopped when it was becoming awkward to keep going unless he was to stand up. Satan regarded Andrew for a moment with a dead, emotionless expression. Andrew once again had the feeling of dread return as he sat there with his right hand stretched straight up in the air. He felt like he was back in school and really wanted to get the teacher's attention.

"Andrew, you can lower your hand, sit back and relax. I will now ask you to please stay seated where you are. I have to excuse myself for a moment."

Satan still very cordial and suave, that's how Satan seemed, suave. Cadwallader was smoove, a solid mash-up of smooth and suave. But Satan was pure unadulterated suave and that trumped smoove. But for that one moment, when Satan excused himself, he looked like he experienced a slight loss of his suave for a fraction of a moment. Satan politely pushed back his chair and stood up. He walked across the room to the door and left.

It seemed to Andrew the door had no more shut, the bolt sliding into its recess, and then Satan came back into the room. He was the personification of suave again. Satan walked from the door back over to the desk with a confident swagger. To Andrew, it looked like a part male model, and part mixed martial arts fighter. He walked back to his chair and sat down as if nothing had happened.

"Sorry about that. I had to make a slight adjustment; these little details can happen from time to time. I also apologize for having kept you waiting. However, I need to have Cadwallader here to witness my ruling."

Satan had no sooner spoke the name when there were three sharp knocks, the door opened, and Cadwallader entered. He walked across the room and stopped at a predetermined point about two feet from the front left corner of Satan's desk.

"Cadwallader I have heard both sides of the issue as presented by both you and the Mr. Andrew J. Wheeler we have before us."

Satan gestured to Andrew as if he were introducing Andrew to Cadwallader for the first time. Cadwallader, who had spent the morning chasing after Andrew, looked at him with a similar demeanor of, *"Nice to meet you."*

"After a signature comparison and performing the" the next sounds that came from Satan's mouth were not words. Instead, he made a piercing sound which made Andrew think of stereo speaker feedback. The horrible squelching sound when a microphone was put too close to a speaker. He involuntarily flinched back with a facial grimace from the sound of it, "test and this Mr. Andrew J. Wheeler failed it. I understand you administer the –once again the stereo feedback sound- test and it was conclusive, but do you agree the" –stereo feedback- and Andrew started to wonder if Satan was doing that on purpose, "test is the most accurate and incontrovertible?"

"Yes, Satan, I would concur the –stereo feedback- is the most accurate and incontrovertible."

Now Cadwallader was doing it. Andrew started to think his ears were going to bleed. Then he started to wonder if he had blood anymore? Was it possible for his soul's ears to bleed?

"As you can see, the right hand of the Mr. Andrew J. Wheeler we have before us does not have the Ring of –stereo feedback- on his right index finger. Neither is he adhered to the contract, nor to my desk. Do you agree with all of those facts?"

"Yes, Satan, I would also concur with those statements."

Andrew started to wonder what all the back and forth lawyer courtroom talk was all about. Then the metaphorical lightbulb turned on in Andrew's head: Satan just said Andrew's right hand was supposed to be stuck to the desk. Andrew looked down at his hand which was comfortably resting on his right leg and not stuck to either the contract or the desk. The proverbial lightbulb started to shine as bright as the sun, and Andrew started to smile. Because, when Satan said he had failed the test, it really meant Andrew had passed it. He had in fact not sold his soul as he had been saying all along and vindication was his. But this information again started Andrew thinking. If he hadn't sold his soul, that would mean someone else did. But who had stolen his soul and tried to sell it in place of their own, and how did they even do it?

"Well, then Cadwallader it would seem we have a problem because the Mr. Andrew Jackson Wheeler here with us now is, in fact, innocent."

Satan turned to Andrew with a whimsical smile and look of relief on his face mimicking the expression Andrew was now wearing.

"Yes, Andrew, we believe that you, in fact, did not sell your soul. Furthermore, until you are returned to your physical body you are now my guest and will be treated with such privilege."

Satan turned back to face Cadwallader. Not missing a beat Satan went from being the polite host and bringer of good news to being what Andrew determined to be the pissed-off ruler of Hell. "And someone is trying to cheat the Devil of his due!"

# 10.

Despite having just been vindicated and told he was a guest Andrew knew this situation wasn't over and he wasn't going anywhere until it was. Not only that, but Satan seemed, and Andrew was going to at the moment stick with his description, Satan seemed very pissed-off! Stuck where he was, in Hell, until the storm blew over, Andrew figured the best thing he could do was to keep his mouth shut and his head low.

Satan leaned back in his chair and strummed his fingers on the armrests several times. He then sat straight up at his desk again and looked around on it as if noticing everything there for the first time. He absently moved the pen Andrew had used to sign the paper from one spot, then to another, and then placed it back onto its holder. He then picked up the piece of paper which Andrew signed his name to for comparison reasons and ripped it in half and placed the two halves into a trash can by the desk. After completing that small task, Satan took a deep breath and turned his attention back to Cadwallader.

"I understand there has been a recent change in the system. I am not pointing fingers or laying blame on anyone's doorstep. However, I need to unwind this Gordian knot, and you good Cadwallader are my sword."

Satan tapped his finger twice on his desk. To Andrew that action must have been the cue, Satan was finished speaking. Because Cadwallader then addressed Satan.

"Sir, I have no excuse for this current situation, nor do I have the intention of fabricating one. I will submit, however, under this new system, this sort of cock-up was, unfortunately, inevitable. I understood better than most the rationale for a new system, but as I stated in the review meeting; with neither simplicity nor disdain does one cast away tradition. There is always a reason why certain actions and tasks are performed in an ascribed manner. As I further stated for the record the human adage of *if an item is not broken do not attempt to fix it.*"

Andrew couldn't be sure, but it seemed Cadwallader was pointing out to Satan that he, Satan, had somehow made a mistake. The weird identity theft situation Andrew was now a part of came about because of a change in Hell? More than that, to Andrew it seemed Cadwallader had been, and apparently still was, against the change. Yes, Satan had told Andrew he was a guest there in Hell. Not just a guest, but Satan's personal guest. But Andrew started to wonder, what would happen to him if a coup broke out?

Despite Andrew's building inner paranoia about a possible violent change and overthrow of leadership in Hell, nothing happened. Cadwallader remained standing where he stood, and he did it with perfection.

"I have full knowledge of all parties involved in our current conundrum, and with your permission, I will bring them to you for your review."

Satan did his thin-lipped smirk again; it seemed playful and boyish, yet at the same time there was sinister and evil vibe to it. His smile made Andrew think of a little boy looking at the wings of the fly he had just caught.

"Cadwallader you keep me honest with myself; you have always been my best!"

Although Cadwallader still stood at perfect attention, there seemed at least to Andrew, to be pleasing glow starting to emanate from Cadwallader at those words of praise.

"I want you to bring me the contract agent first."

# 11.

With impeccable timing for Satan had just finished speaking, Cadwallader presented a perfect bow and walked backward in a straight line from Satan's desk to the office door. When he reached the threshold of the door, he released his bow, turned and exited the office. As Andrew watched the way Cadwallader' exited the room, he thought such an action was many things, but mostly it was just weird. But later, he found out why Cadwallader existed in such a manner. After Cadwallader had left and the door shut Satan turned his attention back to Andrew.

"This should only be a moment. Of course, time is a bit different here, so moments aren't quite the same for you as they are for us.

Andrew was not surprised by that information. He was after all in Hell. There were probably lots of things comparably different between Hell and Earth; Andrew started to feel giddy at such a thought. Despite all his inner suspicions and curiosities, he wasn't inclined to press his amiable-seeming host with needless questions. Andrew sat with a quiet nervous posture and tried not to stare at Satan. Satan was sitting rather comfortably, leaned back in his oversized, upholstered dark leather chair, and gently rocking it. In return, Satan regarded Andrew back with a quite friendly smile.

"You are a passive one. The usual archetype is some pathetic soul crying and writhing as they obsecrate themselves before me."

Satan leaned further back and gestured behind him.

"Of course, I have the curtains opened for effect at that point. But even without a panoramic view of the magnificent entirety of Hell, they're just falling over themselves trying to make some feeble bargain. They start offering me anything to abrogate their contract. However, they always fail to realize they've already relinquished their only item of value to me. In context; they beg. They beg like dogs!"

Andrew couldn't, and didn't, want to imagine that situation. To be there in Satan's office begging for grace and mercy knowing there would be none given. That person, that soul would be cast into the great Absence of Hell for all eternity. Andrew sat in nervous silence across from Satan who once again did his smile smirk thing and added an eyebrow arch.

"Yes, go ahead. Talk. Ask a question or two. I give you permission if it would help. You probably won't say anything which will make me more upset than I already am."

Despite his situation, sitting in Satan's office in Hell, Andrew found he smiled back. He had to concede even if it were only to himself, despite what Christianity said about Satan, he did come across as a very charming fellow. Even with his diatribe about watching people grovel in his office.

"Well, sir. I am just doing my best to hold it together at this point."

Satan gestured his hand in a manner to stop Andrew.

"Please call me Satan. You don't work for me, yet."

The yet seemed ominous, but Andrew just took it in stride and after another calming breath continued, "Okay. Thank you. Satan."

He tried to think of something to say, but nothing would come to mind. As Andrew contemplated a conversation topic, something occurred to him. Andrew decided to jump in, as Satan did offer the opportunity to ask him questions. It was of course not every day a person gets to sit down and have a conversation with Satan, and Andrew was hopeful such an opportunity was not likely to happen again.

"Earlier you and Mr. Cadwallader were speaking in a normal voice. Then you started making screeching sounds that sounded like stereo speaker feedback. I am kind of curious why you did that."

Satan leaned back in his chair and stretched his arms and back.

"You mean -stereo feedback-?"

Andrew was certain his physical response would signify, yes that was the sound. Because the weird piercing screeching high volume sound made his shoulders rise and his head to sink. Andrew was physically trying to get the two body parts to meet. For one to cover the other to block out the sound before the ears started to bleed. But just to be sure Andrew also answered vocally.

"Yes, that would be the sound. What is that?"

"Hell Speak Andrew. It's the language of Hell. The actual words used have no translation in your language. You don't, after all, think everyone in all of Existence speaks your United States version of English, do you?"

Andrew in the privacy of his mind felt sort of naïve and stupid at Satan's comment. Thanks to movies and television show's he did sometimes forget there was more than one spoken language in the world. Despite having had High school French and College Spanish, Andrew still saw the universal language as English. It had never occurred to him Hell had a language. Of course, previous to today, Andrew never knew there even was a Hell.

"You have never heard Hell Speak before so there is no way for you to understand it. Think of it this way: The word Internet is a new word to all planes of existence. It has no comparable word in any other language outside of your English. So all non-English speaking people use the word internet. It is a universal English word which even I use because there is no similar word in Hell Speak. Now the word –stereo feedback- has no comparable or translatable word in any language spoken on your Earth plane, so it is the only word I have to use, just like Internet. You hear what I say, but don't understand it, just like you don't understand anything spoken in Khoisan."

Andrew understood the answer he just didn't know what Khoisan was.

"Khoisan?"

"Yes, the Khoisan language. It's spoken by specific tribes in Southern Africa, the San Bushman for example, and it uses clicking sounds as consonants. It's a shame you don't speak it. I find the language to be fun. Khoisan is an interesting language to listen to. Especially when the speakers are drunk. Or listening as one of them begs for mercy."

Andrew wasn't sure he liked the direction their conversation was once again going. He thought he would change topics before discussion options would start to include the various torture methods employed in Hell and stories about how much fun they were to do to people."

"If you don't mind me saying you have a very nice office. It is somehow familiar and yet not. I just can't seem to place why I think I've seen or read about it before."

Satan leaned back in his chair and gave a broad, toothy smile.

See if this helps".

Andrew noted a subtle change as everything in the room shifted in perception. Satan was still in his imposing chair, but things changed, he looked at Andrew and spoke in a perfect imitation of the classic line.

"*I'll make him an offer he can't refuse.*"

It was amazing! Because what Satan had just said was so amazing Andrew didn't give the next words out of his mouth full consideration before speaking them. Instead, Andrew blurted out a blatant stupidity.

"You have the office from *The Godfather*!"

Satan went from being Don Vito Corleone back to Satan in a blink. This new Satan wasn't the amicable Satan he had just hanging out with and socializing. This Satan wasn't even the perturbed Satan Andrew had been talking with before Cadwallader left the room. Although Andrew didn't think it was the current Satan was the full ruler of Hell Satan. However, it was close enough that Andrew understood why people whimpered and cried and begged. At that moment, Andrew started to contemplate those very options.

"I have the desk and office from *The Godfather*?"

Satan's voice had increased only slightly in volume, but it now had a resonance. It sounded as if there were several of him all speaking at the same time. He paused and stared at Andrew to the point where Andrew thought he was about to burst into flame or worse.

"The Supreme Overlord of Hell, in all of Eternity, modeled his office based on a paltry human idea?"

It was at that moment there were three sharp knocks on the office door, and Cadwallader and another person came in. However, they stopped just over the threshold of the door as Satan had not turned to acknowledge them. Unfortunately, Andrew realized Satan was still concentrating on him.

"You have until this next conversation is completed to contemplate what you just said."

Then he went back to all business Satan. He turned to look at Cadwallader and the other person, demon, with him.

"Come in."

# 12.

They approached Satan's desk, and Cadwallader stopped at his designated spot. But the other person on Cadwallader's right faltered a step and quickly froze midstride and corrected for his mistake. Cadwallader's perfect expressionless expression was one of contempt at such a social error.

"Percy here was in charge of the acquisitions. He was the one who made the contract with the alleged Mr. Andrew Wheeler, Sir."

"Percy, is it?

Satan turned his full attention onto Percy. He was shortish and pudgy looking man. He had dark eyes, stringy looking long black hair and an expression of vacant terror on his face. Andrew made two observations while regarding the new person in the room. The first one was apparently not all Hell beings look suave, or smoove. Some look like normal humans. Which begged the question, why do Hell beings look like humans?

Andrews second observation was the vacant terror on the face of Percy was sort of how Andrew was feeling: What had he said wrong?

Satan looked at Percy. Satan's previous jovial demeanor now completely gone. In its place was a cold, penetrating gaze of someone who was going to get what they wanted. Satan's icy stare also conveyed the understanding of, *if you lie to me I will know it*. Andrew was very happy not to be Percy.

"As I recall you were the delightful little fellow who suggested the new paradigm of soul transactions were you not? Didn't you previously work in administration and filing before this promotion?

Trying to be polite, Andrew turned his attention away from the three. He looked around the office trying to occupy his gaze by studying Satan's office. But his curiosity would occasionally shift his attention to eavesdropping on the conversation going on around him. With a quick glance, Andrew saw that Percy's look of terror hadn't completely resolved itself. Instead, it began to expand into a greasy looking sweat starting to build up on his face and stain around his armpits.

"Yes, sir."

"And again, please feel free to correct me if my memory should fail me, and I speak out of turn. But didn't you say in your very lovely presentation, your new design would increase the speed and efficacy of purchasing souls?"

Satan held up his hand indicating he was not done speaking to Percy.

"And also, the margin of error with your new system was no greater than the one that we had been using for spans? Would both of those statements be correct?"

Even though Satan was phrasing all his sentences as questions and even inviting Percy to correct him if he were to be wrong, Andrew knew they were not questions. Furthermore, Andrew was pretty sure from the tone of Satan's voice, should Percy try to correct Satan at any time the consequences would be;

well Andrew didn't know what the consequences would be, but they would be on a Hell scale of horrible. Andrew tried to divert his attention back to *The Godfather* cigar box on *The Godfather* desk and failed.

The sweating was becoming more perfuse and starting to fully soak into Percy's shirt and suit coat while forming large beads on his forehead.

"Yes, Sir."

Satan became more intense and started asking his questions in a rapid-fire prosecutorial manner. Percy began to wither under the onslaught.

"Did you put together the purchase contract for the soul of a Mr. Andrew Wheeler?"
"Yes, Sir."

"Did you negotiate all the terms and agreements and outline the conditions and consequences?"

"Yes, Sir."

Andrew pondered his blunder while Satan grilled Percy. He looked at the *Godfather* lamp next to *Godfather* lighter. Andrew couldn't help but notice the sweat was now freely running down Percy's face. Percy looked like he had just stepped out of a sauna, or as if he was running a full marathon at high noon in a desert. Satan continued pressing Percy with increased intensity.

"When you presented the contract for signature did the person sign it there in front of you?"

"Yes, Sir."

Satan was not only started speaking faster, but the timber of his voice was changing as well. Andrew thought Satan started to sound like a dramatized television trial lawyer trying to break the hostile witness on the stand. Percy's sweat was becoming more viscous, and with it came an unpleasant aroma. Andrew thought it smelled like a combination of ammonia and burning tires. The smell was enough to break the voyeuristic spell and forced Andrew to turn his head. At the same time, he tried to casually bring his arm up to cover his nose to try and block the pungent and offensive stench. These attempts failed, and his eyes started to water.

"Did you get the requisite drop of blood?"

"Yes, Sir." The sweat streaming from Percy began to change from a sort of clear to an opaque greenish color.

"Did you use the " Satan said something, but again it was -stereo feedback- "when you collected the said drop of blood?"

"Sir?" The sweating and fortunately the smell also stopped.

The human-looking Hell being named Percy who stood in front of Satan suddenly started to crack. Not the whole being, but the face and around the hands and any exposed skin, or what Andrew had originally thought was skin. Watching the faux skin on Percy's body crack answered one of Andrew's earlier questions of why did Hell beings look like humans. Apparently, it was just a form of make-up, and Percy's started to crack making a spider web like fracture lines.

It reminded Andrew of pressing on the thin skin of ice covering puddles of water as they just started to freeze and watching the ice crack. The trick was always trying to get the biggest cracks while trying not to break the ice and let the water out. This thought also made Andrew wonder; how much pressure Percy could take before his ice completely cracked and exposed the water underneath?

More importantly, did Andrew want to know what was underneath?

"You did not use the –feedback- to collect the blood? Where did this drop of blood come from?" Satan accentuated his question by pointing to the dried spot on the soul contract still lying open on Satan's *Godfather* desk.

Percy glanced at the contract to where Satan's finger was pointing.

"Sir, from the index finger on the right-hand sir." The cracks were become more prominent and wider, as they radiated outward across all of Percy's skin.

"How did the blood get from the finger onto the document?"

"Sir the person had their own needle and pierced the coating of their finger and,"

"STOP!"

Satan's command wasn't spoken like a command. He didn't yell it out. In fact Satan barely changed the volume of his voice. It was the tone and the intent behind the command. It was of such intensity Andrew almost wet himself, and it wasn't even directed at him. Of course, he was still working on his ethics blunder, so he had only to wait.

"You said the human pierced the coating of their finger? Not soft easy to poke, rip and tear skin, but coating? I understand what happened now. For the final question before you lose your full composure," Andrew could see Satan look at Percy with disgust. Every human and apparently, every being may not speak English, but a facial expression of disgust seemed to be universal.

"Please Percy, look at my guest and tell me if this is the human who sold you their soul for, let me see here, yes, sold his soul for world peace."

Percy turned and looked at Andrew for the first time. Not knowing what to do, Andrew just sat there in Satan's office chair from *The Godfather*. Satan turned to Andrew and was once more the genial and gracious host.

"Go ahead Mr. Andrew Wheeler you can look at Percy here; it's okay. Although at this moment Percy is starting to show hints of his true nature, you'll be fine. Make sure he has a good look at you, Andrew, because your existence depends on it.

Satan turned away from Andrew and back towards Percy. If Satan were a human Andrew would have thought, he suffered from bipolar disorder. Because once his attention was back on Percy, so was the level of irritation. However, even that was masked by a combination of sarcasm and perfect manners. Even pissed off, Satan was still the picture-perfect definition of suave.

"Percy, be friendly, give this Mr. Andrew Wheeler a little wave."

Percy raised his right hand and arm a bit and gave a slight waving gesture with his hand. That movement caused more of what Andrew was coming to understand was make-up some kind; the fake skin cracked further and started to peel back. Andrew tried not to stare and instead maintained eye contact and gave Percy a little wave in return.

"There we are, you two chaps are now; well Percy what is it? Are you re-acquainted or just now becoming acquainted?"

"Sir" Percy stammered on the sir like he couldn't speak anymore.

Satan sat rigid in his chair. An expression of contempt and loathing burned on his face making Andrew think of the saying, "If looks could kill."

"Stop right there Percy!  I have a guest."

# 13.

Satan looked to Cadwallader, "Please bring Mr. Wheeler the – stereo feedback-.

Cadwallader turned from his spot and Andrew watched as he walked over to the bookshelf, the bookshelf from *The Godfather*, which even the bar cart and leather couch, just like in the movie. Andrew's mental cry echoed in his head, *"What did I say wrong?"*

But on the shelf, was an item not from *The Godfather*. Besides the various books and statues was an odd-looking helmet-like object that sort of reminded Andrew of the "Flying Guillotine" weapon from the cheesy B-grade Chinese martial arts movies he loved to watch.

Andrew loved the Flying Guillotine weapon. It was a crazy looking metal hat or helmet thing with a chain attached to the top. The actual design depended on the movie. The Kung Fu Master dude would throw it out like a Frisbee. With an unerring skill only seen in movies, the Flying Guillotine would land on his victim's head. Once it landed, the weapon would cover the head and clamp down around the unfortunate victim's neck. The Master would yank the chain which would make the guillotine helmet thing return like a yo-yo. Only unlike a yo-yo the flying guillotine cut off the victim's head and brought it along. That would leave a very fake looking headless mannequin spraying blood everywhere.

Cadwallader picked up this similar looking item. He walked over with it and stood next to a now nervous Andrew.

"Andrew, Cadwallader is about to put the –feedback- over your head. It will block all of your visual, auditory, and aroma senses. The -feedback- is for your protection. You will still feel physical stimulations such as heat, cold, pressure, and others; these will not harm you. For even though your soul is here, your flesh body is alive and in stasis in Purgatory. Should you fully hear complete

Hell Speak, more than a single word or two like you have been, or fully see", Satan glanced at the cracking façade of Percy "a Hell Being, your body will whither. That would leave you trapped here for eternity, as my guest of course. But, there would be no way for you to go back to the Earth plane. I don't think either one of us would want that, do you?

Andrew answered by vigorously turning his head from left to right and saying "no." No, he certainly didn't want to remain for all of Eternity there in Hell, even if it were to be as Satan's guest. Andrew had Camille, a job, a home, and a girlfriend waiting for him. Staying in Hell was not something Andrew felt like he wanted to do.

"Please remain seated, and when we are finished speaking, Cadwallader will remove the –feedback-."

Andrew didn't think he was offered much choice. Because first, Satan didn't ask Andrew if he had any questions. Which Andrew did, but he wasn't sure how to phrase them. Second, Satan just gave Cadwallader a brief nod, and Cadwallader put the flying guillotine helmet-looking-thing over Andrew's head. Sure enough, just like the flying guillotine from the movies, it closed up around Andrew's neck. But unlike the flying guillotine from the movies, his head remained attached.

Being almost completely sensory deprived was odd. But suddenly Andrew was happy he had the helmet on. His body or what he thought was his body, but was, in fact, his soul, was surrounded by sensations. Suddenly Andrew felt the sensation of pressure. He started to feel like he was being squeezed in a giant vice. The pressure increased and Andrew was starting to become uncomfortable. Then something new joined in, the pressure remained, but then came heat. Then there was cold. Somehow the heat came back, but the cold remained so Andrew was both hot and cold at the same time as he was being squeezed. Then came a sensation Andrew had no idea how to describe other than the texting acronym of "WTF." Andrew was happy to be wearing the helmet. Because whatever was going on out there, he didn't want to know.

Andrew sat there. While doing his best not to move, he experienced a sensory deprived epiphany. Through a series of synaptic links and mental leaps, Andrew thought of the movie *Raiders of the Lost Ark*. In particular, Andrew recalled the scene at the end of the movie when Indiana Jones and Marion were tied to the light post when the Nazi's opened the Ark. While trying to figure out how they were going to get away, Indiana recalled a discussion he had had about the Ark from the beginning of the movie.

Well, Andrew couldn't confirm that was what Indiana had actually been thinking. But it made sense and from Indiana's, Harrison Ford's, expression, that is how Andrew interpreted it. Indiana had been telling Marcus and the American government agents the stories and legends which surrounded the Ark. About how any army that carried the Ark before it couldn't be defeated. Indiana understood no human could look at the contents of the Ark, the Divine, and live. So, Indiana closed his eyes and had Marion do the same.

Andrew realized the helmet worked in the same way. This situation was just like in the movies. The movies Satan kept copying……. *"Oh, Crap!"*

# 14.

Having had most of his senses shielded Andrew was unprepared when, without any advanced warning, the helmet was lifted from his head. The light of the office was blinding. Andrew blinked hard several times to get his eyes to adjust to the light. He also realized, oddly enough, he had to readjust to the sound and smell as well. Fortunately, the Percy smell was gone. Instead of the putrid stench, there were light floral smells making Andrew think of a flower shop. Those subtle details initially went unnoticed until he was deprived of them.

Cadwallader was putting the flying guillotine back onto Satan's bookshelf, as Andrew was becoming readjusted to his surroundings.

It seemed Percy was no longer in the room. Then Andrew looked over to where Percy had been standing and noticed some of him still was. There was a pile of Percy flesh makeup about two feet away from the corner of Satan's desk. Cadwallader returned from the bookshelf, carefully avoiding the Percy pile, to his spot before Satan's desk.

"Sir, with your leave, I will be on my way."

Satan still seated behind his desk nodded an affirmative to Cadwallader. Cadwallader again gave his bow and backed away to the door, stood, turned with crisp military precision, and left.

The door was about to close when another "person look alike" came in.

"I was told there was a mess to clean up."

The tone was not as civil or respectful as Cadwallader or Percy's, and Satan seemed to hear that as well.

"Yes, my good man, right over there." Satan absently gestured to the pile on the floor. "Please be quick as I have a guest."

"All right."

The person was another Hell Being. Or as far as Andrew knew it was another Hell Being. But this one appeared to be a janitor. He wore a simple gray jumpsuit and carried a broom and dustpan. He was large and sort of dumpy looking. He looked as if he had just put on the human façade, and didn't seem to care how well it looked or fit. This one was also, obviously a servant or worker. Maybe it was somehow a lower class? Andrew made this assumption, by the way, the Hell Being looked and acted. Where Cadwallader, and even to a lesser extent Percy looked and acted sophisticated, this one wasn't even trying. Andrew turned away from the janitor, to look back over at the bookshelf. As he did, Andrew thought he saw the janitor glare at him with an evil, I want to kill you, sort of look. However it was just a quick look, and Andrew figured he could've been mistaken. Besides, Satan had told Andrew that he was Satan's personal guest. So, what did Andrew have to worry about or be afraid of, he had Satan watching over him.

As the janitor was picking up Percy skin fragments, a phone ran on Satan's *Godfather* desk. It had been there the whole time, but just like the brick and brownstone houses Andrew passed every morning, the phone went unnoticed until it did something to be noticed. It was a spot-on replicate from the movie, right down to the old rotary dials and hard matte black finish.

It rang again, a normal average sound of two copper bells being struck rapidly by the small hammer. Satan looked at it, paused a moment, and then picked it up.

"Hello old friend, it's good to speak to you again." Satan relaxed as the person on the other end of the line started speaking. "Yes, it has been a while." Andrew could without the intent of trying to listen, hear a voice on the other end, but it was like no sound he had ever heard.

"Yes. He's right here, and it seems he can hear your voice."

Satan had apparently caught Andrew, sort of, listening to the conversation.

"Yes, that should do it." And Satan was right because Andrew could no longer hear the caller, although there was a lingering desire to try.

"Yes, I have the situation under control."

"Yes. I know this was a cock-up from the normal method. No, nothing like that. No."

Andrew again tried to give Satan an idea of privacy as he sat there listening to the now one-sided phone conversation. However, as Andrew sat there, he heard more of the reason for how he ended up in Hell.

"Of all the stupid things, it was Six Sigma."

*Six Sigma* thought Andrew? He wasn't even sure what it was. He seemed to recall something about karate belts being associated with it; getting a black belt in Six Sigma. Other than that, he didn't know any more about it. Although next time things at work got slow, he would look it up on the Wikipedia.

"Yes, I know it was developed to streamline manufacturing processes."

"Yes, one of the ass-kissers in acquisitions thought they could apply it to soul transactions. They put together a nice PowerPoint presentation and everything."

"What! Your people tried the same thing?"

Satan started to laugh. It was similar to Cadwallader's unnatural laugh. The difference being when Satan did it, the unnatural effect was amplified. It suddenly seemed all of Hell was caught up in the unnatural laughter.

"How did yours go? Of course, just as I figured like ours did. Fortunately, I only permitted it on a trial basis to test it out."

"So yes." Satan sat listening occasionally glancing to where Andrew was sitting as if noticing him for the first time.

"Yes, no. Yes."

"Ah-huh. Mmmm."

Andrew tried not to notice Satan staring, and Andrew continued to try and ignore the conversation.

"Yessss. Noooo!"

"Nope. Of course."

But Satan suddenly kept talking human slang.

"Whatever. Get-Out. Dude!"

Andrew tried just to sit there, trying to pretend to give Satan an idea of privacy as he was on the phone. But Satan kept staring at him. It was a very strange exchange, made even more so now that Satan was talking like he was a human teenager.

"Yes, it does seem to be irritating him. Yes, it is funny."

The conversation paused, and Andrew found Satan staring at him again. However, this time in a contemplative manner, not the mocking expression he had just displayed. Andrew wondered about the topic of their current conversation.

"No. You are right of course, and I had already planned to do something along those lines. Maybe not quite so generous but..."

"Well, I guess you're right. No, No. I agree. Yes, not since Walter Disney. Yes, one of these days we will get our hands on him. Until then. Yes. Bye now.

Satan hung up the phone as the janitor finished picking up the last of Percy's skin and sweeping the remains into his dustpan.

"All done. That it?"

From the janitor's surly demeanor and slovenly appearance, Andrew wondered if the guy knew he was cleaning Satan's office? The janitor still seemed to treat Satan as if he didn't know who Satan was; which Andrew thought would be impossible. The guy was in Hell. Andrew started to wonder why Satan seemed indifferent to the janitor's attitude. Everyone else, well the only other two beings Andrew had met, deferred to Satan in a manner reminiscent of royalty. This one didn't seem to care. Maybe Satan thought it would be impolite or something, to discipline a worker in front of a guest. Andrew watched Satan and wondered what was going to happen. Satan seemed as entertained as he was acerbated, maybe. Andrew continued to do his best and remain unobtrusive.

"Yes, quite all. Thank you."

The man nodded his head in acknowledgment. He turned away from Satan. With his broom and dust bin in hand, the janitor started walking for the door. Andrew watched as Satan's smile went from a combination amused and irritated to a scowl of pure indignation. It was at that very moment Andrew came to understand; you didn't show disrespect to Satan by turning your back to him when leaving his presence.

Without any warning or indication, the janitor stopped moving forward. Andrew noted it wasn't because the janitor's feet had stopped moving; they were in fact still in mid-stride and trying to move forward, but he wasn't going anywhere. The janitor looked down and noted, as did Andrew from across the room, the janitor was now levitating about two feet above the floor.

Satan didn't move. He didn't wave a hand, or gesture in some way to indicate it was he who was behind the sudden change to the janitor's situation. Satan only sat and stared at the dumbfounded janitor. Andrew noticed that once again, Satan had that similar glint in his eye and set to his face. He was once again staring at a fly, and Satan was about to rip off its wings.

The large red velvet curtains along the wall behind Satan's desk parted from the middle and moved to the sides. Now opened, they revealed several grand windows. They were large individual sheets of glass with no frames separating them. Each went from the floor to the high vaulted ceiling. Andrew noted those windows were not part of *The Godfather*.

Like the curtains, the windows slid open. The janitor, who several seconds earlier was about to exit Satan's office through the door, suddenly found himself propelled backward and exited through the open windows. Andrew watched as the janitor sailed out over a balcony, screaming out as he descended into a vast darkness.

# 15.

Andrew sat stunned, bewildered, and a bit terrified. He had just finished listening to Satan's phone conversation. Even though Andrew could only hear part of what was being said; it was obviously about him. Then Andrew watched Satan as Satan threw the janitor out of his office. Not just out the door of his office, but out the window and over a balcony. Satan had just used *the Force*; still stunned Andrew couldn't think of a better description. But what happened did remind him of a *Star Wars,* Darth Vader sort of thing. Satan used *the Force* to throw one of his staff off the balcony of his office out into, Andrew could only guess, out into Hell. Needless to say, despite Satan's reassurance that Andrew was a guest, was, in fact, Satan's personal guest, he was still unsure of his status there. Andrew swallowed down the dry mouth, took the initiative and decided to break the now weird silence.

"Satan, excuse me, but I need to apologize to you."

Satan casually gave his attention back to Andrew. Satan was once again the good-natured, and relaxed Satan. It as if just a moment ago, he hadn't just cast a soul, or some Hell-Being, out of his office, off the balcony, and out into Hell. Satan leaned back in his large leather chair, an open, inviting look on his face, suggesting, giving, Andrew permission to continue.

"Earlier when I spoke, I said you had the office from *The Godfather*. I was mistaken and spoke out of turn. Please excuse my obtuse nature. I meant to phrase my response as, the office from *The Godfather* looks like yours. Since yours is obviously the original."

Satan responded to Andrew's apt apology by giving him an approving smile.

"Good work. I was hopeful you would figure out your continuity gaff. Of course, mine was first! Mario loved it so much he recreated it in his book, with my permission of course. He also insured Coppola depicted it correctly in the movie. The only difference is I have those grand windows."

Andrew was about to speak but stopped himself. He realized he was about to blurt out, once again, some stupid comment, instead of thinking through what he was going to say. Andrew kept his tongue in cheek and mentally processed his thoughts. He didn't want to offend his host, again.

Satan looked at Andrew and raised his right eyebrow, his face reflecting a questioning expression. Andrew was sure Satan understood what had just happened. Andrew had just caught himself from once more, just spouting off without thinking about what he was going to say. Satan then furrowed his brows a bit, leaned his chair forward, opened the cigar box on his desk and took one out.

"What do you think of Hell so far Andrew?"

Andrew watched as he trimmed the ends of the cigar. He then turned it, offering it to Andrew.

"No thank you."

Simple, Andrew thought, polite and to the point. He was glad it hadn't been a pomegranate. Satan nodded and then lit the cigar with a crystal lighter from the desk.

"I guess I don't know. I really haven't seen much of it, other than your office and the reception office."

Satan sat forward. He pushed back his chair and stood up. He walked around from behind his desk to the still open window. Satan stepped out onto the balcony and gestured for Andrew to join him.

"Well come here and have a look then."

Andrew thought about it a moment before going over.

"Excuse my ignorance on this matter Satan. Earlier you said I or I guess it would be my flesh body would die if I fully heard Hell speak, or looked at Hell stuff. Am I allowed to look out there?"

Andrew was still mentally juggling the idea that he was his soul, and he was in Hell. But his body, which was sort of him, if he were in it, was alive and stuck in Purgatory. Satan did his little smile again Andrew started to think that Satan practiced it to make sure it looked just like that.

"You are sharp. I like that. Yes, and no to answer your question, Yes, your body would die from direct exposure to Hell, but just like the –feedback- protected you from the direct exposure in this office, the distance will protect you now."

Then Satan said to Andrew those two words. Two words which sounded even more evil and cliché, especially when spoken by Satan Himself.

"Trust Me."

# 16.

After everything Andrew had heard and experienced up to that point; he figured it would be okay. So he did it. Andrew trusted Satan. Andrew rose from his chair and walked across the office to join Satan on the balcony. Hesitantly Andrew stepped closer to the ornate marble rail and took his first look at Hell. It was like looking out at the moon, the universe. Sure, the moon seemed close, but you knew how far away it actually was. That was Andrew's view of Hell. The height of the balcony didn't seem measurable. Andrew could see down. He could see what he thought was the bottom. But where he physically was located in comparison to what he saw he had no idea. Andrew wasn't sure if a NASA scientist or even Dante would have been able to say.

Andrew could see things, and that is all they were, just things. He couldn't make out any one person or being, or item. He could only make out a mass of something moving. There were lights, maybe fire, maybe something else entirely. There were also voices or sounds. However, these were only whispers, background ambient noise, none of which could be understood or picked out.

Andrew could again feel what he called the "Absence." However, this time it felt diluted and weak from the distance. It didn't have the edge it did while he was in the gateway, or whatever the passage between Purgatory and Hell was called. Andrew thought about that experience a moment. Although he could not, and did not want to confirm it; the Absence he felt in the area between Purgatory and Hell was probably not full strength. Yes, the Absence was beyond horrible. It was awful, and all the other synonyms of awful and horrible, but it didn't feel full strength. Andrew had no conclusive proof to substantiate his claim, other than his brief experience. But even at that weakened level, Andrew knew he never wanted to feel the full-strength version.

Andrew stood there on the balcony next to Satan. Together they looked out over the expanse of Hell. As Andrew contemplated Hell's horrors, he had a little internal and private mental laugh. He thought to himself; this was not his usual Thursday routine. And just as Satan had told him he would be, Andrew was safe. The distance was enough to shield him from the full effect of Hell. Andrew didn't want to think about what it must be like to be down there, at the bottom of Hell. What it must be like to be completely and utterly consumed by the Absence.

"See down there" gestured Satan with his cigar.

Andrew nodded because all he could see was just a non-specific mass of "something." He was sure Satan knew he had no idea to what or whom he was pointing out. Andrew accepted the idea that Satan was both gracious and also grandstanding. He was Satan after all.

"Down there is the little weasel who developed Six Sigma. For doing something like that, there can be no forgiveness. He found that out the hard way. Well," and Satan held a dramatic pause, "developing Six Sigma and that other thing he did. However, I make it a point never to discuss other people's affairs. Those items aside, I think his existence is about to get worse. In fact, I know it."

Satan paused a moment and had a far-away expression on his face. Andrew could see Satan was obviously concentrating on something down in Hell. Andrew once again pretended not to watch, but of course was looking. Then Satan's attention was back with the two of them on the balcony, and he started smiling.

"Yes, that will improve my mood for a while."

Andrew didn't want to know what just happened. But considering Satan said he was now in a better mood, Andrew knew it couldn't have been good. Andrew wondered what the Six Sigma guy had done in life to end up in Hell? Andrew didn't think developing Six Sigma could be considered a damnable or cardinal sin after all. Andrew guessed the life of the Six Sigma guy just became much worse. It was hard to imagine what could be worse than being in Hell, and Andrew decided not to try. Satan casually turned his attention back to Andrew, and away from inflicting further horrors on Mr. Six Sigma.

"You know Andrew, despite all that has happened here these past several spans."

Several spans thought Andrew? *What was a span and how long were they?*

"You've maintained a high level of personal composure. The usual soul collection routine is Cadwallader waits for the person to be outside and pulls up in his limo. The person's soul becomes trapped in the reflection of the paint, or in the windows, and Cadwallader simply drives away. To avoid suspicion, the body continues for a little bit before it collapses and ceases to function. You could think of it as sort of a zombie since those are the current Earth fad at the moment. However, this time the usual routine didn't work. You didn't get pulled in by the soul trapping reflection."

Andrew remembered the hypnotic effect of the trying to see the red color in the polished black paint of Cadwallader's limo and the weird images reflected in the windows. How he kept trying to see them like he was drawn to it, a moth to a flame. That limo was so smoove it could capture a person's soul.

"You even managed to evade Cadwallader several times which is no mean trick. Those were some of the reasons he didn't remove your soul with, shall we say, extreme prejudice."

Andrew shuddered at such a thought. He didn't want to imagine what soul extraction with extreme prejudice entailed. And considering everything he had seen and heard so for, he knew he didn't want to know. The weird handcuff thing had been bad enough. But there were worse ways? Andrew thought of his usual response to a bad situation, "*It can always be worse*," and it was usually true.

Someone had stolen, Andrew's identity. Then his stolen identity was used to sell his soul to Satan. That caused Andrew to spend his the morning being chased by a Hell Being who strived for absolute perfection. Unable to escape, Andrew was captured and almost killed in the stall of a public toilet. Narrowly avoiding death, Andrew was then taken to mind and sensory altering Purgatory. There in Purgatory, he had to leave his flesh body while he, Andrew, was taken to Hell to defend himself before Satan. With whom he was now standing, and socializing in a friendly manner, as they stood out on his office balcony overlooking Hell. Yeah, it can always be worse. There might have been better ways for Andrew to spend his day. But as Andrew once again looked over the railing and down into Hell, it definitely could have been worse.

"Cadwallader knew there was something wrong from the initial contact. But he was constrained by the Dictum of -feedback- in the manner of dealing with it. Cadwallader is my best. When he brought this situation to me instead of the usual arbitration courts, I knew it was serious. That was the reason I was personally willing to hear your request."

Ruling Hell was more complicated than Andrew would have ever guessed. He thought it was just all torture and fire. There were rules to be followed and apparently also a court system. The idea of a court system made Andrew wonder how many people won their cases when it was *Them versus Hell*. But Andrew still didn't understand one part.

"But in the bathroom stall, Cadwallader was killing me. He was extracting my soul, well I guess me, and my body was dying. If he knew something was wrong, why did he do that? Why didn't he just bring me here right away?

Andrew watched as Satan took a long draw on his cigar and blew the smoke out over Hell. Satan was leaning on the rail of the balcony, looking out and watching the blue-gray puff of smoke drift away.

"The Dictum of –feedback-, as I mentioned, is the reason he had to extract your soul. I understand it means nothing to you, but the Dictum is a large part of the rules which govern aspects of this and several other dimensions. Cadwallader could no more break any of those rules than I could. They were established to maintain a sense of balance. Without them, the sum of this and several other planes of existence would degrade and revert to a form of chaos."

Andrew still didn't like or really understand, the answer. But he knew it was the best one he was going to get. Then his usual retort came to his mind, *"could be worse."* Andrew applied his favorite aphorism to his current situation. Yes, it could be worse; he could be joining the janitor. Andrew wondered if the janitor had hit bottom yet. Andrew turned his attention back to Satan who continued to explain the situation.

"So, when you were able to pull the request for arbitration out of your ass, it freed Cadwallader from his legal constraints and his then current course of action. Which at that moment was collecting you when it was not your turn to be taken. Thus, it is strictly your luck and savvy which saved us all."

Andrew felt a sort of personal pride at Satan's complement. He wasn't about to admit the only reason he came up with the whole request for arbitration was due to human resources training. Because to do such a thing; to make that acknowledgment would validate the several hours of education everyone at work had to sit through twice a year. But fortunately for him, the arbitration and mediation portion were one of the few things he could remember from the otherwise tedious, and monotonous training. That part of the class must have been in the morning when he still had some coffee. He saved himself and allowed Cadwallader not to have to kill him. Although Andrew wasn't sure what Satan meant by the whole, "you saved us all" part.

Andrew leaned against the balcony rail resisting the urge to spit. Satan took another drag and flicked some ash off the end of the cigar. He released the smoke slowly from his mouth in a manner which inclined Andrew to imagine Satan was smoldering on the inside. Of course, for all Andrew knew, Satan was smoldering inside. Satan turned away from looking out over the balcony and looked Andrew in the eye.

"Andrew, you have proven yourself to be resourceful. You maintain your composure and discipline while under fire. You learn from your mistakes and correct them quickly. Most importantly, and above all the others, you keep and use your manners. Andrew, what would you say if I offered you a job here? Of course, there would be no going back to the earth dimension, at least not as a full human."

Even though he knew the act was physically impossible, Andrew almost swallowed his tongue.

"There, of course, would be an apprenticeship period. During that time, you would have to work in the Abysmal Pits; I can't show any favoritism after all. But, I know you would do well and move up quickly. I know this is sudden, but what's your gut reaction?"

Andrew now completely understood what it meant to be a deer in headlights. He quickly tried to recover from his initial shock at what Satan had just said. At the same time, Andrew was mentally processing Satan's proposal. Satan turned once again to look out over his domain. He inhaled on his cigar. It burned a deep red, and some of the glowing ash dropped off the end and drifted down into Hell, still burning as it went. Then Satan blew out a ring that began to float up and fade from sight. He took another long drag and repeated the process. As Satan did this Andrew concluded it was to give him courteous time to think about an answer.

Andrew had no idea how to answer. He had just been asked, no, he was being recruited by Satan to join his team. Not just that, but Satan also wanted Andrew's immediate gut answer. Andrew looked around at the office and out over the expanse of Hell. He considered all he had seen, been a part of, and heard. Also, the part about having to work in the Abysmal Pits sounded ominous and really, really, just really horrible. Also, probably just a bit terrifying. Andrew's initial gut reaction was his gut shouting something along the lines of "*Are you fucking crazy!*" Fortunately, Andrew's brain was able to prevent the mouth from shouting out that particular response. Understand Satan was used to just a little modicum of respect, Andrew instead edited his gut response into a more dignified and polite one.

"Thank you of course for such a generous offer Satan. But I will have to decline it."

Andrew waited for his turn to go up and over the balcony. But Satan only smiled and tapped his cigar ash.

"I figured you would. But, there is never any harm in asking."

Then a question came to Andrew. He was about to ask about something Satan had previously said to him, right before the job offer. But before he could there were three sharp knocks on the office door. Andrew didn't have to turn around to know it would be Cadwallader who opened the door.

# 17.

Andrew was correct. It was Cadwallader who knocked, opened the door, and walked into Satan's office. However, this time he did not stop at the threshold to be acknowledged. Nor did he stop at what Andrew thought was Cadwallader's designated position next to Satan's desk. Instead, Cadwallader walked directly through the office, and out to join him and Satan on the balcony.

"Your instructions have been carried out sir."

Satan turned his attention from gazing out over Hell to face Cadwallader. He then glanced over to the doorway where Percy, now once again fresh and human looking, stood with another man.

Andrew's attention shifted from the conversation on the balcony to the office door. The once again human looking Percy was holding another person whom Andrew suddenly recognized. Andrew in a moment of excitement was about to blurt once again his realization; just as he had done when he realized Satan's office was the model for the Godfathers. But before Andrew could once again make an ass of himself he was able to stop himself. Andrew remembered where he was and with whom he was standing. Andrew quickly checked himself and was able to refrain from such an egregious display of manners. With the hand, which was about to point at the man with Percy, Andrew instead raised it over his head, feigned a yawn, stretched his back and returned to looking off the balcony at Hell. Both Satan and Cadwallader watched Andrew's comical save. They were both impressed and amused by his performance.

"He has developed during his stay. There are still some rough edges, but a marked improvement on his part; for a human."

Praise from Cadwallader was high praise indeed Andrew thought. Satan turned from Andrew back to Cadwallader with a business-like demeanor.

"Yes, not too bad at all. Oh, he turned us down by the way."

"Oh, pity, I was looking forward to helping him improve his manners and take them to a whole new level."

Andrew inwardly cringed at the thought of being in a manners apprenticeship under Cadwallader. Within the little bit of time he had been with Cadwallader, Andrew came to appreciate how proper manners maintained a higher level of civility and respect. But under no circumstances did Andrew want to have to go through the rest of his existence like that, with a proper manner's stick stuck up his butt.

Cadwallader continued, "Without much effort, I was able to locate the perpetrator of our current dilemma. Upon my arrival, and after a bit of discussion, he was gracious enough to disclose all his misdeeds regarding this altercation."

Satan looked back into his office. Percy was standing next to Satan's desk holding the person who had started the current chain of events. Satan took another drag from his cigar. It was strong, and the end of the cigar glowed a bright cherry red. He took it from his mouth and looked at the firey ash. He blew the smoke out on around it causing it to produce a flame. As the flame started from the end of the cigar, Satan dropped it off the balcony. As the cigar fell, it started to burn brighter. Andrew watched it go. It reminded him of a shooting star. That was because as the cigar went, it was leaving a trail of burning embers and started to glow brighter and brighter as it went further and further down into the seeming abyss of Hell.

Satan turned to Andrew. "Andrew I'm going to ask you now to stay here. What is about to happen inside my office no longer concerns you. It is for that and several other reasons I say this. Stay here until I ask for you." Then Satan and Cadwallader turned and walked back into Satan's office.

Andrew glanced over at the man who had stolen his identity in an attempt to try and trick the Devil by selling Andrew's soul instead of his own. Which, well, stealing someone's money is one thing, but their soul? Andrew wondered how often something like that, soul thievery happened? Remembering the earlier incident with Percy, Andrew was pretty sure he was the first case. Satan did seem like the kind of person, or eternal being, to let a mistake like that slide by uncorrected. Andrew had to wonder about the morality of the person who would even think of doing something like stealing someone else's soul and selling it. Andrew rhetorically wondered what went wrong with that person's childhood. If a troubled childhood wasn't the reason, then it was probably to impress a girl. Andrew would have never thought of something like that to get a girl. Andrew never considered himself an atheist. He put himself into more of a progressive agnostic who survived a rather boring and to what he thought was a meaningless Lutheran childhood. But Andrew never really knew if he had a soul or not. He usually didn't give it much, if any thought. Most of his contemplative time was entrenched in the modern world of technology. Where the microchip was the wheel, and he was part of the circuitry. He didn't realize what having a soul meant until somebody tried to steal his and sell it for world peace. Something Satan said was stupid.

Andrew realized, as he continued to gaze out over what seemed to be the infinite expanse of Hell, he was continuing to have his religious epiphany. The contemplation had started in the toilet stall of a coffee shop, to continue in the back of Cadwallader's limousine. Now, once again, to be continued while Andrew stood on Satan's balcony looking out over Hell. Even with everything which happened to him today, Andrew knew he would never become a regular church guy. He didn't have that type of personality, and to say otherwise would be a lie and make him a hypocrite.

However, Andrew had come to understand the workings of the Universe in a new way. People had choices, and those choices had consequences of both an immediate and also a spiritual result. Andrew started to think about the direction and choices he had made in life. About how his life would balance out in the end. Andrew started to think about the choices and actions he had made in his life. Sure, he had done some not so nice stuff. But he didn't think any of it was Hell worthy. But, Andrew also knew at the time he committed his wanton act of egregiousness, it felt wrong. Inside he knew he had just done something which caused some part of him feel bad. Andrew now knew it were those actions which put him on the path where he now stood. Well, not where he was currently standing, on a rather nice balcony above Hell, but down it. Down in the Abysmal Pits. He did not want to end up in the Abysmal Pits! Andrew decided at that moment to make sure the final balance of his life would be tipped in the preferred direction.

Andrew then started to think about the consequences for the newest guest in Satan's office. The man was the med tech who performed the blood draw when Andrew had gone in for his physical several days before.

*"Huh, go figure; I guess I know what that extra tube of blood and signature was for"* thought, Andrew.

Andrew pulled himself out of his spiritual revere. He turned his attention instead to quietly eavesdrop from his vantage point on the balcony on the events in the office. Satan had asked, by way of telling, Andrew to remain where he was because what was about to happen no longer concerned him. Satan also informed Andrew it was also was probably something Andrew didn't want to witness. Andrew interpreted Satan's statement to mean, "Please stay where you are but feel free to eavesdrop." Moments later Andrew came to forever regret his actions, because that was not what Satan meant.

Satan and Cadwallader left the balcony and strolled back into the office. Satan with his suave demeanor sat on the corner of his desk. Cadwallader moved to his personally designated spot. Percy with his hand still around the back of the man's neck pushed and pulled the now trembling unnamed med tech forward. Andrew adjusted his place on the balcony. He positioned himself so he could see inside the office, yet also remained obscured from sight in case anyone were to look out in his direction. Satan stared at the man Percy was now forcibly holding up. Andrew had to admit the guy did sort of physically resemble him; about six-foot tall, blackish hair, medium build, brown eyes. At the moment, Andrew, couldn't be sure of how much they looked alike because the guy's face was all puffy and red from crying.

Satan blinked, and Percy released his grip, and the man fell to the floor at Satan's feet. Andrew now understood what Satan had been describing to him early about people in his office facing his judgment. The poor guy had decided to lose his total composure as most people, according to Satan, always do. The physical response was all over his body: The tears; the blubbering lips; the wringing hands; the slack knees, this fellow was about to have a bad day. Andrew also noticed the man's soul was shifting from a normal looking clothed person to the naked amorphous shape and back again. However, Andrew found he couldn't be too empathetic to the med tech's current situation because the poor guy on the floor was almost him.

"Disposition of the body?" asked Satan as he stared at the man like a hungry dog at a piece of meat.

The med tech was prostrate on the floor, crying. With no thought or consideration, Satan casually put the toe of his shoe under the man's chin and lifted his face towards his own. Percy stood beside them doing his best to look tough like he belonged and was part of their gang. Cadwallader maintained his perfect composure and social etiquette.

"I removed the soul directly from the body after a witnessed confession was documented, and confirmed by all concerned parties. I will spare you the details of the exact manner of the soul extraction, but rest assured my reputation is there for a reason."

Still holding up the man's head with his foot, Satan turned away from his prey. That was the only description Andrew could think of; the way Satan burnt his gaze into his new "guest." Satan was the ultimate apex predator and this man, this soul, was now his prey. Satan once again became jovial Satan and smiled at Cadwallader.

"You are the best, aren't you?"

"I am second only to you sir. But to further answer the question; the flesh did not survive the process. There remains no possibility of return, rebirth, or progression until you allow it."

Then Satan did something which would forever haunt Andrew. He understood why Satan had told him to stay where he had been and not to be doing what Andrew was currently doing. Because what Andrew witnessed in the office, what he saw, he was never able to un-see. However, Andrew came to use what he saw as a reminder and guide for the rest of his life. Satan turned back to the man on the floor. Satan's normal polished smile became something otherworldly. The effect expanded to encompass his entire face. Despite turning away as quick as his soul would allow, Andrew still wasn't fast enough, and the sight was permanently etched into his memory. Andrew later learned, even just that quick glimpse of what he witnessed was enough to singe his body back in Purgatory.

Satan's smile went beyond his normal practiced and polished human smile. It went beyond his predator smile. The smile didn't grow into some large cavernous mouth like Mick Jagger or Steven Tyler. Satan's normal smile, his eyes, his face seemed to become a portal which opened through several planes of existence all at once, and the edges of those planes began to enter into Hell, specifically through Satan. Andrew, unfortunately, saw glimpses of things and beings no mortal could look upon and want to continue to live.

After turning away from the office Andrew stumbled to the distant corner of the balcony, catching himself on the rail and closed his eyes. Then a series of screams, human screams, filled with pure abject terror resonated from inside the office. Andrew put his hands over his ears in a belated and futile attempt to block the sound of those screams. Andrew's earlier apathy for the med tech began to crumble. He began to shudder, and tears began to stream down his face. Andrew was shaking and wiping away his tears as he opened his eyes to look out over Hell. Wrapping his arms around himself and with a gentle rocking rhythm, he began trying to convince himself everything would be okay.

Andrew didn't know how long he stood there like that, a mental invalid. But slowly he started to regain his physical and mental control. Just as he was getting himself back under control, Andrew was startled by something flying over him and screaming as it went. There was once again a body flying out of Satan's office and over the balcony. Andrew looked up in time to see it was Percy. He was flailing his arms and legs as he sailed out. Probably at some point, Percy would land somewhere in what seemed to be the infinite expanse of Hell.

*"I guess he went to join the janitor."* Andrew's little light-hearted joke to himself helped. He was now able to calm the majority of the fear and anxiety resulting from what he had just witnessed. Satan had been right earlier when he had told Andrew a smile would help him relax.

"Cadwallader," Andrew heard Satan speaking as he was still staring off into Hell trying to steady his nerves while watching

Percy go; *"huh, you can really see for a long way."*

Even though he knew it was wrong of him, Andrew sort of laughed at Percy. Andrew couldn't help himself. It was just that Percy's arms and legs were floundering about as if he were trying to fly, or swim, or some combination of the two, as he soared over and down into Hell. This brief respite of humor helped Andrew finally get his jangled nerves settled. As far as Andrew could tell Percy never figured out how to fly, and was still flailing and falling when he finally disappeared from Andrew's sight. Inside the office, the screaming had stopped and Satan's attention had turned to Cadwallader.

"Please show our new guest to my personal study. Take a moment to make him comfortable, and then please return. Thank you."

Andrew shuddered at the way Satan said personal study and for Cadwallader to take a moment. It was cold and dead sounding with ominous implications allowing Andrew to cultivate some more empathy for the poor dumb schmuck. Even though it had been Andrew who spent the entire morning running in fear of Cadwallader, and then having to face Satan; his saving grace was that he knew he was innocent. Andrew just needed a forum in which to present his case. But the med tech, Andrew didn't even know his name; *"he had to have realized he was going to get caught, didn't he?"* thought Andrew. Either way, if he didn't already, the guy was about to regret stealing someone else's soul and trying to cheat the Devil.

A hesitant Andrew turned slowly, and with care, looked back into the office. Just in case Satan still had his evil multi-dimensional vibe going, Andrew was ready to turn away again. It seemed safe. He watched as Cadwallader left via his usual manner. Except for this time he "escorted" the guest by dragging the man across the floor as he incoherently wailed and clawed at the carpet.

Despite having his back toward him, Satan spoke in a manner as if he knew Andrew was not over at the edge of the balcony. But Andrew was instead near the door, where he now stood. Standing where Satan had asked him not to be standing.

"Andrew if you are done admiring the view we need to finish our time together and see you on your way."

# 18.

Andrew turned back hoping Satan was normal looking again. He was, and Andrew walked back into the office and returned to his seat in front of Satan's desk. Satan once again was sitting in his chair behind his desk. He smoothed down the front of his suit, making an adjustment where none was needed. Even after everything Andrew had directly, and indirectly, witnessed, Satan was still the picture-perfect definition of suave.

"I have two parting gifts for you, and before you try the human polite refusal thing, do not, it irritates me."

Andrew held his tongue. He was certain Satan was still probably just a little upset about the current events. Andrew certainly didn't want to do anything that would compromise the now seemingly calm and normal situation.

"The first is this." and from off his desk, Satan presented Andrew a business card. The same card he currently held in his hand.

"This is for all the trouble which befell you today."

Satan passed the card across his desk, leaving it front of Andrew.

"Both my opposite and I are in agreement that you are in need of compensation and a degree of consideration. For had this, shall we say, clerical mishap." Satan paused pursed his lips and continued, "Or let's not confuse things with lawyer double-speak. If this serious fuck-up had been permitted to occur, and your soul was taken out of turn, The Dictum of –feedback- would have been violated. By doing so, a rampant causality anomaly would have been created. The result of which would have led to the collapse of our current existence as even I understand it."

Andrew felt sort of impressed at that point. He might have unmade Creation.

"This card is my way of saying sorry about the fuck-up, and like it says, I owe you one. By one I mean one favor, your desire, your wish, your Holy Grail, or Golden Fleece. Whatever single earthly gain your heart should desire."

Andrew thought about that: One wish. One of whatever he wanted. Life was about to become much more interesting.

"Here is a little free advice from me to you. Don't be stupid like my current guest who tried to steal and sell your soul for world peace. For every person who does such a thing, and yes there are people who do sacrifice themselves. They sell their soul to save the souls of everyone else. They think such an act of altruism will save them; they will be granted a cosmic reprieve which negates the contract. Not just clemency, those idiots think they will gain some Heavenly favor for their self-righteous hypocrisy. As you have just witnessed they don't."

Yes, Andrew could attest to that statement. There was going to be no reprieve for the med tech. A flash of the horror Andrew just witnessed flashed in his head.

"As for selling your soul for something as asinine as world peace? I can match every one of those hippies against some asshole who wants world war and destruction. The two always cancel."

Andrew would first never have thought about something like selling his soul for world peace. He was just too much a pragmatist, and not enough of a hippy. Andrew, however, was a bit morally and idealistically disturbed by the idea that there were people who would sell their soul for world destruction.

Andrew considered such an act as disturbing as Satan's multi-dimension smile. Andrew regretted using such an analogy because that fresh memory once more came to his mind and made Andrew shudder. Quietly he took a deep breath and steadied himself.

"Now, this leads into my last part. Go home and watch *Darby O'Gill and the Little People*." Satan made a contemplative look and murmured, "someday Disney." Then his attention was back on topic. "It is a good lesson in common sense and on how to use wishes. You also get to listen to Sean Connery sing."

Now that was something Andrew would have never imagined, Satan telling someone to watch a Disney movie.

"When you are ready, and you have made your choice, call the number."

Andrew picked up the card and slid it into his front pants pocket. Before Andrew could say anything, there were three sharp knocks on the office door. Cadwallader had returned from his appointed task. He entered the room and approached to his usual spot at the edge of Satan's desk.

Satan looked up at Cadwallader with a quite smile. Andrew wasn't sure, but it almost looked like a smile of relief.

"He's all ready Cadwallader. Please take Mr. Wheeler home."

Cadwallader gave a polite nod of his head to Satan. He then turned and smiled at Andrew.

"It will be my pleasure, sir."

Andrew stood up. Out of socially polite habit more than anything else; Andrew was about to reach his hand out to Satan as part of leaving. On a personal level, Andrew hated shaking or touching hands with other people. He thought it was disgusting. Andrew had no idea what the other person had just done with their hand or where it had been. But, there were times when the simple social courtesy of a handshake was expected. Andrew felt this was one of those times. But, as he just started to move his arm, Andrew stopped. He couldn't actually be sure if he heard it or not, but a slight *–aarughmm–* throat clearing sound came to his ear. It was enough to make him pause for a moment. If he had heard the sound, it could have only come from Cadwallader. If Cadwallader had made the sound, he did it to signal Andrew to abort his present course of action. Andrew rethought the good-bye and thank-you handshake. He then recalled his earlier observations of the personal interactions between Satan and his staff.

Andrew turned to Cadwallader and performed a bow of respect and thanks, "I am in your capable hands, Mr. Cadwallader.", and stood.

Andrew then turned to Satan performed a bit of a deeper bow of respect and thanks, "Thank you for your time, patience, and generous hospitality Satan."

Andrew held the bow and walked with a slight left and right awkward weaving serpentine pattern backward to the threshold of the door and stood. Andrew noted both Cadwallader and Satan both gave him approving gazes.

Cadwallader's attention returned to Satan.

"We shall depart now."

Cadwallader bowed in a more crisp and practiced manner and joined Andrew at the door. The two of them turned and exited Satan's office.

As the door shut, Cadwallader turned to Andrew with a perfect smile.

"Well done Mr. Wheeler. Well done."

Cadwallader led Andrew across the reception office and opened the door which would take them back to Purgatory. Andrew approached the doorway with trepidation knowing the Absence was there waiting for him. However, Andrew was relieved to find the return journey from Hell to Purgatory to be both quicker and less agonizing than it had been going from Purgatory to Hell. When Andrew entered the gateway between Hell and Purgatory, he felt what he called the Absence as he did the first time but now it was muted and weak. Over the top, smothering the Absence, was a different feeling. This one was more of an exhilaration of sorts; a warm feeling started to gather round him the further he moved away from the door to Hell.

Andrew understood there was an obvious reason for what he was feeling. But, until a person had first-hand experience of the process of going to, and then leaving Hell, they would never understand. This time in the darkness of the space Andrew didn't need to see where to go, he could feel it. It was like the game "warm or cold" except this game was more "happy or sad." If he felt happy, he moved in that direction. If he started to feel sad, he adjusted his direction until he was happy again. Despite the complete darkness, Andrew was able to take a few short steps forward by following the warm-fuzzy feelings. Then several feet in front of him, Cadwallader who had already walked to the other end, opened the door to Purgatory. Andrew with a happy gait and with an overwhelming sense of relief took his final steps out of Hell. Cadwallader shut the door behind him.

There in Purgatory, still sitting at the government surplus desk with both hands still palms down, was his body. He walked over to himself and wondered what he was supposed to do. It was surreal. He was just sitting there, well not him, because he was him, and his body was not him unless he were inside it. In which case, he would be himself again? Even with his expanded clarity of thought, Andrew's emotions caused him confusion in dealing with his dilemma. He was standing, his body sitting, sitting there with a vapid look on its, his, face. The situation was very weird. Andrew started to feel sad that his soul wasn't inside his body; that his soul and body were separate. Andrew looked away from his body and over to Cadwallader. Andrew was sure his feelings expressed clearly on his face.

"Mr. Wheeler, to resolve your current situation you need only to stand in front of your body, look it in the eyes and relax."

Andrew did as Cadwallader instructed. He walked to the front of the desk bent down and looked himself in the eye. It was quite weird and doing this made Andrew think about looking at himself in a mirror. As he thought about that idea, and without knowing the how's or the why's of it, his soul was back in his body. He was whole again!"

With a stupid smile and giddy feeling, Andrew looked at everything as if it all was new. It was and wasn't the same as before. Now things seemed a bit more muddled, his instant clarity of thought was gone. Now he no longer wished to debate Cadwallader on the merits of having a flesh body, as he had wanted to before. Andrew had prepared himself for the nauseating effect of Purgatory, but there wasn't any. In fact, it looked almost as it did when he saw it with his soul. Purgatory still had its' sort of weird other-worldly geometry and continued to resonate with the odd sounds and the glow. But this time Andrew didn't feel like he was pulled in every direction and dimension at once. Andrew guessed it was the somewhat quizzical expression on his face which caused Cadwallader to explain the situation to him.

"Mr. Wheeler your recent journeys have changed your mortal perception of Purgatory. You have traveled to, and been a part of, something never before experienced by a mortal. Because of these events, you now have a new understanding of existence. You will have to come to accept some of your life's mystery has become lost. After all, you experienced today some aspects of your life which will seem rather mundane. The caveat is, some facets of it will become much more difficult. But I have confidence you will be able to come to terms with the situation."

Andrew sort of understood what Cadwallader had just said. In a fashion, he had died, seen the afterlife, and came back from it. An experience like that will change a person. However, Andrew didn't have the luxury of contemplating the full meaning of his experience, because he tried to stand up, and couldn't. He attempted it again and almost fell over and out of the chair.

Standing up was something he had done so many times he didn't even think about how it was even done. Now he had to force his body even to move. He even recruited his unwilling, and foreign feeling, hands to help push him up. With an effort, he managed to stand, but his legs felt sort of wobbly and strange.

"It feels like my arms and legs are asleep. Like they haven't been used in a while."

Cadwallader, who had been watching the process, removed what looked like a normal pocket-watch from his suit pocket. Andrew was disappointed when Cadwallader opened it. Andrew wanted it to be something crazy with several watch faces, some of them with numbers and hands, while others did not. Instead, those faces would be covered with odd symbols and patterned lights. But the watch was just a watch. Well, not just a watch, Andrew thought, it was a smoove watch. Not every person could pull out a pocket watch with such style and flair, but Cadwallader did. And he did it with perfection.

"Mr. Wheeler, you were vacant from your physical body for two hours and twenty-three minutes of Earth time. Your soul spent one full and two increments of a span in Hell, which would correspond to approximately, three earth days. Of course, your physical body was subject to the progression of time here in Purgatory. That was an exact five moments or a bit past seven Earth days. You are correct in your statement Mr. Wheeler. Your body has not been used for quite some time."

Andrew was at a loss for words. He didn't even want to try and understand what Cadwallader had just said about time how multi-dimensional time worked. Instead, he decided he had to sit back down. One reason was that his legs could no longer stand. The second reason was that, trying to understand and process, how those variations in time worked, hurt his brain. It was easier for Andrew to come to terms with the whole situation through acceptance. That was just how the universe worked, instead of trying to find a rational solution.

Andrew rubbed and gently slapped at his arm and legs to get the feeling back in them. As he did, he also thought if his body weren't in the way, his soul would've probably understood what Cadwallader had just told him. He would have understood all the variations in the time between all the various dimensions. But, Andrew didn't care. Andrew was happy to be whole again. Once he was able to get his body working, he would be on his way home. So, Andrew kept working at his muscles, and soon he was able to wiggle his toes.

"So, it's around noon earth time, Mr. Cadwallader?"

"Yes, Mr. Wheeler, twenty minutes past the hour to be precise."

"That works for me Mr. Cadwallader; that works for me. Shall we be on our way? I am sure you have other errands to which you should attend."

Cadwallader smiled his perfect smile in approval

"Well said, Mr. Wheeler. If you are prepared and feel you can move with confidence, please, follow me."

Andrew put his hands on the desk, being careful not to position them with palms down. He didn't want to chance his soul leaving his body again. Then using his whole body, he pushed, and a lifted and was able to stand. The process was easier when everything worked together. Andrew stood up and stepped out from behind the plain enameled gray government surplus desk.

"Following you Mr. Cadwallader."

On wobbly legs with stiff, shuffling steps, Andrew followed Cadwallader back into the elevator. This time Cadwallader did not turn to stand and look at the back corner. The door which opened into Purgatory. Instead, he stepped in and stood to face the seamless wall, which Andrew knew would become the exit. As soon as Andrew was standing beside him, the back door closed, and the elevator moved to return to the Earth plane or dimension. The seamless wall separated, and Andrew now on steadier legs followed Cadwallader out of the elevator. The were now back on the main floor of the office building. Andrew walked next to Cadwallader down the empty hallway which echoed with their footsteps. They walked to the main, and as far as Andrew knew, the only, doors of the non-descript normal looking office building. As he had done when they first arrived,

Cadwallader pushed the door open and held it for Andrew.

Andrew still had no idea where the building was located. But he was quite certain of where he was. Andrew took a moment and stood on the top marble step. He took in the world as if it were his first time experiencing it. He felt the warmth of the noon sun on his face and arms. He inhaled the fresh spring air. He heard the passive background sound of the wind in the trees, birds singing, distant cars on the freeway, a plane flying overhead. Andrew was home.

# 19.

The limo was still parked where they had left it.  As Andrew and Cadwallader approached the car, the passenger door once again opened of its' own accord.  Cadwallader, the consummate host, gestured for Andrew to enter first.  Andrew stepped into the darkness and took his former seat. Cadwallader then entered and took his customary place in the back seat, his seat.  As he did so, the door closed.  A moment later the limo started, and the two of them were on their way.  Andrew noticed Cadwallader's limo was different this time.

The interior was still wrapped in darkness, so only he and Cadwallader were visible. As far as Andrew knew he and Cadwallader were sitting on milk crates. Comfortable milk crates, but since he couldn't see anything, he had no proof they weren't. But this time he didn't care. The first-time Andrew rode in the car he was being taken to Satan to defend, and he imagined at the time, to possibly have his soul ripped from his body. Yes, Andrew definitely liked the ride more now that he was leaving Hell. *"Funny how stuff like that worked,"* was the bemused thought trailing through his once again fleshy brain. Not quite sure of how his time was to conclude Andrew thought he would ask. Ask with proper manners of course.

"Pardon my forward question Mr. Cadwallader, but where are we off to now?"

Andrew could neither confirm nor deny, but it appeared that Cadwallader was also, maybe just a bit, relaxed as well. Of course, his was done in the usual perfect fashion.

"Mr. Wheeler I am taking you to a local spa which specializes in acupuncture, massage, and seaweed mud wraps. Your body was indirectly singed a bit while your soul was in Hell. The wrap, along with several other treatments will help to reduce the irritation which will soon be developing."

Andrew looked at his arms and hands for the first time since returning to his body. He noticed there were some redness and flaking, and some blotchy areas to his skin. He thought he looked like someone who might be coming down with leprosy. Again, with a shudder, Andrew remembered with horror Satan's otherworldly smile. He had caught only caught a glimpse of it, but he knew some of the damage to his body was a result of his glimpse. Andrew was now even happier he had turned away when he did. Any longer and the trauma to his body, as well as soul, might have been more extensive than some mild scorching and a nightmare image.

"How come I don't feel it now?"

"For the same reason, your legs were unsteady when you first returned to your body. Mr. Wheeler, your soul, and your body have been away from each other for quite some time, and the two, shall we say, need to reconnect. It is a process that will take some time, but the spa will help."

As they quietly lounged in their respective seats, Andrew thought Cadwallader was going to doze off; he knew he wanted too. There was an eerie silence to their ride and of the limo itself. It was all very unnatural, but given what Andrew had just been through, he didn't give it much thought. Andrew becoming lost in his contemplations was beginning to be lulled into a light sleep from the silence of the ride, and he almost missed hearing Cadwallader politely clearing his throat.

"Mr. Wheeler we will soon arrive at your destination where we shall be parting company. Therefore, I will take this time to impart several pieces of advice onto you.

Andrew wasn't sure what to expect. So he remained silent and nodded his head to indicate he was paying attention and for Cadwallader to proceed.

"Mr. Wheeler, first I wish to apologize for today's, as Satan put it, fuck-up. I pride myself on being a perfectionist. Not the paltry human misconception of perfection, but true, absolute perfection."

Andrew wanted to be insulted by the perfection thing, but he couldn't. He would not only accept, but would readily admit, Cadwallader was by any human definition, and conception of the word, perfect. But most of all it would have just been rude to interrupt Cadwallader.

"I understand reparations were offered and accepted not only out of the necessity of balance but also for the sake of courteous apology."

Andrew's thoughts, once again, drifted from Cadwallader to Satan's card now in his wallet.

"Mr. Wheeler, I extend to you a very important piece of advice as a personal act of contrition. Do not hold onto Satan's offer for an extended period. For if you do, you will find it will slowly come to consume you."

Andrew thought it was funny; it was like Cadwallader was reading his mind. Because that was something, Andrew had considered, to keep the card for a rainy day. After all, it was in every manifestation of the saying a "*get out of jail free card.*" If Andrew ever got into a situation he couldn't handle, he could just call Satan. If he decided he wanted a million, or a billion, or even a million-billion-trillion dollars; boom he could give Satan a call and tell him that's what he wanted. It could be anything Andrew wanted it to be, with the slight limitation of it only worked once. There was no, "I want my favor to be infinite wishes" or "I want to be a god." It was a singular offer and constrained by Earthly human things.

To Andrew, it was quite awesome to think about all of the possibilities. In just that brief moment of contemplation, Andrew became mentally consumed with the possibilities of what he could do with the card. Andrew began wondering if that was how Gollum, from *Lord of the Rings*, felt about the One Ring. With that thought in his head, Andrew began to understand what Cadwallader had just said to him. What he meant. Andrew came to imagine himself as Gollum. He was emaciated and filthy, out on the street. Huddled in some dark alley corner, living inside a grimy, smelly cardboard box. There in his claw-like hands was Satan's card which remained immaculate, and he was referring to it as his "Favor." With a physical and mental shudder, Andrew knew hanging onto the card was not a good thing to do.

"Satan presented it to you not out of malice, because of what the card can do to you should you let it. But for what you can do for yourself, with it. The card is a grand gesture, and its intent is to be used. Think of it in your human terms. It is similar to a fish in your refrigerator. It can only remain there for a short time before it goes bad and pollutes the entirety."

Andrew noted Cadwallader was looking at him. Cadwallader was waiting for acknowledgment that Andrew understood what he was being told. It was a perfect look of *I'm waiting, and I look perfect doing it.*

"Yes, Mr. Cadwallader. I unequivocally understand what you have just told me."

Cadwallader nodded and continued.

"Mr. Wheeler I also offer this further advice. Be exact in your phrasing when you do come to a decision. Satan will not cheat you, or alter your choice out of malice or amusement, but because of legal ambiguity or inadequacy. If there is any modicum of room for a legal reinterpretation of an item or clause, something Satan feels suits him better, he will exploit it. Soon he will bring your request to resemble something more ideal for him. Satan is the Overlord of Hell for a reason."

Andrew also well understood the second part. He remembered the bookshelves in the reception office filled with row after row of legal texts. Andrew never did get to see the full length of the soul contract scroll, which Satan and Cadwallader had shown him, although it seemed an impressive length. He remembered Satan skimming over yards of paper saying most of it was all lawyer talk. Andrew was pretty certain there were no legal loop-holes in any of Satan's contracts.

Andrew began to imagine a room in Hell filled with lawyers. They had been damned to there, which of course was the automatic fate of any person graduating from Law School. But there, within the squalor and cramped confines of a horrible room, which in some way would resemble something like the attic courtroom place from Kafka's," The Trial." Only that room was worse because it was in Hell. Andrew imagined that room in Hell. It would reek of sweat and human filth, and no breeze or fresh air ever entered. In that room for all eternity, the twisted and tormented souls of every lawyer, ever, were forced to make iron-clad soul contracts. They wrote those contracts or else. Of course, Andrew didn't have to imagine too hard what the, or else part, would be like for anyone who displeased Satan. Andrew had seen and was still on some level physically and mentally scared by it. Andrew could still see with horror Satan's multi-dimensional evil smile as he looked at the screaming med tech. The man who had tried to cheat Satan by selling Satan Andrew's soul instead of his own. Then there were the fates of the unnamed janitor and Percy, both flying off the balcony of Satan's office to end up somewhere in the abysmal pits of Hell. Such was their reward for lack of respect, manners, and for their mistakes.

Not knowing what else to do. Andrew repeated the affirmative nod of his head and at the same time said, "Yes. I understand."

"I will leave off with the final bit of advice Mr. Wheeler. I will also bid you pay heed to Satan's suggestion about watching *Darby O'Gill and the Little People*. It may sound odd to you now, but you will find it helpful when it comes time to make your choice. Even, if you get nothing else from the movie, you will get to listen to the delightful singing of Mr. Connery."

Cadwallader paused a moment holding Andrew's gaze. They stayed like that long enough to make Andrew start to wonder if he had done something wrong. Or was Cadwallader waiting for Andrew to say something? Then Andrew realized Cadwallader was in some kind of reverie, or swoon, over Sean Connery's singing. Cadwallader blinked several times and was back to being Cadwallader.

"Mr. Wheeler we understand you may feel the need to, and most likely will talk to others, your family or friends and acquaintances about today's events. Please understand we cannot, and would not, deter you from this course of action. Your choice would be an act of Free Will as outlined in subparagraph A, of section four hundred and fifty-two of the Dictim of -feedback-. Thus it remains a decision for you to make. However, understand by doing so, by telling people, such an action in some ways may hurt you, and in others ways, it may help. But, that is how your lives work. It is also for you to come to terms with."

Andrew thought about it a moment and realized once again it seemed Cadwallader could read his mind. It was either he could read his mind or Cadwallader was just very good at understanding how humans worked. Maybe it was both options. Andrew did hear Satan refer to him as "the best." Andrew had thought about how he was going to tell people about what happened to him. He figured he would be questioned by "Hey Susie" and "What's up Bill" from the bus stop about the limo. He had to talk to Nancy about it. She had been there in his cube and interacted with Cadwallader. Also, he wanted to know what they thought happened. Ultimately, and if for no other reason, Andrew just wanted to talk to someone about it. At that time, Andrew wasn't sure what Cadwallader had meant by how talking about his journey may hurt or help him, but he guessed he would find out.

"As part of this action, you must also appreciate the fact of no one you tell will believe your story as truth. Because of this, you should not hold the listener's choice of disbelief against them. The events in which you were involved in today are beyond a normal, and customary, human rational occurrence and experience. Your experiences and tales of these events will be regarded in such a manner by those who hear them. The listener will perceive what they want and then disregarded the rest as fiction. After all, would you believe such a story as truth if it were told to you?"

Andrew contemplated the caveat. Would no one believe him? Andrew wanted to say yes; he would believe such a story because it just happened to him. But what if this had never happened to him? What if instead, it had happened to Monica, or Nancy, or even "Hey Susie." Would he believe any of them? Really, honest to goodness, believe someone if they came and told him the story of how they had gone to Hell and met the Devil.

The logical part of him, which after his soul and body had reunited, seemed to be more vocal, and told him, of course, he wouldn't believe it. Andrew had just spent the morning coming to terms with his theological beliefs. Andrew's acceptance came only because he'd been continuously bitch-slapped by the fact that he had a soul. If none of the day's events had ever happened, he would still be the person he had always been. The quiet, not quite atheist, more of a progressive agnostic, and unsure if he even had a soul. But Andrew's imaginative part won. Although he had to concede such a story would sound crazy, who was he to say it couldn't have happened? The world is a crazy place filled with strange things. However, there was still a part of him, the logical, pragmatic part, which made him think the whole telling people wasn't going to end well.

"Thank you, Mr. Cadwallader. I appreciate your sound counsel and judgment and will give them kind regard when making my decision."

Andrew was very pleased with his response. He thought it was quite eloquent and loquacious. If nothing else his internal Thesaurus and Manual of Style were getting the dust brushed off of them.

Cadwallader arched, perfectly, he left eyebrow and regarded Andrew.

"Mr. Wheeler there may be hope for you yet. We have arrived at your destination."

Andrew hadn't noticed the car had stopped moving. But then again, he hadn't noticed when the car had started moving. After all of the day's event's Andrew didn't think anything could surprise him anymore. The door opened, and although the afternoon sun shone directly on the car, as with every time before, none dare to enter into the interior. Andrew looked out at the sepia colored world. Cadwallader moved himself to his left, and gestured that Andrew should exit the car; he would not be.

Andrew moved from his seat, and out into the light and warmth of the noon sun. Andrews's eyes watered, and he blinked several times as they adjusted to the bright afternoon sunlight. He turned and looked back inside the car. Once again it was just inky blackness where no light penetrated.

"Thank you, Mr. Cadwallader. Have a good day or span, or moment, or."

As Andrew faltered, the inky blackness retreated enough to allow Cadwallader to be once more seen by Andrew.

"Just bid me good journey's Mr. Wheeler as I extend the same to you."

"Good journeys Mr. Cadwallader."

"Good journeys Mr. Wheeler."

Andrew stepped back, the door closed of its' own accord, and the almost cliché limo drove off down the street.

# **20.**

Andrew turned and found himself standing on the sidewalk in front of a very elegant and prestigious looking spa. He took a step forward not sure what else to do, or even how to approach the place. Andrew could only imagine the receptionist's response were he to walk in and say, "Yes, I have an appointment today. It was made by Satan, Supreme Overlord of Hell." Oh yes, that would go over just grand.

After such an introduction, two security guards would appear. They would be stereotypically very large, very muscular, with hard chiseled jaws, slicked back hair and Hollywood good looks. They would casually approach Andrew from both sides. Then with their vice-like hands, they would grip Andrew by his puny and weak arms. His arms would be bruised and crushed by these behemoths as they escorted him back out onto the sidewalk with a shove out the door. They would turn away walking back inside laughing and bragging with the receptionist about how far they were able to toss him out onto the street.

Andrew took another hesitant step forward almost reaching the dark tinted door. Just as he was about to reach out for the handle the door opened. Not expecting it Andrew flinched and to his chagrin there stood a very lovely young lady holding the door, who regarded Andrew for a moment. Andrew wondered if something was wrong because of the look she was giving him. He wasn't sure if it was; *"oh he's no bother just some guy who needs directions away from here."* Or the other option which was much like his first thought but without being thrown out onto the street. Instead, since he was already outside, it would be more of they would walk up to him and use their oversized muscular fingers and poke him in his puny chest, cracking several of his ribs. With aggressive pokes and shoves, they would drive him down the sidewalk and away from the building. Andrew was certain he heard someone inside press the security button for the two security guards to please come to the front and gleefully hurt him.

Then the very lovely young lady spoke with a very inviting voice and welcoming smile, "Please, Mr. Andrew Wheeler, come in. We are expecting you." She stepped back from the door holding it open for Andrew. Apparently, there was a third option that Andrew hadn't thought of or had imagined.

Andrew was still a bit suspicious. However, he had to admit that up to this moment both Cadwallader and oddly enough Satan, had been men, well beings anyway, of their word. Satan told him he was a guest and would be treated as such, and Andrew had been treated in just such a manner. Cadwallader had said he was taking Andrew to a spa, and so he had. Andrew decided to just accept the situation and everything from that moment forward as de facto.

"Everything is ready for you. I was told to assure you that all the expenses have been taken care of, to include your ride home. You are to worry about nothing and just enjoy the afternoon as our guest."

Andrew walked into the spa and embraced the inimitable insanity of the day de facto style.

# 21.

"And no one else was with me?"

It was Friday morning, and Andrew was mildly perplexed by the conversation he was having with Nancy. He was sitting in his cube looking across the narrow hallway at Nancy sitting in her cube. This cross cube chit-chat was their usual mid-morning ritual they had been doing for several years. It was during this time they vented over how poorly the Twins or Vikings were playing, or how much they hated the winter cold or the muggy summer humidity. Other times they raved with enthusiasm about how well the Twins or the Vikings were playing, or how pretty the snow looked as it floated down, or how nice it was to be warm again. It was several years of passive dating which never became anything more than a friendship. And Andrew found he preferred it that way. They were friends, good friends, and good friends were hard to come by. Andrew was glad he hadn't gone and screwed it up.

Of course, Andrew had almost done just that a couple of years earlier when he planned on asking Nancy out on an actual date. He had planned out the entire evening several days in advance and was going to make a casual, "What are you doing tonight?" sort of line over lunch at work. He had made supper reservations, bought theater tickets and everything. But fate vetoed his best-laid plans. That Friday morning as he waited at the bus stop his younger sister Tina called with life problems. Her personal upheavals consisted of difficult professors, finals, and an emotional boyfriend break-up. Most of all how she needed a break from college life in St. Cloud.

The momentous night came, and instead of spending it with Nancy, Andrew and his sister had a nice supper and saw a play. Although Andrew felt a little bit cheated by the Universe, it turned out the Universe had in fact done him a favor. Because Nancy already had plans on that same Friday night. She was going out on a date with a guy named Garland; whom she married later that year. Andrew found out all about their wonderful first date Monday morning when they talked about their various weekend activities. Andrew figured it all worked out for the best; everyone was happy, and they all got what they needed.

Despite her being married, and he involved with someone, Andrew sometimes still found himself *looking* at Nancy. She was blond haired, blue eyed with a milky complexion, she fit into the stereotypical Scandinavian Minnesotan archetype. Andrew recalled how she came into the office one cold winter's day. She was dressed in a heavy, obvious fake fur coat and hat and covered in snow and frost. Her appearance made Andrew think she looked like a fictional character from a Hans Christian Andersen story. In a dramatic voice, just loud enough to be overheard by their surrounding coworkers, Andrew dubbed her "The Arctic Queen."

She never forgave him for that nickname. Because by the end of the day, everyone in the office started adding, "Your Majesty," to every conversation they had with her. Of course, she later got him back, but that was the nature of true friendship. Nancy brushed the errant lock of blonde hair, which continuously kept falling across her face, back up and behind her ears. She did it in such a manner that made Andrew think of her as an anime character and a possible new nickname.

"No, you were alone all morning."

Andrew had come to work on Friday not knowing what to expect. He was unsure of how the events of Thursday or his new appearance would be regarded. His skin had a slight tanned look from his soul's brief exposure to Hell, but no one seemed to notice or to say anything about it. At least he felt normal again. Cadwallader had been right, the afternoon spa was great. He entered the place not know what to expect, or how to explain the situation. While Andrew had been changing in the locker room, he was able to look at himself in the mirror. All of his skin was blotchy, reddish and flaky as if it had been dried out for several days in the desert but without the blistering. He also couldn't feel, or taste, or smell. In fact, he had little if any control of any of his normal senses after his soul reentered his body. By the end body wraps and massages, and facials and all the pampering he felt almost normal again.

But just like Cadwallader had warned him, no one believed anything Andrew said when he told them about his Thursday morning escapades. Andrew first learned this at Al's bar, which resulted in him finishing his beer in semi-ignored silence and then going home. Earlier that Friday morning at the bus stop, no one said anything to him about the events of Thursday morning.

He stood there with "Hey Susie" and "What's up Bill" waiting, eager for them to say something about the limo. They at least had to have remembered Cadwallader's limo pulling up. They were standing right next to Andrew when it all happened. They even stepped away from him when Cadwallader asked for Andrew to identify himself. They said nothing outside of "Hey," and "What's up." Andrew finally asked, casually of course, about the limo that had pulled up yesterday and blocked the bus. They both looked at Andrew confused; there had been no limousine yesterday, especially one which blocked the bus. Andrew passed it off as a news story he thought he heard, and decided to change the subject to the weather. He didn't want to press either Susie or Bill. He didn't know them well enough to try and make a big deal of it.

He would wait for work and try with Nancy.

"So, I guess this may sound weird but, what exactly happened to me yesterday?"

After the fiasco at the bar and getting no results at the bus stop, Andrew was reluctant to go into too much detail about his versions of Thursday's events. He would save that for his supper with Monica later that night.

"Well, you were sitting in your cube sort of working on your computer. I got up to go get a cup of coffee. Just after I walked by your cube, you stood up. You were looking all pale and shaky. Then you took off running out of your cube. You were in such a hurry you knocked over the supply table. Which, by the way, I cleaned up for you. So you owe me,"

Andrew smiled, "any time Nancy. Lunch? You name the place", and quickly Andrew added in jest, "within reason. You know how much I don't get paid, so you may have to borrow me some money."

Nancy laughed, and the troublesome lock of hair fell back across her left eye and cheek. She nonchalantly and probably subconsciously Andrew thought, brushed it back into place.

"I know how much you don't get paid, because it is the same amount I don't get paid, so don't worry about it."

Nancy continued with her narrative about the events of Thursday morning.

"But, after you ran into the supply table you dashed out the main doors toward the restrooms. You didn't come back, and a bit later Phil sent out an email to the group saying you had gone home sick. I started to worry because I tried to call you, later on, to make sure you made it home okay, but you didn't answer."

Andrew wasn't sure how everyone got the idea that he was sick or why Phil sent out an email telling everyone so. Of course, it wasn't all that far from the truth. He had been a kind of sick. As far as Andrew was concerned scared counted as sick. Besides being scared sick, he did almost, and might have for a second, died in a toilet stall at a coffee shop.

"I guess you're feeling better today? A twenty-four-hour bug of some kind?"

Andrew snorted a chuckle and nodded, "Yeah, something like that I guess. Needless to say, I am feeling better today. Almost like brand new."

Nancy laughed her light quite office laugh. This laugh was her usual normal laugh. However, to her chagrin, she had another one. Andrew learned about that laugh one night when everyone from the office went out for a combination happy hour and client bonus celebration. A few drinks and a great joke later, Nancy's out of office laugh surfaced; it was loud and raucous and very infectious. It even had several nasal type snort's to it. It was a good laugh. But not one to be used all the time.

"I guess I might have been delusional as well as having an upset stomach. Because I could have sworn, I was talking to this tallish, smoove looking black man in a perfectly tailored suit. He also spoke with a lordly English accent."

Andrew noticed Nancy's left eyebrow go up, "And what were you and Mr. Smoove talking about?"

Andrew fake coughed and cleared his throat.

"He told me he was here to collect my soul because I had sold it to the devil."

And before Nancy could respond he continued, "At one point you were asked to verify the contract was," Andrew thought it better not to discuss the blood spot because he knew Nancy was squeamish when it came to blood, "in fact my signature and I was who I was. If that makes any sense?"

Nancy's left eyebrow lowered, her right hand came up with a finger pointed in his direction, and the errant lock of hair took its place.

"I'm starting to suspect your twenty-four-hour bug was a case of the brown bottle flu."

Andrew realized Nancy was not going to believe him. Just like the guys at the bar. Just like Hey Susie and What's up Bill at the bus stop. As soon as Andrew mentioned anything to do with Cadwallader and having the soul contract, everyone stopped listening and mentally came up with another conclusion. Even though Nancy had met and talked to Cadwallader, she wouldn't remember or believe it. It didn't matter, and Andrew decided not to pursue the topic any further because he didn't want to labor the subject with Nancy.

Andrew had been told no one would believe him and to not hold their disbelief against them. Besides he also didn't want someone to catch a brief part of their conversation and start spreading a rumor that he and left sick yesterday because he was hung-over. Andrew thought if anyone was going to believe, or even pretend to try to believe him, it would be Monica. After all, she was his girlfriend. According to Andrew's personal relationship guide, there was a supposed to be a level of trust and commitment which came with being in a relationship. He would tell her the whole story that night at supper even if she wouldn't, or couldn't believe him. Andrew knew and prepared himself knowing, it would be okay because she would at least be supportive.

"Back to work, I guess.

Say, how's the InterWeb account developing?" Andrew turned the conversation from the mid-morning banter back to work. Not because it was about time for their break was over, but because he didn't know who was listening.

## 22.

Andrew was sitting opposite of Monica at a table in their favorite Minneapolis restaurant Sol Casa. At the moment, Andrew was a bit unsure of how their relationship was going. He had been contemplating their relationship earlier that very Friday afternoon while eating lunch.

He and Monica had been dating for just over seven months. Although they had a satisfying physical relationship, sometimes Andrew emotionally felt like an emotional outsider to Monica. He lived in a modest sized condo over in St. Paul, not too far from Grand. Monica lived in the upscale luxury condo apartments on the east side of the Central Avenue Bridge in Minneapolis. Monica always insisted Andrew stay over at her place on her side of town. She had only visiting Andrew's place and neighborhood once and then only briefly. Despite these subtle differences, Andrew felt they were making it work.

Andrew and Monica met because of their jobs. Total Package was contracted to develop an advertising campaign for a local high-end department store. Andrew was brought on as a writer for the project. Monica was the head of purchasing for women's fashion. She had, as Andrew came to learn, been a model for the majority of her teen years and into her early twenties. She started modeling at age twelve when, as she said, "my tits finally perked up." But Monica also kept her eyes and brain open and worked her way up in the fashion and design business.

When Monica first walked into the Total Package offices, it became chaos. Andrew along with every other guy and two of the women had to keep from staring at her. She looked like one of the models from a lingerie catalog. Her hair was a dirty blond hair with honey accents. Her makeup made her green eyes flash like emeralds. Her complexion was flawless. Monica walked through the doors of the office like she was on a runway wearing the latest fashion. Everything about her screamed she was completely out of everyone's league so don't even bother.

Several meetings later and everyone had officially gotten to know each other. Which was to say, Monica at least remembered several names of the people with whom she was working. Andrew caught her attention at an account update meeting. He made a stupid quip causing everyone to stare at him in annoyance but put Monica in a fit of laughter. Several one-on-one conversations later Andrew finally found the nerve to ask her out on a dinner date. Soon after that night, the two of them were dating exclusively. Although it seemed mutual, sometimes Andrew felt like he was simply a placeholder in her life until someone else came along. However tonight it was all going to change. This supper was going to be their watershed moment, and Andrew felt positive on how well it would go. Then it got going.

Andrew loved Sol Casa. Besides just being a cool, Andrew thought it would be the perfect place for Cadwallader. Sol Casa also had the best fish tacos, guacamole, and tequila selection in Minneapolis. It was also one of the few places where Monica would almost eat what she ordered. Usually, when the two of them went out Monica would take several small bites of her food and be done. Either that or she would complain about the preparation and send the food back. Andrew guessed the tequila selection helped

Monica with her appetite.

Andrew was undeterred by the complete lack of belief by everyone he had told. He came to understand there was no way Monica going to one-hundred percent believe him. And Andrew was okay with that because he was certain Monica would at least try to believe. Even a simple show of support would be an improvement over all the other responses he had received so far. Then after the conversation, food, and drinks, they would go back to her place for the night with their relationship stronger than ever. Earlier at lunch time, he had a daydreamed, about that very scenario. About how wonderful and emotionally fulfilling the evening was supposed to go.

"Yup, that was how the evening was supposed ta' have gone."

Andrew muttered the comment to himself as the bus dropped him off at the corner of Selby and Dale. From there he was left with several lonely blocks to walk back to his condo. That gave Andrew plenty of time to contemplate all of the mistakes he had made early in the evening.

His only company on his walk were the various house and street lights. The passive house lights backlit the Elm and Oak trees. The buzz of the overhead street lights and their odd orange illumination of the sidewalk. The combination of the lights caused them to cast odd shadow forms across the sidewalk and cars parked along the street curb. As Andrew made his way home, he thought of those points where he should have seen, and possibly prevented his mistakes. He tried to determine where he had gone wrong with the conversation, and in a broader sense the whole evening.

First, maybe it had been the tequila shots for both of them. Second, maybe it had been the second and then the third round of the tequila just for Monica; Andrew was still enjoying his first one. But still, Andrew thought to himself, if Monica had any emotional attachment to him, he wouldn't be walking home right now. If she had cared about him in some way, she could have at least faked believing him. She could have pretended to be supportive. He wouldn't have cared. In fact, Andrew was hoping for that type of response. It would have been the thought that counted. Andrew held off on the big conversation until after the food arrived. Which by then Monica had finished two of her three shots of tequila. Andrew was trying to figure out an opening line when Monica aptly supplied one.

It started when she asked why he hadn't called her on Thursday. Andrew used her opening to test the waters and to gauge his audience response. Andrew asked Monica if she thought he was sick or something like that. It gave him a chance to look for any sign of sympathy. Monica said no. Then immediately wanted to know why he would ask her that? Was he sick? If so with what, because she had kissed him and they were sharing the same bowl of guacamole. Those should have been the signals things weren't going to go well, but maybe the Cerveza and tequila blocked his power of perception. Since Andrew was thinking about it, Cerveza, tequila, wine, well, pretty much any alcohol in some form was always used when dealing with Monica. But, as Andrew continued his walk home so did his mental replay of the evening's events in his thoughts.

He jumped right into it and asked Monica to let him tell her something. However, he wanted to tell it all at once and then she could respond when he was finished. Andrew explained it was because he might lose track of the story. Again, thinking back, Andrew thought maybe it was starting with the line, "Okay, this is a true story. I'm not making this up." That statement was somehow an anonym for Monica which caused her to hear, "everything I am about to say is a made-up, big fat lie and don't believe a word of it." Andrew proceeded to tell Monica everything. Maybe he was old-fashioned, but Andrew felt when two people were in what should be a caring, trusting relationship they were supposed to share stuff. Apparently, Monica didn't see it in a similar fashion. That was one of those, *"your relationship is one-sided"* cues Andrew had missed. However, Monica didn't miss her cue and was right on her mark when Andrew had finished telling her his story. She touched up her red lipstick, leveled her emerald green eyes at him, and began.

"So, you went to Hell for the day. Because some guy, who you say was the med tech from the clinic, stole your blood and used it as well as forging your signature and sold your soul to the devil for world peace.  Which in fact doesn't really work.  Because the devil told you, that for every person that sells their soul for world peace some other asshole would sell theirs for world destruction and the two cancel each other out."

Andrew wanted to respond, to say something in his defense.  But even as the thought registered on his face Monica shut him down.  She raised her hand with a pointed index finger in a gesture of, *"Silence! Now it's my turn."*  Humbled and cowed Andrew held his tongue.

"So, some guy named Cadwallader; nice name by the why how'd you come up with it?  Steal it from a television show?"

Andrew thought her sarcasm might have been a bit thick.  However, they had both been drinking.  Sometimes, well most of the time thought Andrew, alcohol made Monica less inhibited in several ways.   The first one, and it was always the first one; alcohol brought Monica's powers of sarcasm to a higher, more potent and acerbic level.  Andrew found this to be unpleasant, especially when her vitriol was directed at him.

Second, alcohol also reduced Monica's internal and external politeness filter.  From then on, she would start to say pretty much anything she wanted.  She also didn't care if she offended anyone in the process.  The third thing alcohol did, and it was the third one that kept Andrew tolerating the first two, it usually led to some pretty intense sex with Monica.

Andrew was walking along lost in his mental replay of the evening. It was at that very moment of thought he happened to stumble on a raised piece of sidewalk.

"Oh, I'm an idiot."

He said that thought out loud while at the same time his big brain internally, and with a touch of sarcasm replied, *"Now you get it."* A second later his little brain replied with a mournful, *"Not anymore we won't."*

Monica with a single swallow finished her tequila. She then chased it with a drink of beer. Andrew mentally prepared himself. He knew any time now, Monica's politeness filter would be turning off. She was in charge of the conversation at the moment, and since it was only the two of them, any and all comments and retort's would be directed at him. And from her tone and current facial expression, none of them would be pleasant or supportive.

"So, this Cadwallader guy stalks you all morning, and no one else can see or hear him. No one at the bus stop remembers him. No one at your office saw or remembers him despite interacting with him. He tries to kill you in a bathroom stall with a soul-sucking handcuff, and no one comes in during the process. You manage to talk him out of it by repeating some legal shit you remembered from human resource training. He then takes in his magical physics defying limo to an empty office building, but you don't know where. But the office building is not an office building but instead is a doorway or some shit to Purgatory. There in Purgatory, where your soul, is separated from your body?"

Andrew just nodded an affirmative to her question. He knew better than to try and respond or defend himself. If he were to try, it would only cause Monica to bring her voice up in volume so she could talk over the top of him. Fortunately, at the moment the normal background noise of the restaurant, the music, other conversations, and wait-staff service calls, were enough to keep their conversation socially private. The last thing he wanted was for the surrounding tables to stop what they were talking about to listen to Monica pillory him.

"And then you go to Hell to chit-chat with the devil. Who you say is in reality a very nice looking guy with great manners. He's an all-around a decent person despite being the ruler of Hell and all that shit the bible says. At some point, the devil had a phone call with someone, and the two of them decide you needed to be compensated for your mistreatment. Then the devil, oh, sorry, your new BFF Satan, gives you a card that grants you one free wish. Then you get brought back to Earth about the same time left because time moves differently in Hell. You go for a half day spa, thanks for inviting me by the way, because your skin was damaged by your time in Hell."

As Monica said it, as she told his story back to him, Andrew realized how stupid and unbelievable the whole thing sounded. Monica's retelling of his original story had been grossly abbreviated. Even through all the snarkiness, Andrew was forced to admit Cadwallader had been right. The logical, pragmatic part of his brain had been right. No one would believe such a story because it just didn't sound believable. Even to Andrew to whom it had happened. Which seemed ironic because at that very moment he had Satan's card was in his wallet. Andrew couldn't bring himself to leave the card at home, not trusting it to be safe there. But now he could almost doubt what happened to him because of how absurd it sounded. It sounded even more absurd when retold by Monica with her scathing sarcasm. Andrew quickly brought his attention back to Monica before she noticed his brief introspection. Her personal filter was now completely turned off, and it seemed Monica was not done throwing his story back in his face.

"After you're done with your spa day you then go to that trash bar Al's. Then home, then get up today go to work. And then, *then*, you call me to make dinner plans for tonight. Was there any time other than this afternoon when you thought of me in all of that?"

Monica looked at Andrew with an expression of you are such a sad little man. You are so lucky that I give you the privilege to date me.

"Seriously, is your work so boring that you are starting back with trying to write a book again? Is that what this is all about? Did you want to tell me the plot idea for the story? Because I will give you credit, it is sort of original. But you are just grabbing pieces from those nerd stories and movies you like to read and watch."

It was at that very moment when Andrew knew he was going home alone. He was sure no matter what the next words out of his mouth were there was no way Monica was going to believe him. Her counter argument had been delivered with such conviction that Andrew began to doubt what happened to him was real. Andrew thought if it weren't for the slight nagging sensation of Satan's card to remind him his little trip had been real, he would have ceded his point to her. But it had happened. In fact, just the thought of the card started to make him ponder about how to use his favor.

However, the spell of the card was quickly broken. Andrew watched Monica drink her other tequila and signaled the waiter for another one. Which the waiter promptly signaled back, it was on the way. Andrew knew that was one of the other reasons it was nice to go out with Monica. She was always given good customer service. Besides being attention grabbing gorgeous, she always wore something sexy and revealing. If a top didn't show her cleavage, she wore it in a way which would accentuate her boobs. Andrew's memory pushed the thought of the card aside and recalled an image of Monica in a tight sweater with a push-up bra. Then reality came crashing back. There she was across from him currently wearing an expression of, "well I'm waiting, you schmuck." Andrew finally finished his first shot of tequila. The burn of the alcohol helped him to gather up his courage. At the same time, Andrew thought of *"was this really what he wanted in a relationship?"* He responded to his inner rhetorical question with the optimistic answer of, *"this can still work out."*

"I thought of all the people I know you would be the one to understand. I didn't make this up. It's not some fiction. It's not bits and pieces of other stories I put together. I understand it sounds made-up. That's because it's supposed to sound like some, as you said," and Andrew felt just a bit insulted by having to repeat her description, "nerd story or movie."

Andrew could tell it was a losing argument. He knew this because Monica was more interested in watching for her next tequila to arrive than listening to him trying to defend his case. However, that didn't matter to Andrew. Because there was still a small part of him that had enjoyed the poetry and romantic fiction classes in college. His inner romantic, that small voice kept telling him to try. The voice told him that love conquered all, and love was also supposed to be a many-splendored thing. He only had to fight through Monica's inner doubt, and the scales of disbelief would fall from her eyes, and she would see the truth. The other larger and rational part of his inner-self had a good inner laugh at such naivety. That was the part which had become cynical and jaded by the marketing and advertising world. But Andrew didn't surrender and cast his bread upon Monica's water.

"If you really think about it, you can see the absurd logic of the situation. Maybe what happened is supposed to sound like a lie because maybe people just aren't ready to accept the truth of it? I don't know. I just know what happened to me is real. I thought out of anyone you would at least try, just try to believe me."

All of that sounded great in Andrew's head. It was honest. It was sincere. The small inner romantic felt huge again and metaphorically stuck its tongue out at the cynical part. It was because of that honesty he also knew and conceded that it all sounded crazy. But Andrew reminded himself he wasn't looking for total belief. All he was looking for was a simple and honest affirmation. Something along the line of, *"I know your story sounds crazy, but the world is a crazy place and who am I to say it didn't happen."* Then maybe some simple act of affection like a hug or hand squeeze. Andrew just needed a sign of some kind, and unfortunately, he got one. This sign caused the now gloating inner cynic to give the inner romantic the finger.

The tequila arrived, and at least Monica was pleasant enough to not just shoot it back like a freshman sorority girl. From some of the heated stories she had told him about what she was like back in her modeling days, doing tequila shots was just a warm up for other libations. Monica had apparently matured since then. Instead, she took several large sips to finish the drink before setting the glass down.

"I'll tell you what Andy."

Andrew knew she was well on her way to being drunk. He knew this because she only called him Andy when she was at that point. Monica also knew, because he had told her several times, he never liked being called Andy. Ever since the incessant teasing as a child when all the other kids would call him "Raggedy Andy." Every time she got drunk, that's what she called him. Having reached the third level, she would soon start with the lewd suggestions and behavior. At other times Andrew didn't mind all that much because of how the night ended. But tonight Monica's lewd behavior was not what Andrew wanted to deal with.

"If all of this is real, and you want me to believe you then call up Satan right now!"

Monica made an exaggerated and weaving gestured with her left hand towards Andrew's phone.

"Tell him to get his ass up here and bring me the biggest diamond, ev-ver, as payment and apology for what he did to me and you."

She then took her left hand and ran it back through her hair and then down along the side of her breast. With a slight slur beginning in her voice, she continued.

"After that, we will go back to my place, and I will do anything, and I mean anything and ev-verything you want or have ev-ver thought of wanting to do with me. And, and, I can ev-ven call a friend or two if you like."

That was not the sign of belief or understanding which Andrew had been hoping. Andrew thought of something as Monica was finished her slightly slurred, definitely lewd, but overall insulting comment. Andrew thought of the janitor who cleaned up the Percy faux-skin fragments in Satan's office. Andrew recalled what happened to the janitor for the simple lack of courtesy and manners. Andrew wondered if the janitor had landed yet? With a new-found clarity, even with his flesh body getting in the way, Andrew suddenly understood. Satan didn't just expect civility and manners. He required them. What at first look seemed like draconian rules for the express purpose of subjugating the people working under him, they were not.

Of course, Satan's concept of manners was on a much stricter level. The common person outside of European predemocratic monarchies would neither understand nor be used to providing such a level of civility. But to Satan and also to Cadwallader manners were essential above all else. Good manners he now realized were just another form of proper respect. Cadwallader wasn't bowing to Satan out of fear because Satan was lord over him. Cadwallader bowed to Satan, just as Percy bowed, and just as he also did to both Cadwallader and Satan, out of respect. Andrew thought of the classic lines of Otis Redding. *"Respect is what I want. Respect is what I need"*.

This new-found epiphany lit up Andrew's imagination. In doing so, it also brought about a peace accord between his inner romantic and inner cynic. Then the images of the janitor and Percy soaring through Hell were replaced. Now Andrew imagined it was Monica flying off the Satan's balcony. She soared out over the pits of Hell and falling for, well only Satan would know for how long. It really did look like a long way down to the bottom.

Andrew slid back his chair from the table and stood up. He took his wallet out of his coat pocket, opened it and put forty dollars down on the table.

"That should cover my half plus tip."

He put his wallet back in his pants pocket. With one hand he picked up a tortilla chip, scooped a pile of guacamole onto it. He then stuffed it unceremoniously into his mouth. With his other hand, he picked up his fish taco. As Monica watched through glassy eyes, Andrew walked out of Sol Casa for the evening and out of Monica's life for good. Andrew's abrupt exit left a somewhat drunken and now bewildered Monica trying not to shout, but still, speak in a loud and authoritative manner.

"Andy, where are you going? Andy, come back here and get me my diamond!"

When Andrew arrived home, Camille as always was waiting patiently for him. She sat on the shoe rug by the door looking up at him expectantly with her large luminous green eyes and two colored orange and brown calico tabby face. She cocked her head a bit to the left, stared at him and flicked her tail back and forth several times.

"Yes, I know I'm home tonight which is sometimes unusual. Yes, I am happy to be here and to see you."

Camille turned her head a bit and made several meowing comments in return. Which Andrew would have sworn sounded like, "I missed you too."

# 22.

Andrew took a deep finishing breath, "Which is everything up to this point."

Andrew looked down at Camille who was quietly purring. Her eyes were closed. She had a slight upturn to her mouth that made Andrew think she was smiling. He was still gently rubbing her warm, soft white furry belly as he finished. She opened her eyelids and regarded him with her glowing green eyes.

"I know you can't tell me you don't believe me. You're a cat, a very cute and awesome cat, but a cat none the less. So, you have to accept what I just told ya is true."

Camille blinked a smile at him. She then stood and stretched her legs and back. After finishing with that, Camile lowered herself from her place on his lap and down onto the floor. In a casual, nonchalant cat-like manner she sauntered from the living room. Several moments later Andrew could hear digging and scratching in her litter box.

"Huh, I guess she could understand."

Andrew picked up the Satan's card and twirled it around in his fingers. "**I owe you one favor,**" it was mind-boggling to think about it. He sat mesmerized by the card. Just for fun he almost thought about calling it his *"Favor"* with a Gollum-like voice. And then Andrew realized just how easy it would be to transition from goofing around with the card to being consumed and obsessed by it. Cadwallader had given Andrew such a warning. But what did Andrew want? What did he really, honest to goodness, down deep in his heart, and lots of other hyperbole want?

Then the advice of both Satan and Cadwallader came to mind and Andrew remembered what they told him. He found his remote and turned on the TV. The screen came to life. Andrew didn't even know he had the Disney channel as part of his cable package. But as if predestined to happen, the announcer came on to say, "Up next, *Darby O'Gill and the Little People.*"

Andrew could only laugh at the coincidence. He also realized Bruce Springsteen was wrong. Andrew had fifty-seven channels with one thing on.

Even though it was close to ten in the evening, Andrew decided to succumb to the insanity. He got up off of his chair. Walked to the kitchen and grabbed a bottle of beer out of the fridge, the bag of parmesan garlic chips from the pantry. With beer and chips in hand, Andrew went back to the living room. He set them on the floor as he flopped down on the couch. Andrew propped up some pillows and prepared himself for a movie filled with good advice on how to use wishes. Which apparently also had the delightful singing of Sean Connery. Andrew never knew Connery could sing. Andrew only thought of him as Bond, James Bond.

Camille returned just as Andrew had pulled off his socks and lay back on the couch. She assessed the situation looked for a spot and then jumped up onto the couch and curled up next to him. Andrew gave her an affectionate scratch on the back. Camille adjusted herself to also watch, or at least it seemed that way to him.

"I wonder what Walt Disney did that made Satan want to get his hands on him? Which also leads to, how come Satan can't get Disney?" Andrew pondered those questions quietly to himself as the movie started.

Less than two hours later Andrew clicked the TV off. He felt violated. He felt cheated. He felt cheap. But mostly Andrew felt violated!

Why would Satan and Cadwallader set him up like that? Sure, Andrew rationalized they were, of course, Hell beings. Andrew was sure there was lots of evil stuff that goes with, well being the ruler of Hell and his number one go-to guy. But come on! The delightful singing of Sean Connery! That went beyond malicious! What Andrew just experienced was pure unadulterated and unabridged evil!

He had to get that sound and song out of his head before going to bed. He had to get it out before the song became ingrained and burnt into his memory forever. He grabbed his phone and turned on the music. Any song coming out of the small tin-like sounding speaker would be better than Sean Connery singing "*My Irish Girl*" in a barely understandable Irish brogue in full stereo surround sound. People could love or hate iTunes all they wanted. However when you have over a thousand songs at your digital fingertips, and one horrible song stuck in your head; the odds were pretty good one of those thousand should cancel out the horrible one.

As the music continued to play in the background, Andrew got ready for bed and contemplated the wise logic of Darby O'Gill. The man did understand how to use a wish. Well, obviously, it wasn't the character, but the writer or writers of the story who came up with those conclusions. It was past midnight and Andrew was tired. It had been a long two days, and he was very much ready for the weekend. Andrew was getting undressed and putting his clothes in the dirty clothes basket when Camille came into the bedroom.

She had just finished expressing her sentiments about Connery's singing and jumped up on the bed. Before he could do anything, she made her way to Andrew's usual pillow. She climbed on, circled twice, laid down, and promptly closed her eyes. Without any indication of remorse for her thievery, Camille fell into an instant sleep. Andrew quietly laughed at her bold move. It was Camille's usual routine to try and take his pillow before he could get to it. Sometimes it was a race, and they both ended up on it at the same time. But this time Andrew didn't even try. He went around to the other side of the bed and got in.

Andrew pulled back the covers of the bed. Camille didn't even seem to notice. He was about to turn off the music now that Sean Connery's voice was gone. Delightful is what they said: Delightful! Andrew touched the screen of his phone to turn off the music. As he was doing this one song finished and the next one started playing. The idea hit him like a lead balloon. He contemplated the idea as he turned off the music, the lights, and slid between the sheets and pulled up the comforter.

"That would be awesome!"

It was surprising to Andrew how these sudden bursts of creativity and inspiration came to him just as he was getting into bed. That little quirk always irritated Andrew. He wanted to go to sleep. But now he had ideas running through his now very awake brain. Why couldn't he get his inspirations when going for walks or driving in the car like other people? Regardless of when and where he received his insights, he couldn't deny the idea was indeed spectacular but was it do-able?

"But best to sleep on it. That's what Darby would have done."

And suddenly Sean Connery was back and unfortunately; he was singing "*She is my dear, my darling one, my smilin' and beguilin' one; I love the ground she walks upon, my darling Irish girl!*" Andrew forced his mind to sleep and forget. Sleep. Forget. Sleep. Forget. Despite Sean Connery's horrific warbling and Andrew's initial excitement at the idea, he quickly fell into a deep sleep. In fact, Andrew slept so soundly he never knew that at one point during the night, Camille stood on his chest and looked inside his mouth. She was trying to learn where the snoring sound was coming from and if she could stop it.

# 23.

Andrew awoke Sunday morning and knew that was it. That
would be his favor.  He had slept on it for two nights.  He had
contemplated it to the point of distraction all day Saturday.  The
anxious contemplation had caused Andrew to pace around his
house in an aimless fashion wearing only his boxers and a
bathrobe.  At one point, he looked in the bathroom mirror and
thought all he needed were facial tissue boxes on his feet.  His joke
broke the favor related contemplation, and he smiled a bit.
Andrew had turned away from the mirror and went back out into
the living room.  He sat down at the table, and once again became
lost and consumed in contemplative thought.

That Saturday he missed a "fun run" with a group of friends. He had ignored his phone, which didn't matter. According to the caller identification, none of the numbers were listed in his contacts, and no one left a voice message. However, out of reflex, every time the phone rang Andrew found he looked at it. He was specifically checking for Monica's picture identifying her as the caller. He felt like he should call her, but he also didn't want to be the one to have to make the call. He ignored the phone and went back to his contemplation. The pragmatist which he was, Andrew spent the day sitting around his house obsessively making business-like pros and cons lists about his idea versus other options.

Andrew had become so caught up in his task he became oblivious to everything else around him. Trying to figure out why he felt tired, Andrew looked outside to see the sun was gone. He had no idea what was going on. The last time he looked at the clock, it was noon. But now the sky was dark, and it was well past ten. He had done nothing else all day. He wasn't even sure if he had even eaten or drunk anything. Although an empty plate and glass next to him suggested, he had. What Andrew knew he had done was sit there alone at his kitchen table thinking about his favor.

The card had consumed Andrew. An entire day had been lost because of it! Andrew knew he had to ask for his favor and be done. The fish was definitely starting to smell in the 'fridge.

He forced himself to get up from the table. Andrew had to be done with the card and he knew it. Andrew got ready for bed although it felt like he had just woke up. He slept fitfully, tossing and turning trying to find sleep but his brain didn't want to shut down. It kept contemplating choices and imagining the subsequent consequences of those choices. Finally, around one in the morning, he was able to come to an agreement and found rest.

# 24.

Come Sunday morning Andrew knew he was right. His decision was based on the last thing he was thinking of when he fell finally fell asleep. That had been his original idea. Everything else he had thought, all the ideas had just kept him awake. Sure, there were lots of other things, those things which wouldn't let him fall asleep.

The first item on the list was money. But money was as much a trap as any non-monetary item would be. If Andrew asked for too little money, he would worry about spending it all. If he asked for too much money, there would be suspicions about where he had gotten so much of it. After all, how does an average nobody citizen explain why they suddenly have enough money to pay off the National debt several times over to the Internal Revenue Service? He could ask for a sports car, but he would be afraid to drive it. Andrew wouldn't want the car getting damaged or worry that someone would steal it. He could ask for a bigger house, but then he would be stuck with the expenses that came with one. He was quite happy where he was. Andrew knew he was too pragmatic; it was one of his faults. All of those things, the money, the car, the house; they were just things.

Andrew even thought of outside-the-box crazy ideas like immortality or being able to fly or read people's minds. Sure, those were a great imaginative comic book and movie sort of ideas. But in real life would he really want the constant buzz of everybody else's thoughts in his head? As being able to fly? Andrew was sure the first time he tried somebody would try to shoot him down. Either shoot him, or the government would be there to arrest and study him. The rest of his life would be spent in a cage.

As for immortality? Andrew for a fact knew that his biological life was just a step to something more. To be permanently stuck there on Earth would be a curse. The very recent event in his life had taught him a lesson. The all the things, the possessions, and objects, in life were irrelevant. It's what a person did with their life that mattered, not how much junk they accumulated.

Andrew also felt like if he asked for the money or cars or houses, they were all just cheats. He felt unless he earned something he didn't want it. It was okay to need but not to want. Andrew knew that as soon as a person wanted something, they would never have enough. Sometimes he hated being sensible.

But what he decided upon, that idea had no lasting monetary value, so it didn't violate his sense of ethics or morals. It would be a once in a lifetime sort of experience if it were ever to happen again. And if it did Andrew was one hundred and ten percent certain he would never be able to be a part of it. It was something he would be able to look back on and say, *"I did that. I was there."* The problem was how? How did he put it into an articulate and direct fashion? As Andrew lay there, he remembered the advice Cadwallader had given him. Andrew knew there could be no margin for error. He was dealing with Satan. Even a benevolent Satan was still, well, Satan.

Andrew wanted to make sure this request was airtight, that even Satan wouldn't find a loophole. Then the obsession resurfaced about keeping the card for a special occasion, as sort of "get out of jail free," option. But the wisdom of Darby O'Gill once again came to mind. *You never know when you could step off a curb and be hit by a car. So don't sit on your ass, get out there and live your life.* Well, Darby didn't put it in quite those terms, but Andrew's rephrasing was more applicable to his day and age. Also, Cadwallader's comment about the card was like a fish in the refrigerator and how after two days it starts to smell and contaminate everything. Andrew was starting to feel that way about the card. It was enticing, attractive; it did have a certain allure and appeal. But ultimately Andrew was sure even Satan would become annoyed by the fact his card just sitting out there waiting to be used.

Andrew could just imagine Satan sitting there in his Godfather office. He was seated and leaned back on his *Godfather* chair with a cigar and a crystal glass of some odd colored Hell drink. He would look over at Cadwallader who was sitting on one of the chairs next to Satan's desk, also with a cigar and drink. Satan would lean forward and put his hand on the desk and say to Cadwallader in a *Godfather, Don Corleone*-style of speaking.

*"This Andrew that I showed such courtesy and respect. Such was my friendship with him that I presented him with my card. A card that says I owe him one great favor, and he is just sitting on it like some pezzonovante. To keep the man, who gave him this great gift waiting, this is an infama insultare. This Andrew needs to learn respect. He needs to be taught better manners than this. Get me*

*Luca Brasi. "*

In his heart, Andrew knew he shouldn't, couldn't, and definitely wouldn't want to keep Satan indebted to him. The idea of a Hell version of Luca Brasi coming to give Andrew a lesson in respect and manners wasn't even fun to imagine. Luca was fearsome enough when portrayed as a human in the book, but as a Hell being; no thanks.

The morning stupor began to drift from his mind, and the sane, rational solution came to him.

"Just write it down!"

The idea of writing everything down instead of trying to remember what he wanted to say was so simple. Andrew felt stupid for not thinking of it right away. All of Satan's contracts were in writing, which is still the best and still the only legal method. Andrew quit staring at the bedroom ceiling and got out of bed. Wearing only the shorts, he had worn to bed the night before; he walked from the bedroom out into the kitchen.

Andrew picked up a pen and paper from his desk. He was about to start furiously writing down his idea when Camille came sauntering into the kitchen. She brushed against his leg, did a long morning stretch, yawned and made her declarative morning hunger meow. Andrew knew there would be no work getting done until she had her food. He put down the paper and went to the kitchen cupboard where her food was kept. He opened a can and emptied it into her dish.

Camille's food was supposed to be a hairball control formula, and it was indeed hairball control. The food gave her control to hack up hairballs whenever and wherever she wanted. With Camille now momentarily occupied, Andrew also took advantage of the broken reverie to make a morning pot of coffee. While his coffee was brewing, he went back to his bedroom and changed into a pair of sweats and put on a t-shirt that stated: *"I am not a number, I am a free man."* He went back to the kitchen poured what coffee had already brewed into a cup, added a splash of half-n-half and started writing.

Andrew had finished the entire ten-cup pot of coffee. During that time he had hand written three drafts of his request and was now on the fourth version. Besides drinking ten cups of coffee, Andrew had also gone through half of a spiral notebook. The latest version was now six hand-written pages in length. It was at this point Andrew was forced to stop writing. All that coffee was working its physiological magic, and there was an urgent need to go the bathroom. Andrew grabbed his notepad since he liked a bit of reading material for times like these, and went to take care of business.

When Andrew returned, he found Camille had curled up on his chair, typical. *"Well,"* Andrew thought, *"I suppose I could transfer all this chicken-scratch to the computer to make all the editing and redrafts easier."*

Andrew riding his caffeine high sat down at his laptop. He set his notes on his typing stand and started typing. As Andrew's fingers flew over the keyboard, he thought how speech recognition software might be nice. Sure, he enjoyed typing, there was just something about it; fingers pushing the keys as words appeared on the screen. But then there were those boring times like these when all he was doing was transferring tedious notes. Especially for situations like he was in now. It wasn't until his stomach grumbled in protest and possibly thinking the throat had been cut, Andrew realized it was well past noon. He had been working nonstop for over four hours. There was another grumble from his empty and determined stomach. His persistent hunger was able to distract him enough that it broke his typing groove. So, Andrew got up from his desk and started to look around the kitchen for something to eat. He noticed Camille was still curled up and was sound asleep on his kitchen chair.

There was nothing in the refrigerator or pantry cupboards. Well, not exactly nothing; just nothing Andrew wanted at the moment. The downside of not doing anything on Saturday, Andrew left himself without food for the coming week. That was because Saturday was Andrew's usual grocery shopping day. Sure he could get dressed and buy some groceries and such. But Andrew was in the middle of typing up his requested favor. And once again Andrew was consumed by the card. But this was in a new way. He knew what he wanted; he was currently writing it down so he could give it to Satan. Andrew didn't want to take the time to stop and go shopping. He knew here was only one answer to the situation. Andrew decided to get out of the house and let the stink blow off him, as his grandfather used to say.

Andrew grabbed his backpack from under the desk. He packed up his laptop and power cord and headed down the several blocks to his favorite watering hole The Dirty Dog. It wasn't a classy bar; it was a classic bar. The Dog had decent food, but a great beer selection. Also, if he could get one of the booths, it would also have an outlet for his laptop. His mind tried to make a hypocritical analogy between himself and some of some of the people at the coffee shop from Thursday morning. How he was about to become in a similar fashion one of those same "lazy hipsters who monopolized all the tables and outlets just to use the free Wi-Fi." Andrew told his brain if it kept up that sort of rhetoric it wasn't going to get a beer and a cheeseburger. His brain promptly silenced any, and all of the rhetorical comparisons. The thought of a cheeseburger was too, much. The brain then decided some bacon should be added to that cheeseburger. That would guarantee its continued silence.

After a brief hunger driven ten-minute walk, Andrew arrived at the Dirty Dog. It was a St. Paul version of Al's Bar over in Minneapolis. The bar was old, and possibly one of the original buildings still standing around the area. But unlike Al's where people were separated by brick and steel, the Dog had large plate glass windows along the front wall to allow for people watching.

The actual bar was shaped like a big wooden horseshoe stained dark brown. In fact, all the wood in the place, even the floor, were stained the same color. In the middle of the bar were over thirty taps with many craft brew beers from around the country and several European imports. Being located not too far from the local neighborhood, and only half a block from the bus stop, the Dirty Dog was almost always busy. Andrew was lucky, and the Dog was relatively quiet that Sunday afternoon with most of the customers taking advantage of the warm spring air and sitting outside in the patio area. Inside the bar, the majority of the booths were open, including the ones with the power outlets. Andrew's brain once more tried to compare him to the lazy college students, but the smell of food quickly silenced it.

There were a few regulars around who noted and acknowledged his arrival. Andrew never learned or cared to remember their names. Instead, he amused himself by developing mental nicknames for some of the various people based on their looks or behaviors or both. On the corner barstool, next to the patio door was the woman he determined was Frodo or the Hobbit.

She was a very small red-headed middle-aged woman with the stature and features of a hobbit. She also seemed to have a boyfriend or husband on the staff which was probably why she was a regular. She always had the corner stool next to the patio door because besides being a hobbit she was also a chain smoker. And for hanging out in a craft beer emporium, she only drank Miller Lite.

Behind the bar working as the bartenders were "Leo Sayer" and "Opie." Leo Sayer received his nickname because of the jukebox. In the jukebox was a Leo Sayer's Greatest Hits CD which happened to have the artists' picture on the cover. In an unfortunate incident one night the bartender received his new moniker. An overly loud and enthusiastic reaction from a drunken woman, screeched aloud for everyone in the bar and possibly ever person in a one block radius to hear, "Dude you look like Leo Sayer!" It became his instant nickname by everyone in the bar that night. Much to Leo Sayer's chagrin, the name stuck.

Opie, of course, was called such because he looked like the young Ron Howard character from the *Andy Griffith Show*. The two main differences were that the bartender Opie still had all of his red hair and the second difference was he also seemed to be high the majority of the time he was working. Whenever Opie was high, it would become obvious. It was obvious because whenever Opie was high the stoned effect caused him to develop a slight southern drawl and odd mannerisms.

In the kitchen area, Andrew noted Andre the Giant was cooking. The cook Andre was not quite the huge giant as the real Andre the Giant. But this Andre was a big stocky guy with a large blockish head. Second, to Amorina, he was probably the friendliest of the staff which belied his looks.

Waiting tables were "Girl with the Dragon Tattoo" or sometimes Andrew thought of her as the "Dragon Lady." She was pretty, heavily tatted Asian woman who seemed to have the ability and the demeanor to do everything. Which could, and several times did, include physically removing obnoxious customers from the bar. Her no-nonsense "tired of this bullshit" attitude could at times scare some patrons and staff members. Even Andre the Giant gave deference to her. Andrew had the impression she might have lived upstairs above the Dog, but he had no facts to back that up.

Then there was his favorite waitress Amorina. She had become his favorite waitress not just because she was physically pretty and would take the time to talk with him. But because Andrew actually knew Amorina's name, and he was also not afraid of her. Amorina was also very intelligent. Any customer who tried to speak down to her, thinking she was just a simple waitress, soon found they were intellectually outmatched. Besides all of that, Amorina had a certain something about her. Andrew tried to find the right word or description but couldn't so he decided she had an ineffable *je ne sais quoi*.

Whatever it was, Andrew knew he liked her, and it seemed she liked him. Well, maybe more than the average regular customer-server relationship. She was tallish, probably around five-ten or so; Andrew based that off of a comparison to his height. Her hair was brown and shoulder length with matching brown eyes. He was also relieved because she was in the area where he wanted to go sit instead of scary "Girl with the Dragon Tattoo."

# 25.

Amorina noticed Andrew come in. She waved him over to a booth while she walked over to the bar to get a menu and a glass of water for him. Andrew had just sat down and was setting his laptop on the table when Amorina came over.

"Hey Andrew, you looking for something warm and tasty, cool and refreshing or would you like some food and a beer instead?"

Andrew wasn't sure if she said stuff like that to everyone. But she always gave him some creative greeting with a suggestive double entendre. He waved off the menu already knowing what he wanted.

"Hey, Amorina. I found I ran out of food at home so I thought I'd come here for lunch. And I already know what want, besides what you first offered."

He would have taken more time to banter with Amorina, but his mind was still focused on the project at hand. Andrew was concentrating on his single wish. He was putting together an airtight, iron clad no loop-holes, and lots of similar legal hyperbole to describe his one free request from Satan. Instead of a protracted dialogue of the usual bantering, Andrew politely kept it short. His conversation with Amorina was a, "hello, how are you?" and "what's new?" Andrew was prepared with, "already know what I want" ordering of a cheeseburger and fries, and a pint of his favorite beer, "Little Sumpin, Sumpin" to drink. Amorina gave Andrew curt look as she took his order. Amorina left to go put in Andrew's order as he turned on his laptop and got to work.

Andrew hadn't realized he had finished his pint of beer, had eaten about half his cheeseburger and a pile of French fries. He was over halfway through with the third editing of his request when Amorina came over to see how he was doing. Andrew liked Amorina. He liked her from the moment he first saw her. Andrew also found he had become mentally stuck in a redundancy loop because he kept thinking of her over and over again.

Andrew and Amorina had gotten to know each other when she started working at the Dog around six months earlier. After their first several conversations Andrew toyed with the idea of asking Amorina on a date. However, at that time, Andrew was happily dating Monica. Also, Andrew's self-confidence and personal intuition weren't very good. He wasn't sure if Amorina's friendly flirting with him was real or could have been just friendly waitress stuff to get a bigger tip. Not wanting to ruin the relationship he currently had with Monica, Andrew never acted on his initial impulse.

Of course, at that time he hadn't realized what a train wreck his relationship with Monica was going to turn out to be. But maybe not asking Amorina out right away may now work in his favor. Over the months of being a semi-frequent regular at the Dog, he had the privilege of getting to know Amorina without the pressure of actual dating. Which in the language of men the tedious process of dating translated to; *how long before she has sex with me?* The Dog was only a block from the bus stop and Andrew, of course, had to walk by it on his way home. It wasn't as if it was out the way to go there for a beer after work.

Looking at her now Andrew's mind drifted from going over the contract to going over Amorina. Both Andrew's inner cynic and inner romantic came to an agreement and worked together on the appraisal. Amorina was the antithesis of Monica. They were both intelligent and attractive, but that's where their similarities ended. Monica still maintained the anorexic eating habits and weight of a lingerie model. Amorina was a normal weight and had no problem grabbing some cheese and sour cream covered nacho's off of Andrew's plate if the mood suit her. Monica would refuse to be seen without make-up and stylish clothes; "High Maintenance" would be the term Andrew thought of to describe Monica.

Whereas Amorina, at least almost every time Andrew saw her, hardly wore any makeup. Her clothes were usually well-worn blue jeans and some old faded concert shirt from the nineteen eighties and nineties bought at used clothing stores. Andrew once asked Amorina about her shirt with the rock band Queen on it.

Her response was something along the lines of Freddy Mercury had one of the best voices in rock history, and Queen was one of her favorite bands. As for being used clothing, she didn't care because first, it was a Queen shirt. Second, it was cheap. After graduating from the University of Minnesota and not found a real job yet, cheap clothes were all Amorina could afford on her waitress salary. Besides, it wasn't like she didn't wash them first.

Andrew became lost in those thoughts as stood there looking at him, waiting to see if he wanted another beer. Andrew thought Amorina was the picture definition of "Low Maintenance." It was those impressions of her. It was all those nuances. Those behaviors either pronounced or so subtle they could only be perceived by the heart of his inner romantic, which made Andrew begin to appreciate spring.

"How's work going?"

Amorina stood by the table looking down at Andrew. He was sitting in the plain dark stained wooden booth with his computer in front of him. Off to the side, as if forgotten was a half-eaten cheeseburger, a small pile of French fries, and an empty beer glass. Andrew blinked several times to break from his mental reverie.

"Oh, it's not for work."

Andrew instantly mentally chastised himself for not just saying his work was going well. It would have been the simple, easy answer. But no, down the road less traveled once again he went. Andrew wasn't sure how, or if he should try to explain what he was actually doing. Then he had a thought of something different, a possible new way to approach the situation. All the previous times he told people of his adventure they all responded with the same or very similar comment about Andrews's odyssey; no one believed him. But maybe, just maybe his new version might work. Andrew figured there was only one way to find out. Andrew noted Amorina looking down at him with an expression of curiosity on her face.

"If it's not for work what are you working on with so much enthusiasm that you are letting your food get cold?"

Amorina emphasized the cold part by picking up a soggy French fry, taking a bite and making pouty-lipped, droopy eyed, sad looking "this is cold French fry" face.

Andrew took the plunge. There had been a universal response by everyone he had told about his adventure. Well, another response besides suggesting he was a hopeless liar. Andrew was hopeful this new version of the same story would be accepted.

"I'm writing a story, a book."

There it was. Andrew had just thrown it out there, and now he would see how it played out. Hopefully, this time not with him having to pick up his half-eaten and no longer hot-off-the-grill cheeseburger and unceremoniously leave the Dirty Dog as he had from Sol Casa Friday night. Andrew quickly went over a mental replay of that evening and wondered if Monica had made it home okay. Andrew had to wonder if everyone around him were somehow psychic, or if it was just that easy to read his expressions and feelings. Because Amorina made a slightly furrowed eyebrow, half closed eyelid, pursed lip expression at him and asked him why he was alone.

"I can't remember the last time you were here on a weekend afternoon. If ya do come by it's usually in the evening after you spent the weekend with that girlfriend of yours."

Andrew understood the slight edge to Amorina's voice when she said "that girlfriend of yours."

It had been about a month or two of dating Monica when he convinced her an evening over on his side of town, and subsequently staying over at his place, would be fun and different. Up to that point in their relationship, every weekend had been spent over in Monica's neighborhood and within her sphere of influence and prominence. But after some cajoling about how it would be fun, and how she had never stayed at his place or even seen it, Monica agreed. So, on an auspicious Friday evening, Andrew took Monica to the Dirty Dog. She, of course, hated it.

The Dog was not the place for Monica. Especially when she chose to wear a little black dress by Roberto Cavalli and strappy sandals by Manolo Blahnik. Andrew would have never known who made them if Monica hadn't pointed it out to him several times. But the dress, along with the lift from the shoes, left little to and did a lot for the imagination of almost every person in the bar that night. Andrew thought he could see rivulets of drool starting from the mouths of several of the guys closest to them as soon as they walked into the Dog.

Monica had an opposite effect on the women. Their eyes became ice cold, and all of their mouths became drawn tight with thin-lipped scowls. The universal response from the women was because every man in the bar and Andrew even thought that included several of the gay guys, were all now looking at Monica. It hadn't been Andrew's intent to walk into the bar that night with a supermodel dressed in supermodel clothes. But it had been Monica's.

As soon as they stepped into the bar, Andrew suddenly realized why Monica had been willing to come over to his side of town. It was new territory for her, and she was going to lay distraction and ruin in her beautiful and fashion dressed wake. The bar was busy, and no booths or high tables were available. Andrew was able to find one open stool at the bar; Monica sat on it like she was doing it a favor and he stood behind her to the side. Andrew began to realize what was supposed to be his fun planned evening over in St. Paul was not going to be as fun as he planned. Monica and her dress were more of a distraction than a live television broadcast of a high-speed police chase and shoot-out. All the men continued to stare at her with desire, the women with loathing, and Monica basked in all of it.

Andrew ordered a beer while Monica pressed the bartender with questions about the wine selection. To his relief, the bartender was not "Girl with the Dragon Tattoo." Instead, it was "Bald Surly Guy." Andrew had given him this name because he had yet to find a better one. But the name also described the bartender well. He was middle-aged, pot-bellied, seemed to hate his job. Which begged the question "why do you still work here?"

However, on that particular night, Bald Surly Guy did not hate his job. He was in fact very happy to be the bartender. His new-found work attitude was because he spent the brief time Andrew and Monica were at the bar, trying to see all the way into the plunging V-cut down the front of Monica's dress. Andrew realized a fun night at the Dirty Dog was just going to end in disaster. It was going to conclude with either indirect fights between other couples because the guy was looking at Monica. Or it would be a direct fight with some guy coming over and trying to start one with Andrew in hopes of impressing Monica. Andrew finished his beer faster than he would have liked while Monica sort of drank some of her wine. She politely commented, in a not so polite voice, was probably good for that sort of bar. However, not one she would usually drink. Andrew put a twenty on the bar, and the two of them left. Monica with a feigned expression of, "*Oh, were not going to stay,*" then suggested they might like to make a trip over to her favorite bar.

Monica suggested they go back to Minneapolis to the Club Orleans. The Club Orleans was similar to the Dirty Dog. It was one of the older and original Twin Cities buildings. It was a smaller bar and restaurant in the older Warehouse district of Minneapolis. Andrew had to concede it was a nice place. It had a modernized look, but with a cool jazz vibe to it. If Andrew had to describe it, he would say it was solid mash-up of "Blue Train" and "Bitches Brew." The bar was long with a polished patinaed stainless steel top instead of the usual classic wooden one. Behind the bar, there were seven illuminated glass shelves in front of a mirror that went from the top of the back counter to almost touching the pressed tin ceiling. There was an old wooden library ladder which wheeled from end to end. Andrew watched as the bartenders rolled it back and forth to climb to the top shelves for some dust covered bottle with an exotic name.

Andrew noticed all this as everyone else was noticing Monica. But at least this time he didn't worry about having to fight for her honor. Because in Club Orleans, there were several other women who were dressed in similar fashion. However, the designer look wasn't just limited to the ladies. There were several men at the bar looking like they had just stepped off the cover of GQ magazine.

They all hung together and spoke a language Andrew didn't really understand. Andrew in his nicer, but still casual work clothes. These consisted of khaki's, dress shirt, and off the shelf dress shoes from the local discount shoe warehouse. He stood on the periphery and did his best to pretend like he belonged there. Despite feeling out of place surrounded by such self-given style and class, Andrew had to admit the bar had a great whiskey selection. He especially appreciated the collection of Scotch whisky.

Andrew watched a now happy and completely in her element Monica. She sipped a martini and chatted away with the other mannequins. She even occasionally remembered Andrew was with her on the date, which became more so after her third martini. Andrew took an appreciative drink of his Oban and determined that Club Orleans was a nice bar. But it was nothing more than the Dog with lipstick on it. And why put lipstick on a dog?

"We sort of broke up Friday night."

Andrew said the words out loud for the first time. As soon as he said them, the realization of what happened fully hit him. It was strange, thought Andrew. He hadn't officially broken up with Monica. Although he knew their relationship was over the moment, he walked out of Sol Casa. There would be no reconciliation, no let's try and make this work only to have it fall apart again in several months' type of bullshit, and he didn't care. He wanted to care because he knew there was more to Monica and their relationship than his current post-break up animosity was allowing him to see. Andrew cared enough to briefly try to think of a way they might still be able to make it work. But any of those thoughts would just be lies.

However, another aspect of the situation was Andrew was also distracted by the task at hand. Because of this new focus he had just temporarily buried his post-break up emotions. But a part of him knew, if he had truly cared for Monica, for the emotional relationship, not just the sex, he wouldn't be hanging out at a bar writing up a request for a favor from Satan. He would be at home wondering how and where the relationship had all gone wrong. In fact, he wasn't experiencing the post break-up depression, or sadness, or maybe even a mild numbness. If anything, Andrew felt sort of strong and confident. Also for some stupid reason, he was starting to think about waterfalls, sunsets, and holding hands; stupid and sweet inner romantic stuff as he talked with Amorina. He sat there with all of those thoughts colliding in his head. Several reactions seemed to go across Amorina's face at the same time.

"I'm sorry to hear that. I remember her from the night you two came in. She seemed like such a nice, person."

Andrew wanted to laugh at the way Amorina responded to his news. Each sentence had a different inflection to it. Andrew mentally translated her first sentence as a warm surprise of, "*that's great*," the other two were more of a cold, "*Oh, yeah. We all remember that stuck-up bitch.*"

Amorina interrupted Andrew's varied thoughts.

"Okay, you keep working on your story and eat your burger before the grease completely solidifies. I'm going to keep working and go get you another pint of Little Sumpin, Sumpin."

Andrew hadn't expected such a business like, and somewhat motherly response from Amorina. But at least he knew he was going to get to sit there and finish his cheeseburger and not have to leave. Not only that but he was going to get another beer to go with it. Apparently, the new approach was the way to go; simply make the truth into a lie because people will believe it. Why did politics and politicians suddenly come to mind Andrew pondered in a rhetorical way?

However, it seemed Amorina wasn't done. She came back over with his beer and took another French fry from his plate. She took a small bite then pointed the end at him.

"I'm done in an hour. You keep banging out that story." Amorina's use of the word "banging" echoed in the prepubescent child part of his mind with a snicker. "When I'm done, I'm coming back over with a beer for both of us, and you are going to tell me about your story."

Without waiting for Andrew to respond, she picked up his empty glass. She turned her body with a flip of her hair and hip and walked back to the bar while still munching on the fry. Andrew couldn't help himself. He watched Amorina as she walked away; she did it so well.

Andrew finished his final edit about the same time he finished the last of his cheeseburger which had become solid with cold grease. The physical state of the burger was contrasted by the cold French fries which sagged with greasy limpness. But cold food be damned, he had done it. He had written what he felt was a straight forward, no-nonsense request. He had several "*if, then*" type statements which he felt did not violate the one favor only stipulation. Those parts were covered by what Andrew considered to be gray or legally fuzzy areas which could be open to interpretation depending on how one was to look at them. He didn't want any loop-hole type nonsense, so he did his best to make sure there wasn't any.

Of course, Andrew was smart enough to know it was all bullshit. What he had just written would have had trouble holding up to the scrutiny of human lawyers in a human court. Meanwhile in a cramped and stuffy attic room in Hell, which now brimmed with filth and waste. Besides the refuse, there were also giant cockroaches crawling about everywhere. The room reeked with the stench of the damned souls of every lawyer who ever lived. All of them at that very moment were laughing at Andrew's so-called request contract as the roaches crawled all over them. Andrew chuckled at his thought and wondered, what did the world have against lawyers?

Either way, he was done. Andrew unplugged and shut down his laptop and packed it along with all his notes into his backpack. What he had just put together and written on his computer was for Satan only. He sat back in the booth and with what was becoming a borderline paranoid obsessive compulsion, he once more started thinking about the card. Andrew once again started wonder about his favor, and going over the contract while sipping at the last of his beer. Thoughtfully nibbling on the edge of the glass, absently hearing the T-Rex song "Buick Mackane" over the speakers, Andrew slipped into a trance of contemplation.

# 26.

Andrew was lost deep in thought about his favor and Satan's card. He didn't realize where he was until Amorina was once again standing next to the table. She put down two beers and slid into the booth on the same side as Andrew. Amorina moved in close to Andrew and pushed her left arm and legs close to his right side in a casual, "it's crowded in here, and I'm only making room for other people" sort of way.

Of course, they didn't need to make room for more people it was just the two of them, but Andrew didn't mind. Andrew's body had never been that close to Amorina's before, and for the first time, he noticed she smelled nice. Not that Monica ever smelled anything but nice. But Amorina's aroma, her level of perfume was a whispered hint of a fragrance which made Andrew desire to put his face up close and next to her neck to try and get a better smell. Monica's perfume was never so pungent or heavy to be obnoxious to everyone in a one block radius. Hers was more of a statement of, "yes this is the new fragrance from Prada, and I will ensure those around me will know and respect it."

Amorina pushed aside Andrew's empty plate and pint glass and put the new full one in front of him.

"All right. I'm all done working, so you start talking. I want to hear this story of yours."

Andrew told Amorina about his story. He made up fictional names for the people but left Cadwallader as Andrew knew him to be. The same was true with Satan. No one was ever going to believe what he said anyway, so he didn't bother with trying to fictionalize anything. It was a work of non-fiction fiction. But he never told her how the actual story was going to end. Andrew didn't tell Amorina the hero of the story just spent the afternoon in a bar writing out in excruciating detail the request he desired. Instead, he let the story end with the intrepid hero arriving home.

It was an uneventful, anti-climactic ending, but it wasn't too far from the truth. Thanks to Andrew's experiences in Purgatory and Hell much of the world around him had come to seem uneventful and anticlimactic. Over the past couple days, he had started to feel life was mostly wasting time. Andrew found he had to keep pushing those notions aside. Cadwallader was correct; he was better than that.

However, the real conclusion to the story was on his laptop, and it was anything but anticlimactic. Maybe someday he would tell Amorina if the timing seemed right. But today was not that day. Amorina gave Andrew's hand a friendly slap and push.

"The story's good. I like it. The plot's original. Even the parts where you're intentionally telling the reader you're taking elements such as names, ideas, and plot devices from other stories. Those work here. After all, that'd be the intent of the Satan and Cadwallader characters, to obscure the truth from humanity. In fact, Cadwallader probably chose that name just in case you did tell someone. Besides the Satan and Cadwallader character's you'd probably hav'ta include God. Since you can't have one without knowing the other exists."

Andrew started to get excited, and in a good way. Amorina was getting it, she understood. In fact, she was filling in the plot holes on her own. Her rational mind would have rejected the story as truth, just like everyone else had done. But her imaginative part took over and was trying to suggest why the story could be seen as believable.

"Anyway, the borrowing of those ideas lends credence to your story. The intent of the narrator is to try and make the reader not believe what happened to your character was real. They're not suppose'ta believe he went to Hell and had some crazy adventures. That's what's new here."

Andrew noted Amorina was getting caught up in her interpretation of his story. Her eyes started to sparkle, her voice becoming a little bit higher in tone and quicker in speech. It was starting to make him enthusiastic. It also made him think his little odyssey could be made into a book.

"You took a story which has been told before because let's face it every plot idea has been around since people started telling stories. Don't let some editors and publishers tell you your story is derivative. If they do, tell them to go to the movies and then come back and talk to you. The writers in Hollywood couldn't come up with an original idea to save their ass. Those morons couldn't even remake *Point Break*. These are the same type of people who only look at a story with dollar signs as part of the subtext and germane to their needs. If you were ever a fan of *Dr. Who* you would know the movie *The Matrix* was nothing more than a blatant rip-off. In fact, there was a Dr. Who storyline involving a computer called the Matrix from back in the Tom Baker years. And the subplot for the movie *Batman Begins* was taken from the Batman animated series."

Andrew couldn't believe it! Amorina just referenced *Dr. Who*. Amorina just referenced the Batman movie and the cartoon! The only word he could think of after hearing that was "awesome!"

"But *The Matrix* took the *Dr. Who* storyline and re-imagined it in a new way just like you've done here. There are some good twists and turns, and you bring the reader along and make them want to believe in the disbelief. You want them to say; Hey you stole that from the *Twilight Zone*, *The Big Lewboski*, or *Men in Black*. But they will also say, I'm supposed to believe that. I was supposed to see that element in the story because I'm not supposed to believe what happened to the protagonist is real. It's the silly comedy bit. I know that you know that I know. But what you don't know is, that I know that you know, that I don't know what you don't know. So I do know what you know. But never forget; *never get involved in a land war in Asia, and never go in against a Sicilian when death is on the line!*"

Andrew was in love! How much of his life had he missed because of Monica? Well, he had to admit, not much to be honest. They had only been dating about seven months although right at the moment it seemed longer. But this was, it was inconceivable, that is what it was! How did he not see what was right there wearing used concert T-shirts, bringing him beer's, talking and joking with him, and even, occasionally sharing the food on his plate?

Amorina referenced *Dr. Who* and not the new ones, but the classic ones. She at some point had not just seen but also remembered Batman cartoons and the movie. She referenced *The Big Lewbosksi*. And, and, she just quoted from *The Princess Bride*! She also didn't try to explain where her references came from. Amorina didn't question any part of the story he had just told to her, and finally, Andrew understood. Because he had told Amorina it was just a story he made up; she already set her mind not to believe what he was going to tell her.

There would be no demand for proof or accusation of lies. Because Andrew's facts resembled, and in some cases, as he had learned, did come from fiction. It all made sense to him now, and he wondered why he didn't think of this plot device before when telling people about his adventures. Then Andrew thought, maybe he wasn't supposed to until now. The universe was a strange place. But Amorina understood it all; she got it. She was amazing. She just said what? Andrew looked at Amorina with a puzzled expression.

"What do you mean I stole a plot device from *Men in Black*?"

"It's what the Cadwallader character did. You suggested he made everyone forget they saw him. He also made them believe something else similar to what just happen, did happen but missing some the crucial details. That was what the neuralyzer did in the *Men in Black* movies and the cartoon. Which by the way the Saturday morning cartoon was much better if you ask me."

With her statement about watching the *Men in Black* cartoon; she liked watching cartoons! Andrew moved Amorina into a new and much higher category. He wasn't sure what that category was, but he could imagine it. He imagined it could involve lying in bed and eating cereal while watching the cartoon network. That was one of his secret guilty pleasures. He also thought that category could also include the situation where he was down on one knee holding a ring.

But these were not any of the categories he needed or even wanted to consider right now. Andrew first had to present his request to Satan. Then he had to in a formal and hopefully adult like manner, end his relationship with Monica. Andrew mentally joked to himself if he could somehow work into his request to have Satan go over and deliver his break-up news to Monica. But he did a quick double take on such an idea. Satan was the definition of suave and Monica did like a man in a suit. That was a bad idea, a very bad idea even as a joke. Andrew erased the thought and turned his attention back to Amorina.

"Now what you need to do is clean the story up. You need to flesh it out a bit more and watch your grammar when you write it. Also, put it all in a third person viewpoint. Please don't try and shift it back and forth from the first to the third person. That stuff irritates me. I also want some really good detail so give the story some life."

Amorina noted Andrew's furrowed brow look at her last comment. She quickly continued before he could make a defensive comment or question.

"I know you work in advertising. Because of that for you, everything is constructed into a condensed three-word sentence. Or some shit like that. You need to open up. Don't just tell the reader what is happening. But also show them and spur their imagination.

Amorina wasn't just right. Andrew knew Amorina was very right. Andrew had taken a beating in his creative writing class because of the professor, Dr. Nelty, kept knocking points from his papers for lacking detail. Andrew could still hear Nelty's favorite phrase, "word paint." He kept telling Andrew to "word paint the room." "Word paint the characters." It wasn't enough to just give them names; he had to give them life.

Andrew wanted to hate the class and call it silly. He actually wanted to call it a lot of things, and often late at night, he did. But he couldn't hate it. That was because the class was part of his degree and he needed it if he wanted to graduate. He also knew the reason he hated it. He hated it because growing up he learned to hide that part of himself. Andrew made a point never to go around talking about his wild imagination to friends or family. Andrew never told anyone of his love of science fiction and fantasy stories. He didn't want to be labeled as a nerd or geek like the other kids who were brave enough to be themselves. And in full and open secret confession on the topic, there were also female reasons. The girls, or at least the cute girls he was inclined to be attracted to, would never openly talk about *Star Wars* or *Dr. Who*. He believed they hated not just the genre, but also anyone who did like it. If you wanted the girls, you made compromises.

But there in his Junior year of college, he wanted to make sure he did well in the class. Andrew sucked it up and let his imagination come out to play. What helped him was, unlike High School, he only saw the other people in the class once or twice a day. In fact, he and didn't even know most of their names. They were just other people in the class. That helped to reduce the chance of constant ridicule and being ostracized.

With the initial help of a couple of beers, Andrew was able to break free of his inhibitions. He let out his creativity run amok, in a controlled fashion. Dr. Nelty was impressed, and Andrew's final paper and grade for the class were both A's. Andrew took a drink of his beer and Amorina did the same and then continued.

"Really make them think Satan's office was the model and idea for the office of *The Godfather*. Because that's sort of cool in its own way. Now I really wonder if the author, that Coppola dude really did sell his soul to the devil."

Andrew chuckled, and Amorina looked at him with a slight questioning smile of "what?"

"Mario Puzo wrote the book *The Godfather*. Francis Ford Coppola adapted a screenplay from it and made the movie."

Andrew finished his sentence with a smile and a double eyebrow raise. He hoped such an expression would suggest it wasn't a critical correction of Amorina's mistake, but more of a fun, *how come you didn't know that I do,* sort of response.

Amorina's response was to furrow her eyebrows and draw her lips together in a look of feigned anger. Andrew knew her anger was feigned because he could see the laughter in her eyes.

"Sure, pick on the poor waitress. She ain't got some fancy college English degree and work for some big highfalutin advertising company in Minneapolis. She don't know nuthin' 'bout dem books'n words'n such. All she knows about is how to give people drinks and sometimes can make change."

Andrew laughed as Amorina said all of that while poking out her bottom lip and making herself sound like some stereotypical television hillbilly. Then she changed back to

Amorina.

"Oh yeah, and besides those things. I can also diagram the three different stages of the biochemical synthesis of $C6H12O6$, or what you call glucose, into adenosine triphosphate. And, and I might add, I can say it. So, I got that going for me."

Andrew was impressed Amorina was able to say all that with her voice cracking with the laughter which was apparent on her face. He took the last drink of his beer and prepared his response. He knew it was a chance, but he was going to see what would happen. Andrew decided he wasn't going to live a life of wasting time. He figured it was about time to use the same level of confidence which allowed him to face Satan and Hell and to save his soul.

"Well, I guess you need a Prince Charming to write you a fairy tale. One where you are swept off breathless and starry-eyed to his castle to live happily ever after. Where you won't have to say" Andrew thought about saying adenosine triphosphate but decided not to, "say such big crazy words anymore."

Amorina looked at Andrew with a deep, serious regard for a moment. She took the last drink of her beer without breaking the eye contact and set the glass back down on the table. Andrew thought they seemed to be staring at each other for a very long time. With the moment broken, there could be only two outcomes. It was either going to end in a big Hollywood-style kiss, which

Andrew thought would be okay. Or it was going to be a stinging Hollywood style slap, which Andrew definitely decide would not be okay. Either way, Amorina had Andrew starting to feel a bit like Percy must have been feeling when Satan had been staring him down.

"My birthday is June twenty-second. I am having a small party here in the back room starting at eight. "You" and Andrew noted she emphasized the word, you, to mean a singular only him and no one else, "are invited. I'm not seeing anyone right now, and I don't want to be a rebound girl, and I don't think you want that either. So, let's give it a month or so, come to my birthday, and we'll see about starry-eyed castles."

Before Andrew could respond in any way, she leaned forward to the point where their noses almost touched.

"As for not having to say adenosine triphosphate anymore. This University of Minnesota graduate with a Bachelor's degree in biochemistry finally got a job. Finally, after almost a year of applying everywhere. Thus, I will be saying ATP all the time. I will also get to say other tongue twisters like ethylenediaminetetraacetic acid, phospholipid bilayer, and reverse phase liquid chromatography."

She then gave Andrew a quick kiss on the cheek.

"And with that, I am calling it a night because I start work in the morning at a real job just like you."

She slid out of the booth where the two of them had been very cozy. At least it had seemed that way to Andrew, and he had liked it. He grabbed his backpack which contained his laptop and all of his notes and slid out as well. They both walked to the door when Andrew realized he hadn't received, nor paid his bill for the food and beer. Andrew's sudden stop caused Amorina to turn and inquire what he was doing.

"I forgot to pay. Hey, you didn't bring me my check?"

Amorina looked at him with an odd, oh yeah; I was supposed to do that sort of expression on her face.

"I think it was around twenty-five dollars with a big fat, generous tip for your hot waitress."

Andrew almost dropped his wallet because of the hot breathy voice Amorina used on the last half of her sentence. He had a response for her. In fact, he had several responses some of them verbal a couple of them were not. But he would keep his rhetoric to himself for the time being. He could wait and should wait a month as Amorina stated. He didn't want her to be just a rebound girl.

He slid thirty-five dollars on the bar and tried to catch Opie's attention. From the vacant expression on Opie's face and his bloodshot eyes, Andrew wasn't sure if Opie was seeing him or some crazy Aztec temples and dancing bears. Leo Sayer came over before Opie could get his legs moving in Andrew's or any other direction. Andrew slid the thirty-five dollars towards him.

"According to Amorina, this should cover my bill. The rest is for her."

Leo gave Andrew an odd questioning look of, what are you talking about?

"She took care of your tab at the end of her shift, didn't she tell you?"

Amorina was standing nonchalantly over next to the door as Andrew looked over at her. She was waiting there with a feigned expression of "I don't know what you are looking at me? I'm just standing here waiting for you."

Andrew took back all but a five and told Leo it was for him and Opie to split. He put the other money back in his wallet and walked to the door where Amorina was already exiting out onto the sidewalk.

He had prepared several varied comments when they paused outside to go their separate ways. Amorina's car was in the parking lot about ten feet away to the right. Andrew had to turn left to walk to his place. Instead of citing some trite platitude, Andrew decided to keep it simple.

"Thanks for lunch. I owe you."

Amorina smiled with a genuine warmth and affection. It was a type of honest openness Monica rarely displayed unless she wanted something or was drunk. Andrew started to wish that Earth time moved as fast as Hell or Purgatory time.

"Tell ya what. Make me a character in your story when you write it. Give me really big boobs and make sure I kick some ass."

Amorina smiled and mimicked the double eyebrow raise he had given her earlier. Before they could drag it out into a normal Minnesotan goodbye; which meant they would stand there talking for at least another half hour. Amorina gave him a quick peck on the cheek turned and walked to her car.

Andrew still feeling sort of silly by the effect of her kiss, watched her walk to her car. Watching her go was not just to watch her "go" which even in the waning light of the setting sun was still very nice. He told himself he wanted to ensure she made it the ten feet to her car safely. He, of course, believed his own lie. Amorina got into her car and started it. She turned to look at him and gave a wave of her hand in a gesture of bye and thanks. As Amorina's car left the parking lot and headed down the street, Andrew turned and made his way back home.

# 27.

The walk back to his home was good. The cool evening air and the little bit of exercise helped to clear his head and let his body process the beer. He also used the time while walking the several blocks back home to keep his courage up. He was still feeling strong after a successful afternoon with Amorina. Andrew needed those strong feelings. Because he knew when he arrived home, he had to make the phone call. There couldn't be any waiting for the next day or next weekend. He wasn't going to sit and go over his request, and over it, and over it, until he went blind, stupid or both.

Andrew's normal inner voice became in tone and inflection the blockish and military one of R. Lee Emory as the Drill Instructor from the movie *Full Metal Jacket*. This new voice then started shouting, *"You are going home and calling Satan, or I will personally rip your head off and shit down your neck and piss in your skull! Do you understand your filthy maggot?"*

The first thing Andrew did when he got home was to gently drop his backpack on the floor and then with a mild urgency speed walked to the bathroom. His body had been very efficient at processing the several beers during his walk home. Andrew's quickly filling bladder made the last half a block more of a slow jog, instead of a leisurely pace. Having to no longer worrying about soiling himself, Andrew picked up his backpack and put it on the kitchen table and started to unpack everything. As he was taking out his laptop, he almost dropped it when his phone started to ring. He was surprised by the sound of it. After almost an entire day without the buzz or chime or ring of his cell phone, Andrew had forgotten all about the stupid thing.

Even though no one had been there to see him flinch in fright from the sound of his phone, Andrew felt the need to defend himself from himself. In his defense, he pointed out that the phone hadn't rung for the entire day. Not being properly conditioned by the sound it was only natural he might overreact to the sound of the ring tone. Thus, in conclusion, any embarrassment the phone may have caused was only a natural reaction. Also, because his mind had been occupied with other thoughts, the sudden sound of the ring would have made anyone react in a similar fashion. Andrew knew it was a lame defense. But it was the only defense. However, besides being the defendant, he was also the judge and jury. So, he ruled in his favor.

He looked at the caller identification and saw the picture of Monica. He thought back to their supper the other night. He hadn't left that night because she didn't believe him. Up to earlier that afternoon with Amorina, no one believed him. Andrew could understand and accept that part, the not believing his story of wild inter-dimensional adventure. But it was Monica's sarcastic condemnation and complete lack of support which still stung on a certain level.

Maybe that was part of what Cadwallader had warned him about, the telling of the story of what happened that day. He had said, "in some ways, it may hurt you, and in others, it will help." The situation with Monica was turning out to be both. Now that it was over, Andrew could look back and see what a train wreck his relationship with Monica had been.

She was controlling and used her beauty and status to manipulate people around her, which included him. But despite the superficial appearance Andrew had come to find there was a person underneath those polished fashion clad layers. The problem was it usually took alcohol to bring that person out. Sure, it was fun, really uninhibited fun, but ultimately Andrew didn't want a relationship built on a shallow emotional connection, sex, and alcohol.

He also tried not to be petty. For one reason, it would make him just as shallow as he had just been accusing Monica of being. For another reason; Andrew couldn't think of another reason not to be petty. Because, please, waste his favor on her; after the way, she treated him that night. Andrew let Monica's call go to voice mail. He would call her on Monday and let her try to manipulate him into apologizing for walking out on her Friday night. Then by refusing to, Andrew would let Monica break-up with him. It would just be easier that way and with significantly less drama. Andrew also thought he owed Monica, and so he would give her the break victory. But ultimately and secretly in his heart, Andrew knew that he broke up with Monica. Not that he was being petty.

As far as Andrew was concerned, he had over the past several days been through enough drama to last him the rest of his life. In that same train of drama and relationship thoughts, he also came to understand why Amorina said to wait a month before she would go out on a date with him. Because even though Andrew could at the moment be callous about ending his relationship with Monica, he knew there would be some post break-up fallout. He knew there would be times when he would think of the Monica. Times like when he heard a certain song, or when eating pizza. Another one of the few foods Monica would eat. Andrew realized he was going to need some time for those fresh memories and feelings to start to fade.  Without warning the voice of R. Lee Emory was there to break the mood. *"You limp-dick pansy-ass!  Stop your sniveling about little Suzy Rotten Crotch and get to work!  I got a shit on deck, and your neck is just begging for it!"*

Andrew set his laptop down at his small flip top desk, plugged in the power and printer cords and powered up.  As the computer and printer came to life with their whirs and beeps and flashing lights, once more Andrew mentally started to go over his requested favor.  About to once more slip into obsessed paranoia, Andrew realized the card was once aging getting to him.  It was either the card or his over active self-conscience making him hesitate over what he had decided would be his favor from Satan.

Whichever mental insecurity it was, even if were a combination of the two, it didn't matter. The doubts, the continued reading, and rereading or his express desire and the contemplation of it were as much a trap as the card itself.  Andrew knew he had to be done with it.  He had to get rid of it or else he might actually turn into a Gollum-like thing he had imagined before.

He opened the file and printed it out.  The request was three pages long.  It was good.  Andrew was fully confident he had covered every aspect, every point, every counterpoint, every possible loophole Satan might try to exploit. At the same time, Andrew imagined he could hear the Hell lawyers laughing as they skittered about on their cockroach legs. Because Andrew knew Satan did have those lawyers, Andrew had a fallback choice. Just in case Satan disagreed, stating Andrew's request violated the one favor rule. True, it was nowhere as awesome. However, Andrew's second option would still be something he would never get to have under normal circumstances. Plus, it didn't violate his self-imposed rules or moralities. Andrew thought about that thought for a moment, the idea of self-imposed moralities. The first that thought came to him was in Hell. When he realized in life, there was a moral, or conscience choice to everything he did. Yes, Andrew knew he could have asked for money. But what was money? What it do for him that if he were to try; to truly put forth the effort and try? What could money give him that he couldn't earn on his own? Money was nothing. It was a way to keep score in the game. To make sure everybody would love the winner and want to be like them. But Andrew wanted more than that, and his conscience agreed with their choice.

The moral choice not withstanding, Andrew started to get clammy palms. He didn't know why he should be nervous. After all, Satan gave Andrew the card. Satan told him to call the number when ready. Even knowing those facts, Andrew still felt a bit of nervous about making the call and giving Satan his requested favor. It felt like he was about to step off a cliff blindfolded. Believing because he couldn't see the ground he wouldn't hit it. Suddenly Andrew knew he had to make the call because the R. Lee

Emory voice was once more in his head yelling. *"Do It, Do It, Do It!"*

Andrew took a deep breath and stepped off the cliff. Andrew picked up the card and called the number.

# 28.

There was a ringing on the other end, once, twice, which then coincided with a knocking at the door. Of all the dumb luck! Andrew had no idea who would be coming over, and he hoped it wasn't Monica! Andrew didn't know what to do. He quickly wondered if it was possible to hang-up on Satan and not be killed. But was the knocking at the door just serendipity or was it somehow card related?

Fourth ring, more knocking, conundrum increasing. Andrew kept the phone to his ear and answered both the phone and the door.

"Hello."

The voice on the other end and the person standing at the door spoke in unison.

"I was wondering if you were going to answer."

There standing with an air of casual indifference at Andrew's front door was Satan. He physically looked just like he did when they had met in Hell. The only difference being Satan now wore a stylish black pinstriped suit with red tie.

Andrew canceled the call. Satan stood there in the doorway looking at Andrew with his jovial half smile and half smirk. Then after several seconds of looking at each other Satan broke the awkward silence.

"So, shall we discuss business here or are you going to invite me inside?"

Andrew hit himself on the head with the palm of his hand.

"Oh, sorry. I wasn't expecting you to be at the door when I called, and then you answered." Andrew stepped back, "Please, welcome." Satan did a slight bow of acknowledgment and thanks and entered.

"Anyway, it just surprised me is all."

Then Andrew realized a minor detail.

"You don't have a phone! But you answered? How?"

Satan's' half smile was joined with a head tilt and a double eyebrow raise.

"Andrew, after all, you experienced you called me here to ask such a meaningless question?  Is that to be the favor of which you ask me?"

Andrew wasn't sure if Satan was joking or not.  There was still something about him that Andrew couldn't place.  Was it his look, his clothes, the way he talked?   Andrew caught himself thinking and staring again, which was hard when dealing with someone who insisted on impeccable and flawless manners.

"I'm sorry Satan.  As I said I'm just a little taken aback. I wasn't sure how this was going to work.  Please, let's go into the living room and have a seat where it's more comfortable than standing here."

Satan nodded his head in approval and gestured for Andrew to lead the way even though the single couch and wing back chair were no more than four steps away.  Andrew gestured Satan toward the leather upholstered wingback chair.  Several years ago, Andrew had given it to himself as a gift.

Andrew had been out window shopping along the shops on Grand Avenue. He was daydreaming, looking at furniture after just signing the deed for his new condo. He saw the chair and didn't think much of it. It looked stodgy and of exacting posture. It looked like something Colonel Mustard might sit in as he thought about killing Ms. Scarlet in the library. For fun, Andrew sat in it, and it was love.

Andrew's love affair with the chair was short. Their break up was quick and to the point, because he saw the price. There was no way a relatively new college graduate, who after several months at their new job and just bought a home could afford a thousand-dollar chair. Andrew was still using the folding card table and chairs from his old apartment as his dining room set.

Andrew stood looking at the chair with sad break-up remorse. As he did the sales person came up and gave Andrew what was probably their standard sales approach. "So where do you want me to deliver it?" Andrew admitted to the man there would be no way he could afford it unless the store were offering a half-off discount and also a layaway plan. The sales associate in a polite and off-hand manner informed Andrew the store was hiring seasonal holiday help. Which besides being part-time and getting to negotiate the work schedule, also offered an employee discount of forty percent.

Andrew was quick to fill out the application. He started the following Saturday and worked weekends and a few evening shifts from October to the end January. By the time the season ended he had earned and saved enough money to by not only the chair but also the footstool to go with it. Now he was offering it to Satan to sit on. *My world has truly become a strange place*, thought Andrew.

"Please, the chair is quite nice if you like."

"Thank you, Andrew."

"Can I offer you a drink or a snack of some kind?"

Satan looked at Andrew with what was apparently a thinking expression.

"Since you are offering, you don't happen to have any Scotch whisky do you? I would certainly entertain a dram if some were available. But only with the concession that you join me."

It was as if Satan knew what was in his house. Andrew did, in fact, have a lone bottle of Glenfarclas twelve-year-old single malt Scotch whisky. Like the chair and several other pieces and items in his home, the Scotch had been another gift to himself from himself. This time it had been for the past Christmas since it seemed Monica had forgotten or neglected to get him a present.

Andrew had bought her a simple, but he thought sophisticated looking, gold chain and earrings. There had been no indications from Monica about Christmas plans so Andrew waited for what he thought would be the right moment. Christmas Eve, they sat on her couch with only candles for light. They sipped champagne and looked out over the semi-frozen Mississippi river, and the snow and frost covered Minneapolis skyline. Andrew thought it would be a perfect romantic moment for him to give her the gift.

Monica took the wrapped box with feigned enthusiasm and surprise "Oh thank you. I didn't know we were giving each other gifts." Andrew watched as Monica opened the wrapping at the seams. She peeled back the weak points where the paper was taped together. She then undid the carefully folded paper. Taking her time, trying not to rip it. As the paper slowly came off, Monica noticed the box was from a jeweler. Suddenly there was a genuine interest in his gift. The glow of genuine emotion began to show on her face and her smile. Monica's genuine response quickly returned to the feigned reaction when she opened the box and saw what was inside. "These are so nice and thoughtful" was her less than enthusiastic response.

Andrew had been willing to go along with the whole "*I didn't know we were going to exchange gifts*" lie. But her honest reaction upon seeing the gift bothered him. It bothered him because, during one of the several business meetings he and

Monica had been in together, she commented on how much she liked the necklace and earrings on the model in the pictures. Andrew had spent several days tracking down where the jewelry had come from just to get it for Monica. It bothered Andrew because he thought he had done something special for her and once again she rewarded these efforts in her usual manner. As Andrew was taking the bottle down from the cupboard, he once again imagined Monica going over the balcony and down into the pits.

"Funny you should ask Satan; will a Glenfarclas twelve be acceptable?"

"That would be delightful Andrew. Thank you."

"How would you like it?"

"Neat, please."

Andrew didn't have any fancy glasses. He just normal, everyday glasses he had bought at a local department store when they were on clearance. It wasn't that Andrew thought of himself as cheap or even frugal. He was stuck in a pragmatic world of his making. He had mentally rationalized why should he spend a lot of money on something which he was going to break eventually. He could get expensive plastic glasses which were never supposed to break, but he hated the look and felt of them. The situation resulted in Andrew buying inexpensive glass, glasses. Which Andrew on occasion, did break. However, he didn't feel bad about it when he did. So Andrew considered the situation as a win, win. However, Andrew did have his favorite glasses. These were the ones he used for special occasions. Andrew had to conclude no occasion was going to get quite more special than this one. That was unless of course, God happened to suddenly knock on the door and want to join them for a dram. This speculative and sarcastic thought actually and truly made Andrew pause from what he was doing for a moment and look at the door.

Andrew took down two of the old jelly jar glasses. They were part of a set his mother had saved from years ago. Back when he used to love peanut butter and jelly sandwiches. The glasses were Smuckers Grape Jelly half-pint jars which had various Looney Tunes cartoon characters enameled onto them. Andrew poured what felt was a socially generous amount of Scotch. Somewhere between two and three fingers, into each glass and took them back to his living room. There Satan was sitting nonchalantly in the wingback chair. His legs crossed at the ankles and was casually looking around Andrew's apartment. Andrew handed Satan the glass with Bugs Bunny on it. Andrew kept the one with the Road Runner for himself. Satan accepted glass, looked at it and smiled.

As Andrew sat down on the couch, Camille sauntered into the living room from the bedroom. She took a brief moment to stop and stretch and yawn and to let Andrew know she had just woken up from her before bedtime nap. She chose a spot on the floor between Andrew and Satan and sat down. She regarded the two of them and finally set her quizzical cat expression on Andrew of, "Who is this? Why is he here? He smells different." Satan gave Camille a bemused turn, and then he also looked to Andrew. Not knowing what else to do Andrew introduced them.

"Satan this is Camille. Camille this is Satan. I was telling you about him before. He is the nice," Andrew faltered; was Satan a person, man, being, ruler of Hell, all the above? How did Andrew present Satan to his cat of all the unreasonable weirdness in a manner which wouldn't seem insulting to Camille or Satan?

Andrew cleared his throat and restarted.

"He was kind enough to help me resolve the mess I was in earlier this week."

Camille usually very cat-like in her manners, such that she ignored all those around her and did what she wanted, actually paused, turned and looked at Satan. She then did her eye-closing-cat-smile thing at him as if to say "Thank you" and to Andrew's surprise, Satan did it back. Camille then flipped her very long and very furry tail and sauntered into the kitchen for an evening snack.

"She's a lovely animal and very intelligent. You are lucky she allows you to stay here."

Andrew wasn't sure if that was a joke or not. So, Andrew responded with what he felt was a suitable answer.

"Well, I do pay the bills."

As Andrew sat down on the couch, Satan raised his glass up towards Andrew's glass.

"Well then, to paying the bills."

"To paying the bills."

Andrew touched his glass to Satan's and took a light sip of the Scotch. He savored it knowing that bottle was going to have to last until Christmas. The Scotch was heavenly thought Andrew with a touch of bemusement. He never really knew how he had developed a taste for Scotch, but once he had it, he knew he liked it.

"Aaah that is refreshing" exclaimed Satan. "One of my guilty pleasures about visiting the Earth plane is the chance to enjoy this bonnie nectar."

Satan took another lingering drink of the Scotch and just held it in his mouth for a time before swallowing it.

"Not a bad one either. My compliments on your taste in Scotch, Andrew."

"Thank you, Satan."

"Well if we are ready now, I believe you called me here for a specific reason. I will admit it didn't take you long to come up with something so it must have been on your mind before we ever met."

Andrew wasn't sure if what Satan suggested was one hundred percent true. Although he had to admit it was one of his "what if" and "oh that would be cool" day dreams. Like when riding the bus and seeing the lottery sign declaring the next jackpot was one hundred million dollars. In that idle moment, he would contemplate about the things he would do if he won all that money. Well, it seemed he had in a way won the lottery. But instead of just money, he won a single wish. Just like the lyrics of the song.

"Yes. I wasn't sure how to present it, so I wrote it down to make sure I didn't stumble over a detail or forget something."

Andrew retrieved the three-page request from the table where he had set them when he had first called Satan. He brought the pages over and handed them to Satan and returned to his place on the couch.

"Well, very nicely put together. Cadwallader would be proud of your professionalism and presentation."

Andrew felt both a reluctant and respectable sense of achievement from Satan's praise.

Satan began reading, and Andrew started to become nervous. He wasn't sure if everything was right or not. Had he made sure to cover every detail? Did he remember to put down the thing he wanted? Did he go too far in the request?

Those and another thousand million crazy paranoid thoughts broke free from their mental prison cells and were running riot through his brain. Andrew's rational brain soon became embroiled in a battle with the paranoid thoughts for control of the mouth. Andrew knew from the first-hand experience Satan did not like to be interrupted and would consider such an action to be of poor manners. The alcohol was not helping his brain with the inner battle of maintaining his self-control. Satan had just finished reading the second page and had turned to the third when Andrew's sane and rational brain was defeated. It fell before the invading paranoid army, and the nervousness got the better of him.

"I want to let you know, I understand this may be outside of, shall we say, the spirit of the favor. As it entails several different items that equal the whole. So, if you feel this isn't kosher in any way, I do have a backup request. Which I would also be very happy with receiving."

Satan continued his examination of the pages; neither acknowledging Andrew had spoken or was even present in the room. He finished and lowered the papers and regarded Andrew, who was sitting on the couch with a flush expression after just finishing his spasmodic episode of oral diarrhea. Satan's facial expression was one of a bemused "Oh, you were saying something" which led Andrew to quietly lean back on the couch and have another, a slightly longer, drink of his Scotch. The pleasant burning helped him to clear his mind and get the rampant paranoid thoughts back into their mental cells.

"Andrew I must say this is a, well I am for a moment at a loss of human words to express myself,"

The stereo feedback sounding speech coming from Satan wasn't as pronounced as it was in Hell. The sound was subdued in tone and pitch, but it was still quite annoying and irritated Andrew's ears. At that point, Andrew thought it was all over. What he had asked for was stepping way over the line and Satan had just become pissed off. It was all over. Andrew was going back to Hell and over the balcony. Then the feedback sound stopped, and Satan continued,

"Fucking brilliant! That's the human expression which will work here: Absolutely Fucking Brilliant!"

Andrew picked up his glass to take a relieving drink of Scotch. At the same time, Satan also picked up his glass, leaned forward and clinked his glass against Andrew's.

"This will take a bit to iron out the wrinkles but nothing out of the ordinary; I will accept your request and honor our agreement. At the end of that evening, I will consider all debts equal and paid in full. The Universe will have balance once again."

Satan took a drink of his Scotch and Andrew did the same. Apparently, the deal had been struck. Andrew wasn't about to be taken back to Hell. Instead, Andrew was going to have his wish come true.

"I will put together all the details and send you the requisite information and parcels."

Andrew wasn't sure, but to him, it actually seemed that Satan was happy. He might also have been just a bit excited about what Andrew had asked for and didn't say anything about the "if-then" clauses he had included as part of the main request. Satan's happiness, at least it seemed that way to Andrew was a genuine in-good-spirits and all around great-to-be-alive, a normal human style of happiness. Which was a contrast to the Ruler of Hell getting my jollies by torturing and tormenting you for all eternity as I Force throw you off my balcony into the abysmal pits of Hell. Of course, to Satan, those two concepts were probably one in the same. Andrew started to realize there was more to Satan than Andrew, or possibly any other human may have realized.

They each had at least a finger and half of glass of Scotch remaining in their glasses. Andrew knew it was usually considered polite manners to entertain a guest, especially if your house guest happens to be Satan, ruler of Hell. Not sure what else to do or say Andrew tried a bit of small talk. In retrospect, it seemed like something really stupid to say. However, as he learned in his writing classes; just start putting the words down on the paper. Even if they start out as shit, they eventually give rise to flowers.

"How's the weather?"

Inwardly Andrew groaned at such a stupid question and silently decided to fire his brain. Satan looked at Andrew with a bemused smile at his attempt to entertain a conversation.

"Well, it's about the same as always. Just the way I like it. How about your weather? Staying comfortable here in the flesh dimension?"

Andrew could tell Satan was now humoring him with the banal chit-chat about the weather. But, and to Andrew's relief, he was doing it with a normal smile. It was not the weird evil multi-dimension one that started to burn the flesh on his body.

"Not bad. It's pretty nice for late April. Not a lot of humidity yet."

"Oh, yes I've heard a lot about that."

Satan was now playful with his dialogue. He made his otherwise soft British accent to sound like more of the exaggerated Minnesotan style.

"They always say it's not da heat. It's da humidity that'll really get ya don't ya know."

Satan smiled and took a drink of his Scotch and Andrew did the same.

"Sorry, Satan. I guess I didn't know how, or what else to say. It's not every day I have guests over, especially, well rulers of other planes of existence much less."

Satan smiled his soft half smile, his blue eyes twinkling a bit. It made Andrew wonder how Satan ever came to rule in Hell. He seemed like a decent enough guy or being, as long as you didn't piss him off; sort of like the Incredible Hulk.

"Oh, don't worry about it, Andrew. It's all in good sport, and I do understand you are a bit out of sorts over this. Well this," as Satan gestured quietly with his glass to both himself and Andrew, "and having just separated from your girlfriend."

Andrew coughed at that statement. How could Satan have known about that? Understanding it was a stupid question, Andrew left it better unsaid and just nodded in agreement.

"Yeah, not great right now, but life has its little ups and downs."

Satan did his head nod again. Andrew felt like their chit-chat, and small talk wasn't going too bad. He would ask a stupid question, and Satan would give a bland, banal response. The situation was like being at Thanksgiving or Christmas with all the aunts and uncles and cousins and nieces and nephews, in-laws and out-laws. All of whom you barely know and don't care about but once or twice a year you put forth the effort, buck-up and play along. You make conversation and ask about the weather and smile like a jackass the entire time.

"Andrew," Satan took a sip and relished in the taste; *he loves his Scotch*, thought, Andrew. "As pleasant and genial as your small talk is, please, as I stated before there is very little you could say that would in truth offend me. So please set aside the clichéd platitudes. I would prefer it if you actually talked to me. Please ask a question or two. I have freely extended the offer, so there is no charge. If nothing else it will possibly be a more interesting conversation then what I am sure is about to become something about the boils on your great aunt's arse."

Andrew had to laugh at Satan's comment. Even Satan chuckled a bit.

"There we go. Think of this as just two regular blokes sitting around enjoying a wee nip. After all, in the big scheme of the Universe isn't that all we are? Relax."

"Alright, I will do my best," replied Andrew.

With the Scotch providing a bit of courage and social lubrication, Andrew took Satan's offer. He let lose some of his anxiety and fear and jumped in.

"But about the whole, not upsetting you comment. In Hell, I incorrectly said your office looked like the office from *The Godfather* and you, well, I sort of thought I was going to burst into flame or something."

Satan smiled in response to Andrew's comment. It was that same practiced and perfect smile, and Andrew knew he hadn't gone too far with his comment.

"That was a test, plain and simple. I wanted to see how you handled yourself."

Satan calmly sat in the chair, crossed his legs and gestured toward Andrew as he continued.

"You were already in a situation which was beyond normal human imagination, and faced with someone whose position and status over you was inimitable and absolute."

Andrew hadn't realized it was a test. All he knew was he had to find the solution to his mistake before he, well possibly tossed off the balcony. That thought kept coming back to Andrew, tossed, Force thrown, whatever, off of Satan's balcony down into the abyss of Hell. Andrew sort of figured the reason must be because he definitely didn't want that to happen to him. His fixation with Satan's balcony having been mentally rationalized with poor grammar Andrew decided to press forward with a new and more intriguing conversation topic.

"Why would you want to test me?"

"I asked you to come and work for me, do you remember?"

Did Andrew remember? How could he ever forget? It isn't every day a person gets a recruitment pitch from Satan to join his team and work for him in Hell.

"You held your demeanor and manners in spite of, what for you at that time would have been an unimaginable situation; you were in Hell. You showed true metal that day, and you should remember that in your dealings here on Earth."

Andrew did have a question for Satan. Well in truth he had lots of questions; he even had questions about his questions. But Andrew wasn't sure if he wanted the answers to any of them. When he thought about the myriad variety of questions and gave them a hard introspection, he wondered if they were even good questions or just rhetorical ponderings. They would just be more of the same banal "how's the weather?" crap. Andrew pushed and prodded at them, and soon all of that mental noise and jibber-jabber type questions started going through a separation process. In the end, there were several of them which were successful in passing through the various grades of Andrew's mental sieve.

Of those questions, he already knew one of them was off limits, although it was very intriguing to him. But, Andrew had already learned Satan did not gossip about other people's situations. Of course, since the one involving the med tech did directly involve him, so he did learn about the whole "sold his soul for world peace" thing.

However, Andrew was just a little more than just curious about the deal with Walt Disney and why Satan couldn't collect on it? The words, *"Yes, one of these days we will get our hands on him"* still resonated in Andrew memory. In that sentence, there was one word in particular which stood out; it was the "we." Satan had been talking on his phone to someone. Andrew was almost one hundred percent sure whom that other person was. But it was the word "almost" that kept him wondering. Since Satan had told him to ask a question, Andrew decided too.

"In your office, your phone rang; the person you were talking too; if you don't mind me asking, was it God?"

Satan took a taste of his whisky, his eyes regarding Andrew from over the top of the glass. Andrew thought he might have gone over the line with the question and hopefully, if Satan didn't want to answer it, Andrew hoped he would just say so. Andrew most certainly did not want to upset his guest with what might be construed as an impolite, or too personal of a question.

Satan once more did his Scotch appreciation smile, finished and then with a very serious face looked straight at and into Andrew's eyes.

"Yes, it was."

# 29.

Andrew's rational mind once more experienced a jailbreak and went a bit crazy from the idea. God and Satan talking to each other over a phone. It seemed unbelievable. Yet Andrew was there and witnessed the conversation. It was just difficult for him to wrap his pragmatic or imaginative mind around. Not just the whole talking on the phone thing, but God and Satan were chatting like buddies.

Andrew caught Satan watching him as he was contemplating this new information in his mind. Although Andrew said nothing in response, his reaction was written all over his face. As Andrew's philosophic and theological mind raged out against what he was just told, Satan sat calmly and let Andrew deal with it for a bit.

"You are having difficulties with the answer, aren't you?"

Andrew calmed his mind and steadied his voice before responding. "Yes, and I'm not sure why. It seems almost reasonable, but it's the *almost* part that keeps me off balance."

Satan nodded at Andrew with a yes, I understand sort of look.

"It's your body, your flesh. It gets in the way and causes some problems in intellectual and philosophical understandings. Remember your initial reaction to your arrival in Purgatory?

Andrew wasn't likely to forget it. Besides making him sick and giving him a headache, it had caused him to forget how to breathe. It wasn't until Cadwallader helped Andrew's soul to leave his body, Andrew couldn't think of a better word or phrasing other than "helped"; afterward he could understand Purgatory and could see it for what it was. But even trying to think back upon it now, to try and hold a mental image of it started to give Andrew a headache.

"Then why do we, humans that is, have bodies? It would seem sort of clumsy and unnecessary."

Andrew wasn't sure why he asked the question. Although, he was sure the whisky he was drinking and the several beers he had drunk earlier weren't helping him with his self-control. And again, with his preternatural abilities, Satan responded. Here responded with what Andrew thought was a very apt and an uncomfortable insight into his psyche.

*"Scoticis cupam habet veritatem"*

Andrew looked at Satan with a slightly befuddled look. He knew it wasn't Hell speak because it didn't sound like a microphone being put next to a speaker. He suspected it was Latin, and not the illy-say, upid-stay, ig-pay atin-lay of his youth.

*"Scotch whisky is true."*

As Satan translated for Andrew, he also took a small sip of his whisky. "Andrew, I understand your question and the dilemma it causes and let me say now, without any animosity either intended or perceived; because that is how the system works."

Before Andrew could respond, or even think of a comment, Satan put up his right-hand gesturing for Andrew to wait and listen.

"And before you ask your next question. Please let me also suggest this to you. Your Christian-based theology, well, to be honest, the majority of all of the human religious dogmas and philosophies. They may have a few core concepts, and well how should I state this? They are wrong."

Andrew wanted to say something, anything. What Satan said couldn't be right. He was Satan after all, with the evil and the torture and the fall from Heaven and all of that. All of the religions of the world made a claim there was an ultimate good and an ultimate evil. Sitting in his favorite chair in his home drinking his Scotch was the Ultimate Evil.

As Andrew processed these new iconoclastic revelations, the words of Cadwallader came back to Andrew. Once again, he knew the words were true because he, Andrew, had lived it; Satan was always fair. But could someone who is considered evil also be fair? What was evil? Was it just a human perception?

Besides, if Satan was the epitome of evil, what did that make the man who stole Andrew's identity and attempted to sell his soul? That act would be considered evil. Therefore, would it mean the person was also evil? Or were they just a normal person who committed an action which human society would consider evil and that person was being punished for it? Is evil to be countered with a greater evil? Or was it possible there could also be some element of good in the person despite their evil actions? Once again before Andrew could bring his comments out into the open Satan gestured for Andrew to remain still and wait.

"Always remember what the physicist Isaac Newton rationalized in his law of motions. For every action, there is an equal and opposite reaction. His principal is sound. But he lacked the expanded imagination and experience to see it all the way through. Your current universe and to that matter, the sum of all existence demands balance and will accept nothing less. You should understand this better than most considering what brought us together here now."

Andrew's brain started to formulate thousands of questions and retorts. So many he thought it was going to explode. Satan was right. Andrew had been there. And as far as he knew, he had seen and heard and experienced more than any other living person, ever! But all that didn't matter until the facts were spoken out loud and were laid out before him. This situation, this conversation was just like when he told Amorina he and Monica had broken up. The moment Andrew walked out of Sol Casa he knew their relationship was done. But the truth of the situation didn't hit him until he said those words out loud. Now once again he was being bitch-slapped with an undeniable truth and once more he had to come to terms with it. But, before Andrew could go into a complete manic philosophical question overdrive, Satan took the last lingering, satisfying drink of his Scotch and looked at Andrew.

"Do you know Quentin Tarantino didn't know it's true? When he wrote the dialogue for his movie."

Andrew didn't know Satan watched movies. Ultimately what did Andrew really know about Satan? All Andrew could ascertain at the moment was Satan was changing the topic by leading him to ask a specific question. Andrew appreciated this because it gave him something new to focus on other than the theological shit-storm going on in his head. Out of relief, polite conversation and being a bit inquisitive and about to possibly get another slight glimpse into the workings of Satan and Hell, Andrew took the bait.

"What lines were those?"

"In the movie, *Inglorious Basterds*, when the characters were in a bar to meet their German contact, the movie star and double agent Bridget von Hammersmark. Right before the shoot-out with the Nazi Gestapo officer Major Hellstrom, the English officer, Lieutenant Hicox said *there is a special rung in Hell for people who waste good Scotch*".

Satan smiled a whimsical daydream type of a smile.

"Andrew, did you know there really is a special rung in Hell for people who waste good Scotch?"

Of all the odd things to come to learn about Satan and Hell, that particular piece of information was probably, in Andrew's estimation, probably the oddest and sort of the coolest of all. Andrew could only smile in response, eternal torment for wasting good Scotch.

"I will keep that in mind every time I have one."

"With that, I will be on my way."

Both Andrew and Satan stood, and Andrew gestured for Satan to precede him to the door. They walked the several feet, as Andrew went to open the door, something Satan had said came to him. It was about the Universe demanding balance. For every action, there must be an equal reaction. The idea of balance was so simplistic and yet staggering to Andrew. From the grand scale of the universe down to the even a smaller more intimate scale, equilibrium must be maintained.

"Satan I thank you for personally stopping by tonight. I very much enjoyed our conversation even though the discussion seemed more one-sided; you talking, and me listening. I am not sure if you are interested but, if you would like as a remembrance of this evening, you are welcome to keep the Bugs Bunny glass if you like."

Satan paused and looked back at the glass sitting on the coffee table in the living room and then at Andrew. Andrew was not sure if it was the correct thing to do. If he had overreached his conclusion; he had been drinking quite a bit that day. But it felt right; it felt like the "balanced" thing to do, to at least make the offer, the gesture.

"You would have been a brilliant associate, just brilliant!"

Andrew wasn't sure what to say. Satan's enthusiastic response to Andrew's offer of the glass was not what he was expecting. He thought it would be something more along the lines of a polite, "thank you but no" sort of thing. Not an exclamation about brilliance and being an associate. It would have been the second or third time Satan had suggested Andrew would have done well if he were to go work for Satan in Hell.

But even as one very small part of Andrew sort of entertained the idea; if a person was going to go to Hell wouldn't it be better to go on your terms? But simultaneously the other, the much larger and rational part of him replayed over and over the mental image of the janitor and Percy going over the balcony and falling; Andrew still wondered if they had hit bottom yet. Then there was a flash of his imaginative re-enactment of the balcony scene, but instead of the janitor or Percy, he had put Monica into it.

Once again over the railing, she went. Only this time the imaginative re-enactment changed. This time as she went up and over the railing, Monica was now flipping him off as she went and shouted something about faking it.

"Yes, Andrew I would appreciate the glass as a keepsake of this evening."

Andrew went back and picked up the glass for Satan and handed it to him.

"It was a pleasure Satan and good journeys."

Andrew didn't perform a full bow as he had done before but he did a simple Japanese sort of "Hello/Goodbye" type of bow. It was after all his home, but the bow was not just another way of saying "goodbye" since as Andrew had learned before, Satan did not shake hands. The slight bow was also an act of respect.

The person before him wasn't some self-proclaimed royalty. They weren't someone who said they were better than the average person because of their family history. The being before him was the Eternal ruler of Hell. And maybe, just maybe, he did earn a bit of respect because of it. How did the Rolling Stones put it, "...*if you meet me have some courtesy, have some sympathy, and some taste. Use all your well-learned politesse, or I'll lay your soul to waste.*"

"Thank you, Andrew, and good journeys to you as well."

Much to Andrew surprise, Satan did return the bow. Although Satan's bow was more of a slight head nod. But it was an acknowledgment. Satan accepted his glass and walked out the door. As he passed through the doorway, he turned his head back slightly towards Andrew.

"Cadwallader will be contacting you once again. He will bring you any items related to the fulfillment of the contract."

"I'll be expecting him. Thank you."

Satan didn't say anything, he just held up his right hand and gave a simple single wave as he walked down the one, two, three steps to the sidewalk, turned left and walked down the swept clean association sidewalk and then out the gate and onto the littered public one. Andrew stood in the doorway and watched until Satan was no longer in sight.

Andrew stepped back into his home, shut the door and decided to pour himself another, small, Scotch. It was a bit late on a Sunday evening, and already having drunk more than usual, not just for a Sunday, but in general. However, Andrew needed another drink to help him unwind. To make the best of the situation, he took his glass with one finger of Scotch to the bedroom. He quickly changed out of his clothes and unceremoniously climbed in before Camille could take her normal place on his pillow. Andrew took a deep introspective sigh and sipped at his Scotch. He was careful not to waste any.

# 30.

It was Friday afternoon and five days since he had given his request to Satan. It had been a long week, and Andrew was ready to go home for an uneventful and hopefully down-right boring weekend. The previous Sunday after finishing his Scotch Andrew slept until his alarm informed him it was time to get up. Fortunately, the alarm had a snooze feature which would allow him another ten minutes of possible sleep.

However, his second alarm did not have a snooze button. Besides waking him, the radio also woke Camille, and once up she did not go back to dozing. She only understood it was time for her breakfast. Despite the alarms ten-minute reprieve, Camille gave none and walked over and onto Andrew.

She stood on his chest and looked him in the face and told him he needed to get up because it was time for her breakfast. Faced with an unstoppable force; no matter what he did Camille would just come back and harass him. Andrew got out of bed a bit slower than usual on that Monday morning and engaged in his normal morning routine which he had done several hundred million thousands of times before. But Andrew paused a moment because he felt something different. Before he could mentally drift into his normal morning contemplative thought about having to vacate his warm bed something stopped him. It was a feeling or lack of one.

Andrew thought about it and realized the feeling which was now missing had started after he came back from Hell. He had felt anxious, disquiet even fearful of people. That fateful Thursday of the previous week and his untoward adventures had left him paranoid. Now the feeling was gone. In fact, he felt good despite having drunk far more alcohol than he usually did, especially on a Sunday night. Then the answer came to him. He no longer had Satan's card.

Just the thought of it being gone, his request made and not to be undone. This fact brought an aura of relief. It brought mitigation from the effect of the card on him. He was just average every day Andrew again, and he was happy. Because of this, Andrew looked forward to his day. He gladly stepped back into his own personal, and redundant life. Even the lack of sleep and a bit of a hang-over didn't deter him or his good mood.

But that had been Monday morning, and now it was Friday afternoon, and Andrew was waiting at the Nicollet Mall transit stop for the Metro bus to take him home. The week had gone much smoother than he would have thought and all the little details from his adventure had resolved themselves without further incident.

The break-up with Monica went almost verbatim to Andrew's preconception of it. Monica called Monday morning and demanded an apology. Andrew in returned feigned some level of outrage as to why should he apologize after she insulted him.

Of course, Andrew knew deep down both of them were at fault for what happened. But Andrew didn't want to prolong the phone call any more than he had to, so he just played his role of angry boyfriend. Monica continued her tirade, and he for the most part ignored her. Andrew ignoring Monica was, in fact, true. He blissfully continued to work on a project as she verbally attacked him. Several of the lines she used against him were good. They were descriptive and full of true emotion. He quickly wrote them down on a notepad for a possible future narrative. He sent her a silent, and mental *thank you* as she called him an asshole.

The break-up continued with Monica saying something about him being petty and childish. There was also something about what he did Friday night is what she expected from of someone like him. Mostly what Andrew heard were blah-blah yak-yak and venomous diatribes. Finally, the phone call and their relationship concluded with a, "better if you never called me again." Their break-up was made all the easier because he was never allowed to keep anything at her place and she had never stayed at his. When Monica hung up, their break-up had come to its ultimate finale, and there would be no encore.

Andrew took a deep breath, leaned his chair back and looked at the ceiling tiles a moment and sighed. Although Andrew had wanted their relationship to end. In fact, on a certain level, he needed it to end, and so he did nothing to prevent it. After their fight in Sol Casa Andrew knew their relationship was not what he wanted in life. At some point, what they had together was going to implode, explode or and because he knew Monica, it would be a combination of the two. The sooner it happened the better off they were both going to be. But he was also going to miss being with Monica, and it wasn't about the sex, although his thoughts did seem to always wander in that general direction. He would miss her for the happiness she brought to him even though it wasn't very often, and maybe that's what made her special to him.

There were those special times when Andrew was able to get past the armor of her physical beauty when he was able to get to the real Monica. To the Monica who had fun, let her guard down and included him in her guilty secret pleasures. Many of the weekends he spent with Monica went the same way. She would wake them up at nine every Saturday morning to be downstairs in the fitness room for her spinning and yoga class. She would drag Andrew with her; telling him it would be good for him to get some form of exercise once in a while as well.

Andrew feigned his reluctance, got dressed and went along. He guessed Monica knew he was only faking his reluctance to this morning ritual. In fact, Andrew was positive Monica knew he didn't mind coming along. She knew this because as he rode an exercise bicycle, or jogged on a treadmill, she strategically placed herself in the yoga class, so Andrew always had a good view of her. His favorite yoga moves, as he learned from an internet search of the various yoga poses and their names, were called "Happy Baby" and "Downward Facing Dog." After their workout and yoga visual foreplay, they went back up to Monica's place for a post-workout workout. They would then enjoy a leisurely and relaxing shower which could sometimes it would become more than a shower.

Their afternoon routine differed depending on the weather and the season. Sometimes the he and Monica went for a walk along the river. Other times it was window shopping at some of the local boutiques. There were even times they went to the movies. And during all of this, they were just an average couple out and about and held hands the entire time.

No matter how those days began, they always ended the same. They would order a spicy sausage and pineapple pizza from their favorite pizza place, Pizza Amore'. They would get it "to go" and take it back to her place. Monica would get undressed and wear only a bathrobe. She said she loved the feel of the warm, soft fabric on her skin, and of course, Andrew didn't mind. The two of them would lounge on the couch with the pizza, a bottle of wine, and watch the fashion channel for the rest of the night.

Andrew had to smile and also felt a warm tear run down his cheek at that memory of Monica. Even after their break-up, she was still able to make him both happy and sad. If only there had been more of those special moments rather than the volatile ones, like at Sol Casa, he might have fought harder to make their relationship work. With one more introspective sigh, Andrew turned away from staring at the ceiling, brought his chair forward, took a sip of coffee and figured out how to work childish into a tagline.

But that had been Monday, and Monica's phone call had been the most dramatic item of the week. Andrew looked at his watch to check the time and then looked down the street to see if the bus was in view, and then back down at his watch. As he looked up an almost cliché long, almost cliché black, almost cliché limousine pulled up to the bus stop. Everyone else at the bus stop looked at the limo, then at their various watches and phones, then down the street for the bus, back to the various watches and phones, and then at the limo.

The almost cliché' black tinted back window lowered and a voice called out from within the inky darkness.

"Mr. Andrew Wheeler?"

Once again, a now familiar pompous English lord sounding voice called out from the dark and empty looking interior of the limo.

"My records indicate there is a Mr. Andrew Wheeler in this group. Would Mr. Andrew Wheeler please be so kind as to step forward?"

It was phrased as a question, but spoken as a statement and Andrew could only smile as he walked towards Cadwallader's smoove limo.

# 31.

As Andrew approached the car, the window closed and the door opened. Without any hesitation, Andrew climbed into the limo where no light dared or was permitted to enter. The other people at the bus stop watched as Andrew disappeared into the darkness of the back of the car and the door closing behind him. Andrew had no doubt all of the people at the bus stop just forgot what they had seen.

"Hello, Mr. Wheeler. How do you fare these days?"

Cadwallader was seated in the perfect center of the back seat of his limo. Andrew had taken the front seat opposite of him. He was as Andrew remembered him to be; Cadwallader was perfect. "I'm doing quite good Mr. Cadwallader. How have your journeys been?"

For some odd reason, Andrew enjoyed the dramatic formality of speech and manners which Cadwallader displayed and expected of his guests. Even if his guests were his quarry and he was bringing them to spend their eternity in Hell; with only one exception of which Andrew was personally aware.

"Mr. Wheeler, I have been engaged in my assiduous efforts to return the soul transaction process to its original conception so as to preclude another incident such as the one which befell you."

Even with his English background, Andrew had to start rummaging through his dusty mental thesaurus to keep up with Cadwallader. Andrew recalled how Cadwallader had admonished him when they first met, about Andrew's improper use of grammar and the English language. Andrew guessed he was once more being tested by Cadwallader, or at the least being forced to again be proper in his speaking and word usage. Two could play at this game; at least Andrew hoped."

"Mr. Cadwallader, would it be zetetic to intimate any other vitiate emanating from Percy's erroneous modification of the original conception of soul transactions have all been ameliorated?"

Cadwallader's face lit up at Andrew's question. It was an expression, a perfect expression, of satisfaction.

"Thank you, Mr. Wheeler. That was an exquisite sentence which was worthy of our conversation. I applaud your efforts."

As Cadwallader responded to Andrew's question the inky darkness inside the limo receded. The darkness which had previously prevailed inside the limo receded to proper shadows among the recesses of the seats and floors. For the first time, Andrew was able to see the full interior of Cadwallader's limo. The inside of the car defied all of Andrew's preconceived notions or imagination of how it should look. He wasn't sure what to do, how to express his thoughts. Should he say anything or should he act like it was no big deal and just keep talking?

It was normal. The inside of the car was just a normal looking, well Andrew would concede it was perfectly normal, but none the less, normal looking interior of a limousine. It had deep burgundy leather seats, black carpet, and burgundy wood accents in the doors. That was all. Considering how the outside of the limo was so cool with the shifting reflections and soul trapping craziness Andrew had no idea what to expect from the inside.

Whatever it was he had imagined it to look or be like; normalcy was not on the list.

"Mr. Wheeler I will ascertain from your visual response you find the interior of my car to be unsatisfactory in some way?"

Andrew didn't know what to say. Well, he did know what to say, he just wasn't going too because Cadwallader already knew what he was thinking. But, then again Andrew knew Cadwallader and Satan both appreciated honesty; it was a type of proper manners. Andrew was just going to need tact as well as proper manners to answer Cadwallader's question.

"Mr. Cadwallader I was simply not prepared to receive an invitation to view the full interior of your exceptional car. My initial outward and observed expression was one of surprise at such a gesture. My overall opinion on the matter, and for what it is worth, is the interior is subtle in character and does not distract from the car as a whole."

Andrew was quite happy with how he pulled that one out of his ass.

"Mr. Wheeler you have indeed come a long way from our first encounter. Although you find the interior features of my car to be normal in appearance, let me assure you there are other subtle nuances here that I chose not to reveal. That privilege is for me alone. Besides, I like it, and that is all that matters, especially since it is *my* car."

Andrew laughed at Cadwallader's response. It was honest and to the point; no one could or would want to argue with him over it.

"Mr. Wheeler as we are almost to your destination let us attend to the business which brought me here today."

Andrew, just like before couldn't tell the car was even moving much less knew he was getting a ride home. Although it didn't take a rocket surgeon to know a man standing at a bus stop with a bunch of other people at four-thirty in the afternoon was almost assuredly going home. Cadwallader reached into his suit coat as he did the first-time Andrew met him, only this time he didn't bring out a scroll. He instead brought a large manila envelope and handed it across to Andrew.

"This is for you from Satan. It has all the requested materials for the fulfillment of your request. I will add you did quite nicely in your approach and presentation of said request."

Andrew took the envelope being offered by Cadwallader and held it on his lap.

"Thank you, Mr. Cadwallader. I found your advice to be quite insightful with how to put it all together."

"You are quite welcome, Mr. Wheeler. Ah, I believe we are at your destination. Enjoy your evening."

The car stopped, and the door opened. Andrew looked out to see they were in front of the Dirty Dog. Andrew had mistakenly thought Cadwallader was taking him home. Andrew could only surmise that once again Cadwallader knew what was on Andrew's mind. On his way home from the bus stop Andrew was going to the Dirty Dog. He was meeting Amorina, to share a beer and nachos, and hear about her first week at work. That thought reminded him of his manners. As Andrew exited the car and stood on the sidewalk, he turned back quickly before the door could shut. Once more Andrew looked into the inky blackness where no light would dare to enter.

"Mr. Cadwallader, as we are at a bar and I am going to have one, would you care to join me for a drink? It would be both my treat and my pleasure to host you."

The prevailing darkness receded to expose Cadwallader reclining in the back of his car. The darkness receded a bit more to show Cadwallader already had a drink in his hand. Andrew knew it was completely for his and only his benefit, the darkness dissipated just enough for him to see a feminine arm and hand, pale skinned with long red fingernails loosening Cadwallader's tie and unbuttoning the top buttons of his shirt.

Across from him, where Andrew had just been sitting, there was a long dark skinned, lithe, feminine leg stroking Cadwallader's leg with its foot. Andrew knew better than to ask how? That must have been one of those "other subtle nuances" Cadwallader had mentioned. Andrew could only smile at Cadwallader. He was the definition of perfect smoove.

"Mr. Cadwallader as I see you are quite satisfied where you are, I will simply bid you good journeys."

The darkness began to once again gather around Cadwallader, and he slowly began to fade from Andrew's sight. As he drifted into the darkness, he lifted his drink in a polite gesture of thank you for the invitation, but I am quite comfortable right here.

"And good journeys to you also Mr. Wheeler."

Andrew stepped back, the door closed and Cadwallader's limo drove down the street. Andrew tucked the envelope into his backpack and went into the Dirty Dog where Amorina was waiting to tell him about her first week at her new job. As they sat and talked Amorina never asked Andrew about the limo. Andrw also knew better than even to bring it up. Andrew didn't mention it because he wasn't sure if Amorina or anyone else in the Dog had seen the car or even if they had seen it would they remember seeing it. But mostly Andrew didn't say anything about it because it didn't matter.

# 32.

Andrew had to push through the crowd. It was spectacular in scale. Everyone was standing in line, or queue as they called it there in England, waiting to get through the doors of the Royal Albert Hall. It reminded Andrew of the airport and waiting to board the plane. Everyone passively pushing and budged into line so they could board before someone else. Because of course, they had to get to their assigned seat first.

For the first time, ever in his history of flying, Andrew didn't care about boarding the plane. In his request, it had stated should his request to take place in another city or a location which would require air travel that airfare or ticket be provided. However, when he checked in at the ticket counter to drop off his suitcase the ticket agent politely informed him his original assigned seat had been upgraded to first class. He had not thought to ask for such a luxury and was now wondering how it happened. *Was Satan still trying to recruit him?*

The very nice ticket agent also pointed out he had been approved for the "pre-check" security line and the agent pointed to the sign where Andrew was to enter for the security checkpoint. Not having flown for a while, not since all new security measures were put in place, Andrew was amazed by the level of it all. He had read and heard news reports about all the questionable body scanners. Or the overly aggressive and personally violating opt-out pat-downs. There was also the body scanner and then a pat down anyway. Also, everyone had to take their liquids out of their bags or else. It seemed to be an overly aggressive way of processing passengers just to make them think they were safe. But since Andrew rarely flew anywhere, he had yet to experience the new system for himself. It seemed he wouldn't have to either.

Andrew walked up the TSA agent, presented his boarding pass and passport, the agent looked at both pieces of information, looked at Andrew, looked at the boarding pass and passport again, did some scribble on his boarding pass and told Andrew to proceed. The next security person informed him he didn't have to take off his shoes and only had to take the liquids out of his bag before they went through the x-ray scanner. Andrew was quite happy to pass through the metal detector, retrieve his belongings waiting on the other side and be on his way.

During his quick pass through security, he noticed several people receiving physical pat-downs by agents with several more waiting their turn; apparently, they didn't think the scanners were safe. Other people were engaged in some awkward dance routine as they attempted to put their shoes back on while also trying to put their belongings back into their carry-on bag. Then there was the line forming to be put into the body scanner machine, and several agents over in the corner just watching the process and pointing at the people. Andrew looked at the overly complex confusion of the situation and wondered why the TSA just use dogs?

Andrew meandered through the Minneapolis airport to see what else was new while making his way to the gate for his flight. After boarding and getting settled into his seat the very polite stewardess introduced herself as Irene and asked him if he would care for a glass of champagne or other drink before take-off. Andrew sat back in his surprisingly comfortable and spacious First Class window seat. Which unlike the middle section where two seats were next to each other, there was only one seat next to the window, so Andrew didn't have to worry about a chatty neighbor. To both, his pleasure and delight his seat with the press of one of the several buttons provided a roller type massage and the press of another button transformed the seat into a bed. Andrew had to admit as he sipped at his, actual glass, not plastic, but a real glass of champagne that first class was pretty nice!

Of course, the one slight problem was all the other passengers boarding in First Class passed by his aisle seat. By doing this, they all provided Andrew with gratuitous and unwanted close-up views of their asses as they would stop and go in front of him. He thought of it as an ass smorgasbord. Of course, another side of the situation was if it wasn't their asses, it was their crotch or over-hanging belly fat. Well, there was nothing he could do about it except lean back take another sip of his champagne, put on his headphones turn on some music and ignore the world around him. Amorina's birthday was in a week. He should bring her something from England. Maybe a classic rock band concert shirt for her collection.

Now, once again he was in a similar situation. Andrew had to wonder if life was destined to be nothing more than standing in line and waiting. Andrew made it to the door and presented his ticket which made the very large, and not large because of fat but more like an over-muscled professional wrestler, man to look at him twice while scanning the barcode. The light turned green, Andrew's stomach returned to its relaxed state.

"That'il be prob'bly ta best seat in'a house ta'night mate. How'd ya score that?"

Andrew was very conscientious of the line growing behind him, and he didn't want to block the rest of the people from getting in. But of course, they weren't going anywhere until the tattoo covered behemoth, and probable human being was going to let them. So, it really didn't matter. Andrew had several responses come to mind, some of them snappy, some stupid, but instead he thought he would just tell the truth.

"I asked Satan for it."

The man laughed thinking it was a stupid quip but apparently still funny to him anyway. He responded with one of his own, which made Andrew start to think.

"You an 'eryone else mate. Enjoy the show."

Andrew once again experienced a type of epiphany, a loop-hole which he hadn't considered before. How many people would have, and probably did sell their souls to be at this concert tonight? Something like that never came to his mind. As he walked into the concert hall, he looked around at all the people he was going around, excusing himself to, pushed through, and stepping in front of as he found his seat. The show was sold out as Andrew knew it would be. This was a unique moment in history. A concert like this would be similar to the passing of Haley's comet, the moon landing, discovering water on Mars, but far cooler than any of those.

Andrew looked at the faces in the crowd, heard their voices, and he knew in his heart, he was one hundred percent certain there were people in attendance who had sold their soul for tickets. Andrew wanted to have empathy for them. He honestly did. He had seen a small part of what was in store for those people; from being thrown off the balcony to the absolute loss of love and hope, the Absence which comes from being in Hell.

Andrew wanted to feel bad for them but he couldn't. Because Andrew knew that no matter what he had asked for there was going to be a price. It didn't matter if it would have been for something as simple as a sewing needle or as big as being President of the United States. The Universe would have exacted a balance to his request. Andrew also knew people were going to do what they wanted, which was the trap of Free Will. He didn't force them to make their choices and neither could he stop them, their lives were their own.

And Andrew decided he did not feel bad for those people. But, despite his declared apathy, there was a small part somewhere down in his heart or soul, or where feelings and emotions came from, some pity and empathy did reside. So he did feel sad for those who made such a choice. And that made Andrew the person he was.

"I see you found your seat. Is it to your liking?"

Andrew had been caught off guard and jumped at the sound of the voice speaking to him. Andrew had been so lost in his thoughts he hadn't noticed Satan come up next to him and take the seat on his left. Satan was once again exceptionally dapper looking in his usual suit and tie.

"Perhaps we should have announced ourselves so as not to have startled the poor fellow."

It was Cadwallader speaking now. He was next to Satan. Andrew was starting to wonder what was going on.

"I didn't know. What are you both doing here? How?"

Andrew started to stumble again mentally. His brain was still trying to resurface, after being caught so deep in thought. Caught up in the contemplation about, well, about life, the universe, sort of everything. Andrew, surprised when Satan and Cadwallader sat down next to him. Andrew once more became as flummoxed as he was the first time they had met.

"It is almost sad to see him verbally flounder about like that wouldn't you say, Cadwallader?"

"Quite so Satan; and he had come so far in such a short time. Perhaps after tonight's performance, he should return with us for further instruction?"

Andrew knew they were teasing him and sort of serious at the same time. He wondered about the state of his life where he somehow came to understand some of the mannerisms of Satan and Cadwallader better than most people. *"How pathetic am I?"* Andrew wondered. As the concert hall was almost at full capacity, Andrew found himself adjusting his voice to the roar of the noise around them to make sure he could be heard.

"Please, gentlemen, excuse my less than eloquent response to your greeting. I was, shall I say, gathering wool and did not hear your approach."

Satan and Cadwallader exchanged looks and nodded back at Andrew.

"He does recover well though after the initial shock; quite adaptable."

Satan turned to Andrew.

"And there is no need to shout. We can all hear each other just fine."

The idea that shouting wasn't necessary hadn't occurred to Andrew. It just seemed the obvious thing to do since it was becoming quite loud. Then again, Andrew remembered with whom he was speaking. That realization reminded Andrew to remember his manners.

"I wanted to thank you for the upgrade in the flight and the hotel. I hadn't expected to be in first class, or in the full suite with car service."

Satan nodded his head.

"You are quite welcome of course, but neither Cadwallader nor I was directly involved in those changes. Those came from Percy. He is currently in the process of, how shall I say this; he is making amends for the error of his ways. He hoped you would appreciate it. It was his way of saying sorry."

Andrew didn't want to think about what the "making amends" meant on a Hell scale. But the concept of Universal balance came to him again, and Andrew tried to imagine what making amends might entail.

"Well, I don't know if it will help his situation or not, but I did and do appreciate his efforts."

Satan made a slight nod and pursed his lips in the inflection of giving it some thought.

"And maybe I will consider some of his errors to be, slightly, amended."

Then Cadwallader leaned over in an obviously faked clandestine manner towards Satan and pretended to conceal what he was saying.

"Should we prepare him for what's next or see how he responds?"

Satan looked at Cadwallader, then back at Andrew, then back at Cadwallader with over dramatized movements and facial expression. His over-acting was done with such flair Andrew almost thought Satan was trying for a bad acting award.

"I love a good surprise myself."

Cadwallader smiled his perfect smile, and for a moment there was even a perfect glint of light which flashed in his eye.

"Excellent."

Andrew was just starting to wonder what they two of them were talking about when he felt rather odd. It wasn't a feeling he had ever felt before, and he wasn't sure how to express it. He tried to think of it in simple terms. Ideas and expression with which he was familiar. He thought of the first times he had sex; or the taste of some food that was amazing and drove his taste buds and brain to desire more; those were still not adequate.

He thought of happy and amazing childhood memories of playing with puppies and kittens. How soft and warm their fur was, and the pure exuberance of playing with them. Great events in his life like High School and College graduations. The flash of Amorina's kiss; from the first one she gave him on the cheek to a deeper one they had shared before he left and the warmth it brought about within him.

What he was now feeling were all of those memories and positive emotions amplified to an extreme Andrew didn't think could be possible. With a sudden realization, he understood what it was. He was at that moment feeling the opposite of what he felt when he first entered Hell. That was the total loss, the great Absence. Now he was flush with, with everything. If the Absence was the overwhelming loss, Andrew now experienced suffusion of everything positive and good in all of Existence, it was a Presence, and it took his breath away. Then he felt an awareness which came with the Presence and Andrew became awed because he understood it could mean only one thing.

Andrew started to shake. He hadn't moved and was still looking at Satan and Cadwallader and the two of them at him. Cadwallader's perfect smile became almost too big to be contained on his face, and he burst out laughing his very imperfect and unnatural laugh. Satan's smile didn't change much, but it did change just a little. It took on a slight tight business like edge to it. At the same time Satan broke eye contact with Andrew, looking past Andrew and nodded his head, not much, just a slight dip, to someone Andrew now realized was on his right side. Satan's gaze came back to rest on Andrew.

"Go ahead and relax. From your expression and once again old boy trust me. If you could only see your expression right now. You know who just sat down next to you.

If Andrew had been terrified before, when he first learned he was being taken Hell, he now felt that terror amplified by, well he didn't know how much because infinity doesn't end. It was pretty much terror, horror, awe, intimidation; the complete thesaurus of all those related words but on an infinite scale. He didn't know why he should be any of those because he felt as if were wrapped in a soft, warm blanket made of the Presence. The singular piece of knowledge he was one hundred and ten percent sure of, and right at that very moment Andrew knew it would, in fact, be possible to achieve one hundred and ten percent because he knew sitting next to him was God.

# 33.

Andrew, unsure what to do sat frozen. Then from his right side, he heard a quiet voice with an English accent; apparently, the English ran the entire Afterlife.

"It's alright Andrew I'm not going to bite your head off. I literally have others to do that for me."

Andrew had to laugh despite his theological terror; he had to laugh. Those were some of the first words Satan had spoken to him. They weren't funny then, but they were funny now. And Andrew started to laugh.

"That's better" commented Satan as tears of laughter started coming out of Andrew's eyes.

Cadwallader even chimed in on the moment.

"Yes, Mr. Wheeler does seem a bit more right in color; he was a shade too white a moment ago, even for him."

Andrew started to regain his composure although his shoulders and belly still had some occasional spasms. Not sure what to expect, and with a subtle, friendly eye and head gesturing from Satan which suggested he should turn and introduce himself. Andrew took a breath and turned to the other deity sitting next to him to say "Hello."

Andrew didn't know what to expect. What would God look like? Would He be the classic Michael Angelo depiction with the long gray and white hair, the flowing beard, and the robes? Or would He be something along the lines of what Satan was, a suave looking human male in an impeccable suit? No matter how God was to appear to Andrew, he was certain that appearance was just a façade as were Satan's and Cadwalladers. However, God didn't quite look like anything Andrew had thought. Who Andrew saw was a normal looking older man.

God was so average and normal looking that it was almost un-average and un-normal. He was casually dressed in faded blue jeans and a light long sleeved shirt with a sixties style paisley print. He wore round black rimmed glasses. His hair was medium in length. He had a short, close-cropped beard that could have been nothing more than several days of not shaving, all of which was salt and pepper looking in color. God looked at Andrew with a soft smile and gave him a little wave with his right hand.

"Hello, Andrew, fancy meeting you here tonight."

Andrew swallowed several times in an attempt to try and produce some saliva which would help his tongue to no longer be stuck to the roof of his mouth. While he tried to get his mouth to function Andrew returned God's little wave which also helped his hand to relax and not shake as much. With one more solid try his mouth was finally able to get enough moisture to allow it to function normally once more.

"Ahh, yeah, I, err, I mean."

God looked past Andrew and over to Satan with an amused look on his face.

"He is quite loquacious, isn't he? I'm glad I didn't have anything to do with him."

Satan's body moved with a closed mouth laugh.

"Don't try to lay the blame for him on me. That is certainly not my department."

God smiled a pleasant soft smile at Satan's retort.

Andrew wasn't sure, but it seemed God and Satan were joking around, joking around about him. Who was, Andrew questioned, lucky enough to get to sit between the two of them? He tried once more to get his brain and mouth to function in a proper and coherent manner.

"Sorry about that. I guess I am still not used to all of," and Andrew paused looking back and forth between God and Satan, "well with all of this. It is quite a lot for a just a quiet simple human from Minnesota."

Andrew watched as God and Satan looked at each other and with a shoulder shrug, head tilt, eyebrow raised expression of, "yes, he is only human."

"I don't mean to be invasive and pry into each of your affairs, but why are you all here? I didn't think something like this would be an interest to", and again Andrew paused not sure how to finish his sentence, "well to you guys?"

This time all three of them laughed. As they did, they looked at each other and Andrew. Andrew wasn't sure what to make of their laughter. It wasn't the big belly laughs from earlier. It wasn't a pity laugh like you are such a puny, insignificant thing. It wasn't a condescending laugh like who are you to question Us?

Andrew realized what type of laugh it was; it was a, "are you kidding me, do you think I would ever consider missing something like this" sort of laugh. The three of them God, Satan, and Cadwallader got themselves back under control. Which Andrew thought was good, because it seemed while they were getting their chuckles on, odd things started to happen around them

Nothing significant as to draw direct attention. However, there was some odd, otherworldly sort of glow coming both God and Satan. Andrew also noticed the people sitting around and behind them started to act oddly. Some of the people started laughing as well, a couple of people started crying, one person seemed to drift off and stare mindlessly up towards the ceiling with a sort of serene look on their face while another started to drool and clutch at their hair. Of course, for all Andrew knew those people could have been on various forms of drugs as well, he had no proof either way. But he did notice once God and Satan settled down so did the people around them.

"He is a funny one. You were right about him."

God then turned from Satan and looked at Andrew with a serious look.

"It was a very good thing you were so quick thinking that day in the loo otherwise none of us would be here right now doing what we are doing."

Andrew wasn't sure how to interpret that comment, especially from God. Apparently, Satan wasn't exaggerating nor over dramatizing the situation had Andrew's soul been taken out of turn. Andrew hadn't been sure about the unmaking of all creation; thinking it may have been more of a locally defined and contained event. Maybe something along the lines of only unmaking Hell or something. But to hear it from God made Andrew considered the situation from a new perspective. Once more the idea of Universal balance came to Andrew.

The Universe would have sought to balance itself apparently for an event which wasn't supposed to happen or had happened out of turn. To Andrew's speculative and admitted mental limitations, if his hypothesis were correct the Universe would have tried to compensate for something which wasn't supposed to happen. It would have done that by possibly unmaking all the events. Andrew started to feel a headache at such a thought and decided to concentrate on something less existential, like sitting between God and Satan at a concert.

"Either way, "continued God, "it didn't happen, and here we all are. I must admit this was a good choice. I very much approve. As for thinking, we wouldn't be interested; no one misses a chance to attend an event like this."

Satan agreed with God.

"Yes. Even I was a bit surprised by it. Although putting an event of this size togeher took a bit of doing on my part. There were all those pesky last-minute details. There were the negotiations with booking agents. Then the threats of evisceration of said booking agents. Then the negotiations with record label agents. Then the threats of evisceration of said record label agents. All that normal sort of thing when dealing with executives in the music industry. But it all came together quite lovely. The boys were eager for a chance to reunite and play together again, and here we all are."

God looked casually over at Satan with an impish grin.

"Yes, you may have done all the work for tonight, but I believe I might have had just a little something to do with the band's original formation back in the day."

Andrew noted Cadwallader and Satan both nodded in agreement. Satan back to face God, "I thought for a moment at first he might have done the usual thing and asked for a bigger nob, providing exact measurements and diagrams and the lot. This choice is clearly much better."

God laughed a light and understated laugh at Satan's comment.

"Yes, you're quite right there. The human male is quite concerned about the size of their "chap." Such a pity really if they only took a moment to see the grand scale of life."

Andrew was once again the source and butt of the jovial exchange of jokes and slights between God and Satan. He couldn't do anything more than to laugh along with them. It would seem that God, Satan, the Universe; the total sum of existence seemed to enjoy a good joke and a laugh. Andrew could do nothing more than to sit back, relax and laugh along with them.

Then, without warning, all the lights went out at the Royal Albert Hall. The capacity crowd responded to that action with a deafening roar. Andrew, seated in the center seat in the first row could hear movement on the stage.

There were some fumbling sounds and voices, the sound of a bumped microphone, an amplifier being plugged in, several thuds from the drum kit. Then the stage burst forth with an explosion of energetic life; light and sound and heat and the stadium erupted into an explosive fury as a reunited Led Zeppelin ripped into their bombastic opening song "Rock and Roll."

# ABOUT THE AUTHOR

Once again, I will not bore you third person details about me. I am neither that interesting or that exciting. If you don't want to believe me, just ask my cats. Oh, look, another bit about me. I like cats. I wonder what gave me away. Sorry, I'm also inappropriately sarcastic. That unfortunate habit has gotten me into trouble more than once. I will not go into detail, but once it did involve me telling someone to eat a Habanero pepper, they did. Besides that, I'm an average guy who does average stuff. To learn more about what it means to be an average guy listen to the Joe Walsh song, "Ordinary Average Guy." I wish I was as exciting as the guys in that song. So, does my wife. All that aside. I hope you liked this book. I am currently sitting at my desk in my bathrobe and slippers and working my next book. So, please stay tuned.

www.ingramcontent.com/pod-product-compliance
Lightning Source LLC
Chambersburg PA
CBHW020532020726
47494CB00006B/1734